I0557029

Praise for *Charting the Course*

"Wahl's skill at conveying emotion and faith at pivotal moments had me spellbound. I enjoyed the twists in this story, and I loved the unfolding of story themes. *Charting the Course* made me think about how the choices parents make can affect their children, and more importantly how important it is to forgive others and let go of the hurts in our past."

~Theresa Linden, author of award-winning contemporary West Brothers series.

"Leslea Wahl is one of my favorite authors. Her works are considered teen fiction or YA fiction, and, being a former teenager, I love the contemporary, sweet-first-love, adventure stories that she writes. *Charting the Course*, which features Liz Kennedy, who was a supporting character in the book *Into the Spotlight*, is one of my favorite books of Wahl's so far. Part of what makes her books so enjoyable is that she creates strong female protagonists who are so easy to relate to. Another factor I appreciate is that Wahl constructs realistic settings. You feel like you're in the story your-self. *Charting the Course* is set on a cruise ship sailing the Caribbean. If you've ever had a chance to go on one, you'll recognize so many typical cruise scenarios, those things that make cruises so much fun. There are a couple of interesting twists in the story that I didn't see coming and I loved the ending. Whether you're getting ready to depart on your next cruise or are planning a staycation this year, *Charting the Course* is the ideal book to bring with you. It'll be a hard one to put down!"

~Amanda Lauer, award-winning author of the YA Heaven Intended series and *Anything But Groovy*

Other Titles by Leslea Wahl

The Perfect Blindside
eXtreme Blindside
Where You Lead
Into the Spotlight
To Serve and Protect

Contributing author in CatholicTeenBooks anthologies:
Secrets: Visible and Invisible
Gifts: Visible and Invisible
Treasures: Visible and Invisible
Ashes: Visible and Invisible

Charting the Course

Finding Faith, Book 2

LESLEA WAHL

Copyright ©2023 Leslea Wahl

Cover illustration copyright © 2023 Elaina Lee/For the Muse Designs
Formatting and Interior Design by Woven Red Author Services

All rights reserved. No part of this book may be reproduced or transmitted in any form or by any means, electronic or mechanical, including photocopying, recording, or by an information storage and retrieval system-except by a reviewer who may quote brief passages in a review to be printed in a magazine, newspaper, or on the Web-without permission in writing from the publisher.

All characters in this work are purely fictional and have no existence outside the imagination of the author and have no relation whatsoever to anyone bearing the same name or names. They are not even distantly inspired by any individual known or unknown to the author, and all incidents are pure invention.

Copyright information for the songs referred to in *Charting the Course*:
Somewhere Over the Rainbow: Document Number: V2224P563
On My Own: Registration Number: SR0000244631/1997-04-11
Can't Help Falling in Love: Document Number: V9921D929, Registration Number: EP0000158445 (1961)
Every Breath You Take: Registration Number: SR0000303802, Publisher Number: A&M Records 0694931692
Living on a Prayer: Document Number: V2332P406
Piano Man: Registration Number: SR0000024765
White Christmas: Document Number: V9974D533
You've Got to Pick a Pocket of Two: Registration Number: SR0000213936
L-O-V-E: Registration Number: SR0000017781

To my family: the strong faith, deep love, and amazing adventures we share inspire me daily.
So many incredible trips.
So many wonderful memories.

Chapter 1

"Merry Christmas! And welcome to the most magical ten days of your entire life!"

I stare at the perky blonde lady in her crisp white uniform. Maybe the longest ten days of my life. Or the most annoying ten days of my life. But I can pretty much guarantee that the next week and a half will not be the most magical.

I respond with a slight smile—she has no way of knowing that ever since my parents' divorce, holidays have lost their magical appeal. Shuffling between Mom's home in Minnesota and Dad's place in Illinois, pretending all is well, does not make for precious memories.

And this one will be particularly straining, ten days alone on a cruise ship with my dad—and his old high school classmates. What a stupid time for a class reunion. Who would want to spend ten days, over the holidays, with the teenage acquaintances you've spent decades trying to forget? Apparently, my father.

I tuck a strand of dark hair behind my ear, hitch my bag higher on my shoulder, and continue following Dad as we make our way onto the ship. I've yet to understand exactly why he wanted me to join him on this Caribbean cruise. While I've always dreamed of such an exotic vacation, him bringing me on this cruise with his old buddies, defies all logic. Over the years, our infrequent time together has not been fun weeks of togetherness. When I do see him, we generally just do our own thing. Which means not only will I be spending the week on my own, but I'm also going to miss all the fun of the Christmas break back in Minnesota. He probably doesn't even know that I always look forward to all the time-honored traditions that my best friend, Josie, and I have created over the years—my favorite being our annual sleepover followed by a day of sledding and snowman building sometime between Christmas and New Year's.

Get real. Josie will most likely spend the entire break with Ryan. The two love birds are nauseatingly inseparable. As soon as the thought pops into my head, a massive dose of guilt wells within me because I know it's not true. Before Christmas, Josie went out of her way to make time for our other holiday traditions. She made sure all our must-see movies were watched, our gingerbread houses decorated, and our present wrapping extravaganza fulfilled.

I'm jerked back to reality as some young boys bump into me, knocking my bag off my shoulder as they scamper past us on their way up the ramp leading to the cruise ship. Their mother offers a weary apology as she hurries after them. A man, who I presume to be her husband and the father of the little ruffians, strides past us. With his phone plastered to his head, he's completely oblivious to his stressed wife and out-of-control children—clearly Father of the Year material.

Dad wraps his arm around my shoulder as I readjust my bag and then leads me up the gangplank. "You've been sulking long enough. Time to have fun."

"Yeah. Sure." Bring on the fun.

As we enter the ship, we're welcomed by the beaming staff. I politely nod but don't even hear their greeting because the opulent promenade demands my full attention. Three levels of balconies, adorned with tiny, glittering lights, tower above me. The long, fully enclosed hallway has the feel of a European street lined with fancy shops and cafes, elaborately decorated for the holidays.

Dad steers me through the crowds of happy vacationers to the elevator and down to the floor where our rooms are located. I follow him along a narrow hallway, past countless doors, until we locate our two rooms. I use the key card to open my door while Dad checks out his adjacent room, then step into my home for the next ten days. Not too shabby. It's roomier than I expected.

Not as big as my room at home but larger than the walk-in closet I feared. And look at that—a balcony.

I pull open the sliding glass door and step out, despite the not-so-impressive view. Since this side of the boat is tied to the dock, all I see are guests being herded through lines like cattle being led to the slaughterhouse and onto the boat. Right across from me is the fake backdrop where all the passengers patiently wait for their first photo memory of the trip. No doubt ours will look like a mug shot. I tried to muster up a smile, but despite years of acting, faking excitement proved to be too difficult because I'm still baffled why Dad wanted me to come on this ten-day trip with him.

When he first mentioned it, Mom hesitated and grilled him to make sure he wasn't inviting his girlfriend along. Mom, who can be a fierce protector, remembered what a disaster my summer with him and his barely-older-than-me girlfriend had been. After assuring her that it would just be him and me and two hundred of his classmates, she agreed, then eagerly booked a flight to visit a girlfriend in New York. Neither caring about my preference of how to spend the holidays.

The three of us spent an awkward Christmas together yesterday in Chicago. But at least it was lucrative for me. They'd gotten me all kinds of new cute clothes for the ten days in the Caribbean. Technically, Mom had purchased my vacation wardrobe, and Dad had shelled out some money. Luckily, they were both on their best behaviors. After hours of stilted conversation and prolonged silences, Mom left for her hotel fairly early, under the pretense that I needed to pack all my new outfits. Then Dad and I caught an early flight this morning for Miami.

I sink into the lounge chair on my mini deck and pull my phone from my backpack. Soon we'll have no service, so there's no time to waste if I want to send any final texts. First, I send a quick one to Mom to let her know we've boarded. She's probably on her flight, so I'm not surprised when no immediate response appears. Next, I text Josie.

I'm dreaming of a white Christmas.

Just like the ones you used to know.

Josie types back in our musical theater dialogue that we've perfected over the years.

Although didn't you technically have a white Christmas? I'm

pretty sure Chicago is rather snowy this time of year.

I grin.

Fine, I'm dreaming of a white day after Christmas.

Miami isn't a winter wonderland?? Shocker.

Seriously. Who wants a tropical heatwave during the holidays? That's not natural.

I wait while she responds.

I'm pretty sure it didn't snow in Bethlehem when baby Jesus was born. So maybe you're the one having the more traditional Christmas. So…how was Christmas with mom and pop?

Josie knows just how much I was dreading spending the holiday with both my parents—a first since their divorce eight years ago.

Ehh…We're all still alive.

And how are you?

I stare at those four little words. How am I? That's the million-dollar question. Only Josie knows how much it hurt when Dad walked out on us. And how I've never truly been able to forgive him. In the aftermath, Mom was such a mess that I felt the need to hide my feelings from her. But Josie was always there for me through all the tears and anger. It's better now, but I'm still waiting for the childhood pain to disappear. I take a deep breath and type.

I'm okay. I made it through a whole summer with him. Ten days should be doable.

I'll be praying for you!

Thx.

Maybe this is a good time to try those prayers I suggested.

My shoulders sag with a sigh. Josie keeps trying to get me to go to her church youth group with her and Ryan. But always being the third wheel is not my idea of fun. And then there's her new-found enthusiasm for the faith, which I don't really get. Ever since the summer and meeting Ryan, she's become more involved with the church. I thought maybe it was a passing phase, but it seems to be the real deal. Before the trip, she even gave me a little prayer card with a novena to pray for healing a family. I know she means well, but my family may be beyond repair.

> Yeah, maybe. Hey—good news is I pretty much got a whole new wardrobe for the trip.

Sweet!

> BTW, how's your head?

The day before Mom and I left for Dad's place in Chicago, Josie and I had gone ice skating. My best friend had one of her "Josie moments," slipping, falling, and taking out a slew of little kids in the process. Luckily, no one but Josie had gotten hurt.

> Oh, it's fine. Ryan brought me over a gallon of ice cream to make me feel better.

> Spumoni?

Of course!

> Your Prince Charming knows you well.

Yeah, he's a keeper! Hey, please try to have fun—okay?

She's been trying for weeks to get me excited about this trip. Visiting my dad is never the easiest time. We always struggle with what to say to each other—but lately, it's been even more strained. Our summer visit was such a disaster that I went home early. Maybe he's trying to make up for that catastrophe with this trip.

> All right.

That's all the excitement I can muster.

> Take lots of pictures.

Will do.

So long

> Farewell

Auf Wiedersehen

> Goodbye

I smile at our signature signoff—my last text for the next ten days. I turn my attention back to the happy vacationers as they stream up the ramp. Josie had a life-changing vacation during the summer. She came back focused and full of confidence. If not a little delusional. That's when she and Ryan came up with this crazy idea of making our school less cliquey. While their intentions are honorable—who wouldn't want to change the hierarchical tier system in our school?—there is no way it will work. The popular crowd is too proud of their status to ever willingly let it go. So, while Ryan and Josie keep trying to implement their idealistic vision, I remain realistic.

I don't know what craziness they are preaching at that youth group, but the change in Josie in such a short time is a little concerning. Take the novena, for instance. I'm pretty sure the only other person I've ever known who mentioned praying a novena was my great-grandmother. In fact, that's exactly what I told Josie when she handed me the little pamphlet. But she just laughed and explained that novenas are simply structured prayers that ask certain saints to pray for us. I guess that's not too weird. I dig through my bag until I find the little pamphlet. The front is a picture of the Holy Family. Joseph has his arm around Mary, and they are both gazing at their little bundle of joy with pure love and devotion. For the first time, I read the fine print: the novena lasts nine days and begins on the first Sunday after Christmas. Today. Okay, Josie—this one's for you.

I open the brochure and read the first prayer. I stifle a laugh when I read, *Help me and the members of my family to love, listen to, support, and accept one another.* Clearly, my family will need the assistance of the entire Holy Family to achieve that goal. I stumble through the prayers and end with a sign of the cross like Josie always does. *Okay, Lord, it's up to You.*

"Hey." Dad steps out onto my balcony.

I shove the novena back into my backpack. "How'd you get in my room?" So much for privacy.

"We have an adjoining door."

Super.

He runs a hand through his touched-with-gray, sandy-blond hair. "I knocked, but I guess you didn't hear."

"Guess not." I know I should be nicer, but when it comes to my dad, sulky, sullen Liz immediately emerges.

He stuffs his hand in his pocket, pulls out a phone, and holds it out toward me. "I got you something."

I stare at the small device in his hand. "What's this for?"

"I've heard nightmare stories about people who try to use their phones on vacation and rack up outrageous charges from international calls and roaming fees. But I thought it would be good for us to have a way to get ahold of each other, so I bought us each a prepaid phone. Plus, it takes photos!"

"I thought I'd just use my phone for photos only."

"But now you won't be tempted to send them or post them." He inches his outstretched hand closer to me.

A twinge of annoyance flashes through me. Thanks for the vote of confidence, Dad. Although, he may have a point. I finally take it. "Thanks."

"I added my number to your contact list."

"You've thought of everything."

He nods, happy with my less than heartfelt statement. "Well, since our luggage isn't here yet, want to go up on deck for the bon voyage party?"

"Sure. Sounds fun." I manage a little half-smile—I think.

I lead the way to the door, then stop and turn toward him. "Do you have your room key on you?"

He pats down his pockets, then gives a sheepish grin before retreating to his room. I'm unable to control the roll of my eyes. Dad isn't necessarily absentminded, but he certainly has a tendency to leave things laying out and forget them.

Up on the deck, we wedge our way through the crowd to find a spot along the ship's railing. Before too long, the bullhorn of the ship blasts, and the boat slips away from the dock.

Dad's arm circles around me. "Bon voyage!"

"Bon voyage!" I half-heartedly echo along with all the other passengers. I lamely wave at the workers on the dock who look bored to tears. How many times have they seen hundreds of strangers waving at them as their boat leaves the dock? Who started this silly tradition?

The crowd begins to filter away from the railing. Dad and I turn to leave, practically toppling over an elderly woman standing in front of us. She's about a foot shorter than me, and since I'm not gifted in the height department, that's pretty tiny. Her white hair is perfectly styled, and her oversized sunglasses almost hide her entire face. She's dressed in a crisp white pantsuit and probably wearing her weight in gold between her many gold rings, bracelets, necklaces, and earrings. The afternoon sunlight gleams off the precious metal, practically blinding me.

The woman flashes us an equally bright smile. "Are you ready for a wonderful vacation?"

"Yes, we are," Dad cheerfully replies. "Are you?"

She tilts her head to the side. "Yes. I am definitely ready for an adventure." She touches my arm. "How about you, dear?"

I force my gaze off her bright red lipstick to my reflection in her designer shades. "Yep. I'm ready. Ready for a magical ten days." Ready as I'll ever be.

"Oh, there's someone serving champagne." Dad squeezes my arm. "Can I get a glass for you?" he asks the lady, his simple question oozing charm.

The miniature octogenarian shakes her head. "Thank you, dear, but none for me."

His smile flashes toward me. "I'll be right back." With that, he disappears into the crowd.

And so, it begins.

My gaze shifts to a large family walking by, all in matching neon green shirts. An elderly couple leads the group, which consists of bouncy little children, talkative middle schoolers, and pairs of laughing adults. A baby sleeping in her daddy's arms is even dressed in the festive attire. At least half of the group has red hair, ranging in color from fiery to dark auburn. The words printed on their shirts confirm the obvious; the Desmont family is enjoying a family reunion.

Envious longing floods through me as I watch them cross the pool deck like a line of ducklings. Another thing I'll never enjoy—a large, happy family. Heck, I'd even settle for a small, happy family instead of my broken, dysfunctional one.

"Are you traveling with your family?"

I'm startled to see my diminutive geriatric friend still standing beside me. "Um…Nope. Just me and the old man."

She taps my arm with her wrinkly, age-spotted hand. "Make sure you use plenty of sunscreen on that beautiful fair skin of yours."

I nod. "Will do."

"Well, I'm sure I'll see you around, dear. This ship might be large, but it's not that large." She turns and gracefully glides through the crowd, past a whining little kid tugging on his mom's arm.

"Mo-omm."

"What?" The woman snaps, and she yanks her arm free.

The boy swoops a chunk of hair out of his eyes. "You said we had to leave our devices at home."

She nods. "That's right. We're having a nice family vacation."

"Well, why doesn't Dad have to follow the rule?"

The mother and son both turn to look at a man standing beside them, looking out toward the ocean. White wires snake from his pocket up to his ears.

The woman yanks the earbuds out of his ears. He turns to them bewildered, then glances at the earbuds in his wife's hand.

"Peter! We agreed to leave our phones in the stateroom."

"I did. I just downloaded a lecture or two onto my old iPod." He pulls a small little device from his pocket.

The woman's face turns an unnatural shade of red. Surprisingly, steam doesn't start shooting out of her ears. The polite thing would be to turn away, but it's like watching an accident; I want to avert my eyes, but I just can't.

"We agreed that we would leave work behind for the whole week." Her raised voice draws looks from various passengers. "I can't believe you brought along a lecture to listen to."

"I didn't technically agree." He winces at the icy glare aimed at him. "I promise listening to a few lectures won't interfere with our trip."

Her eyes narrow into slits. "That's how it always starts. You listen to one of your colleagues' lectures and then you have to send a reply or do some research or look up an article or something. Well, not this time." She grabs the iPod from his hand and tosses it on the lounge chair next to them. "We are going to have a fun time and make some wonderful memories if it kills us," she hisses between gritted teeth. "Now, I want a cocktail to start this enjoyable vacation."

The husband stares at his wife for a moment, then nods. "One cocktail coming up." He dutifully makes his way toward the bar while his wife and son turn their attention toward the distant horizon where we're headed.

Well, maybe I'm not the only one with a dysfunctional family.

～

After Dad and I scope out the whole ship, I'm satisfied there are enough places to keep me occupied during our days at sea. Once we finish the tour, we swing by our staterooms to change into something more suited for the cocktail meet and greet for his class reunion. But as luck would have it, my suitcase has not arrived yet. So, while Dad's all spiffed up in dress pants and a nice yet casual untucked shirt, I'm stuck with the jeans and t-shirt that I've been wearing since five a.m., Chicago time. I don't even have deodorant or a hairbrush to try and look presentable. I can just hear it now, "Oh, Wade, you didn't tell us your daughter was a gypsy. How very bohemian."

He insists I look fine, so nixes my plea to skip the dumb shindig. Despite his bald-faced lies, I dutifully traipse along anyway. The first stop inside the large lounge is a table for our nametags. Next, Dad steers us toward the bar for a little liquid courage. My father is nothing if not predictable.

I take a sip of the soda he hands me, then set it back on the bar. Figures. How hard is it to remember that your only child hates root beer? Dad takes a swig of his drink, then scans the room. The bartender looks at me with one raised eyebrow.

"Could I please have a cola?" I answer his silent query.

He nods and pours me a new drink.

"Hey, I see Pat Holliday. I'm going to go say hi."

"Cool. I'm going to take my *cola* and go sit by myself in that lounge chair over there."

He squeezes my arm without even looking at me. "Okay, great. Have fun." He strides toward a group of people.

I settle into the comfy chair to people-watch and enjoy the live piano music. The handsome dark-haired musician ends one song and begins another. Sadly, the beautiful tunes are largely ignored by the growing crowd.

Middle-aged men with thinning hairlines and widening waistlines shake hands with each other. Groups of ladies, who look far better than their male counterparts—plastic surgery much?—give each other fake squeals of delight and air kisses. Is this what my high school class will succumb to one day? I can only hope that justice will be served and the jocks and princesses of our cliquey class that terrorize everyone on a daily basis will fall victim to the cruel hands of time.

As more guests filter in and the crowd grows, it's easy to tell the spouses from the classmates; they all look how I feel—bored out of their minds, wondering why they agreed to this trip. How many of the poor souls are like me and didn't have much of a choice?

"Is this the teens-who'd-rather-be-anywhere-than-here section of the room?"

I look up to see a guy my age standing in front of me. Tall, muscular build, dark hair—cut very close on the sides and back with slightly longer waves on top—flawless olive skin, undeterminable ethnicity, nicely dressed, eyes with ridiculously long eyelashes. Cute.

I motion for him to sit down. "Yep. But be warned—I've noticed a lot of bored spouses eyeing this designated section."

"Thanks for the warning. I'd better sit while I can." He lowers himself into the comfy lounge chair next to me. "Do you come here often, or is this your first thirtieth high school reunion?"

Good-looking and witty—this boy has potential. "Do you flirt with all the girls you pick up at your parents' social gatherings?"

He grins. "Just the ones who are incredibly underdressed."

I'm unable to stop the little laugh that manages to escape. He's right, of course, but I'm surprised he actually pointed it out. I reach for my soda. "Just my luck, a modern-day Henry Higgins."

He arches an eyebrow. "Does that mean I should call you Eliza?"

My eyes narrow as I take a sip. I never would have pegged this preppy guy to know the characters in *My Fair Lady*.

He shrugs. "My mom is a little obsessed with Audrey Hepburn."

Apparently, he's a mind reader. "Who isn't?"

He leans back, scrutinizing me. "You know, you remind me a bit of her."

I lean back and cross my arms. "Who? Audrey or your mom?"

His deep laugh could only be categorized as charming. "Definitely Audrey." His head tilts to the side. "You think I'm joking, but I'm serious—fair skin, dark hair, slender, poised. If it weren't for the unusual choice of clothes for a cocktail party, you could fit right into *Breakfast at Tiffany's*."

"Now you're just showing off. I'll only be impressed if you can name one more Audrey Hepburn movie."

He strokes his chin. "Is this a bet of some sort?"

I shrug, coyly looking at him over my raised shoulder. "Sure. I'll tell you my name if you answer correctly."

"Hmm…well, I would like to know your name." He leans forward, his forearms resting on his thighs, and concentrates on his clasped hands.

Before he has to declare defeat, Dad approaches with a tall, pasty-looking gentleman with thinning wheat-colored hair.

Dad points at me with the index finger of his hand that's holding the whiskey glass. The ice rattles. "Tad here just said he should introduce his son to you."

Dad playing matchmaker. What could possibly go wrong?

Tad nods. "And here you've already met."

I look between pasty Tad and this cute guy I've been flirting with. The two of them look *nothing* alike. Wow. Never would've guessed that connection. Wonder what his mom looks like. She must possess the exotic, dark genes that make this boy so handsome.

"Tad and I were tennis partners back in the day. We even played on a league together before you were born, until he moved to Virginia." Dad pats his old friend on the shoulder.

Tad reaches out his hand. "Nice to meet you, Liz."

"Liz!" Tad's son exclaims. "Guess I win the bet by default."

Way to go, Dad. "It's hardly a win when you couldn't complete the dare."

The two ex-tennis partners exchange a confused look.

"Cole, ready to head to dinner?" Tad asks his son. "Your siblings are probably anxiously waiting for us."

Cole? Wouldn't have guessed it. Coles should be blond and blue-eyed.

My verbal sparring partner stands. "Sure." He looks down at me. "See ya later, *Liz*."

"Not if I see you first, *Cole*."

He begins to walk away, then turns back and grins. "I hope you enjoy your holiday. Even if it isn't a Roman one."

I cover my mouth to hide my smile at his Audrey Hepburn reference. *Roman Holiday*. Well played, Cole. Maybe this cruise won't be so excruciating after all.

Chapter 2

The good news is that my luggage arrives before dinner, so I can finally wear one of my new outfits—a super cute sundress with matching sweater. Thank goodness because the swanky dining room is decked out with luxurious rugs, crystal chandeliers, and a gorgeous grand piano. Hardly the place for jeans and t-shirts. The bad news, however, is that Dad and I have been assigned to dine every night with three married couples. He's excited to catch up with his old track teammates, but that means I have to converse with seven adults every evening. Joy.

Even though he introduced everyone to me, I only partially paid attention, so forgot their names almost immediately. I've instead come up with nicknames for them like Josie and I used to do. Mr. and Mrs. Tex Mex live in Texas and own several taco restaurants. The high school sweethearts are aptly dubbed the High School Sweethearts. That leaves Mr. and Mrs. Mismatch, a know-it-all balding lawyer and his much younger second wife. Too bad Dad's not still dating Cassie. She and this pampered sorority girl would get along great.

The High School Sweethearts immediately begin reminiscing with Dad and the other two gentlemen. Mrs. Mismatch opens her purse and pulls out a shiny compact to check her makeup. Apparently happy with the results, she slides out of her seat and flits away without a word to anyone, leaving her purse and compact on her chair—discarded and no longer of any use to her, just like the rest of us. She makes a beeline to another table. She and another woman air kiss, then begin chatting. Watching them increases my annoyance level. They act just like the prima-donna popular girls at my school. Guess some people never grow up.

That leaves me alone with Mrs. Tex Mex. She looks like a nice enough lady, but there are few things I hate more than idle chitchat with people I'm never going to meet again. I mean, what's the point? I re-read the menu until it's memorized, then have to relinquish it to the waiter when he appears.

After we place our orders, the high school buddies continue their conversation, and since I have nothing else to occupy my time, I return Mrs. Tex Mex's smile. If we're going to be sitting here every night for dinner, I may as well pretend to be social.

"It's nice of you to accompany your dad on this trip," she says.

I fiddle with my napkin. "I didn't have a lot of say in the matter. Divorced parents sometimes think these kinds of things will make great bonding moments."

Her eyes widen, and she nods slightly. Her gaze turns back to the others. Apparently, my stellar conversation skills have turned her away already. Way to go. Guess I can pass the time by counting the petals on the flowers in the table centerpiece.

However, as the others discuss their old teachers, the monotonous walk down memory lane must be even duller than I assume because she turns back to me. "I suppose coming on a thirty-year reunion cruise isn't really the way you wanted to spend your Christmas break."

"Wasn't my first choice."

She leans close like we're co-conspirators. "I'm with ya, girlfriend."

I grin. "You didn't jump at the chance to relive your husband's glory years?"

She reaches for her wine glass. "Hardly. I wanted to visit our daughter and her husband in Colorado for a ski vacation, but Matt kept bringing up this trip. Seeing how much it meant to him, I couldn't say no."

"You deserve a prize for being such a good wife." I pick up my soda.

"Well, here's to surviving the next ten days." She clinks my glass with hers, then glances at the empty seat. "So, you think Miss High Society will disappear every meal?"

The soda in my mouth nearly spews across the table. Mrs. Tex Mex may be cooler than she looks. "Yeah, she may have deserted us for good." My gaze takes in the rest of our tablemates. "And even worse, our table's dinner conversations may never advance to include us."

She also looks at her husband and his friends, deep in conversation. "Oh, well. Guess we'll have to find our own topics to discuss." She takes another sip of wine. "You know, I met your mom years ago before your folks were divorced. She and I hung out for the day while the men golfed. She's great." Her gaze shifts toward me. "I was sorry to hear they had split up. I always wondered why."

I shoot her a thankful smile. That question has haunted me for years.

"By the way, my name's Linda. I don't know about you, but I'm terrible at remembering names."

I have a feeling that's not really the truth, and she knows I didn't pay attention to the introductions. "I'm Liz." I'm also pretty sure she *was* paying attention and already knew that.

"So, Liz, what grade are you in?"

"I'm a junior." Time to brace for the usual boring twenty questions.

A mischievous gleam sparkles in her eyes. "So, in thirty-one years, when you have one of these reunions, what three classmates will be seated at your table?"

My mind immediately tries to picture Josie and some of our theater friends in three decades. What would they look like with graying hair and laugh lines around their eyes? Will Josie still be so clumsy? Most likely. What about me? Who will I be in thirty years? Hopefully, someone much different than I am today.

～

The first full day on the ship is spent at sea, cruising toward the Caribbean, which seemed like a great day to sleep in. However, my mind and body were stubborn and decided not to cooperate with this plan. So, after a quick breakfast, I find myself on the pool deck claiming a front-row lounge chair.

After lathering up my delicately fair skin, I lay back and enjoy the warm rays. Ahh…the perfect way to spend the day.

"Hey, kiddo. I was looking for you. I tried calling but you didn't answer."

I shield my eyes to squint at Dad—the shadow hovering above me. "Hey. Yeah, I forgot to bring the phone with me. I did knock on your door, but you didn't answer, so I grabbed a bagel and came out here."

He rubs his slightly stubbly chin. Vacation Dad equals unshaven Dad. "I figured you'd sleep in, so I went down to the workout area."

We stare at each other for a moment. "So, any plans for the day?" I ask.

He glances around. "Not much. Maybe I'll head back to the room for a shower and check out the itinerary."

I close my eyes and resume my relaxing-at-the-pool pose. "Well, you know where to find me."

The elusive sleep must finally make an appearance because the next thing I know, I'm startled awake by drops of frigid water.

A slightly rotund man beside me shakes his head like a dog, sending more water my way. He looks at me, then stops, mid-shake. "Oh. Sorry."

I remove my sunglasses to wipe off the drops and very politely keep my snarky comment to myself. After all, he could be one of Dad's friends.

He lowers himself into his lounge chair with a loud groan and tosses his towel between us where I set my items. I glance down. Sure enough, his enormous flip-flops, watch, hat, and water bottle are intermixed with my sandals and bag. What a space invader.

Note to self: tomorrow find a more isolated deck chair.

I yank my bag out from under his wet towel and turn to place it on my other side. Although, from the looks of my neighbor on the left—a little boy sitting cross-legged, dripping ice cream all over his chair—my things probably won't fare any better over there. I shift to one side of my lounge chair and set my bag safely next to me.

The pool deck has certainly become more crowded while this bathing beauty became sleeping beauty. Most of the lounge chairs are now occupied with sunbathers, and the pool is filled to capacity with splashing children.

"Would you like a drink, miss?"

My attention is drawn to a lady in white shorts and a white collared shirt standing in front of me, an empty tray in one hand.

"Oh, sure, something frozen and tropical?"

The woman smiles, her white teeth in stark contrast to her dark complexion. "I bet you'd like a Miami Vice."

"I'll give it a try." A girl could get used to this service.

As I wait for my drink to be delivered, I become a silent observer, watching the families around me. Everyone seems to be laughing or smiling, enjoying each other's company. None of them look how I feel. Alone.

The boy next to me with the dripping ice-cream cone stuffs the rest of his treat in his mouth. He wipes his sticky fingers across his bare chest, leaving four shiny streaks. Ew. I scoot a little further away.

"Mom," he whines toward the woman with the enormous beach hat on his other side. "Can we go play putt-putt now?"

Her attention remains plastered on the book she's reading. "Let me finish this chapter first."

"*Please*?"

"Why don't you go cool off in the pool." She flips the page, never even glancing up at the boy. It doesn't take a genius to deduce from the shirtless hunk on the front cover of her paperback that she's reading some trashy romance.

"Fine," the boy mutters. He takes a flying leap into the pool, sending droplets of water everywhere. Nonplussed, his mom turns another page.

I shake my head. Okay, maybe I'm not the only one on this ship with a neglectful parent.

A short medley of musical notes wafts through an unseen speaker, shifting my attention to the front of the pool. Four tropical-shirt-wearing Latin men in their late twenties with various instruments are set up beneath a giant screen.

The tall one with thick, wavy dark hair, who looks a little like the guy on the cover of my lounge chair neighbor's romance novel, leans toward a microphone. "Welcome to paradise."

A few people clap, but most are so engrossed with their loved ones that they don't even seem to notice them.

"We are The Mambo Boys and will be entertaining you this morning." He then turns to his bandmates and nods his head, his dark hair gleaming in the morning sun. The catchy beats of a famous Latin song overpower the chatty background noise and squeals of children. I lean back, enjoying the lead singer's smooth, polished voice. That's more like it.

As I enjoy the music, I scan the area, focusing in on my server picking up several frozen concoctions at the bar. My tastebuds tingle. When she turns and walks toward me, a familiar face standing at the bar catches my eye. Dad. He's leaning against the counter, one foot on a metal foot bar. He's angled slightly toward a woman his age with wavy blond hair. He tells her something, then grins and lifts his drink. The woman tosses her head back in laughter, then touches his arm. My stomach churns. There should be laws against flirting in front of your children.

"Here you go, one alcohol-free Miami Vice." The server hands me my beverage.

I take a quick sip. An explosion of coconut and strawberry flavors fills my mouth. "Delicious!"

"Enjoy."

"I will, thanks." Forget Dad. I'm sitting by a beautiful—if not overly crowded—pool. I have a delicious beverage in hand, fabulous live music to enjoy, spectacular views, and warm weather to work on my tan. Who needs anything or anyone else? Not this girl. I lift my glass to toast myself.

"That looks tasty." The romance-reading mom stares at my drink. She fans herself with her book. "I could use something to cool me down."

She sets down the book and makes a beeline to the bar. Her son notices and scurries after her. He yells, trying to get her attention, but his little voice is lost amid the live music. My heart aches for the poor kid. If only she were as interested in him as in her book.

Before I know it, my drink is finished, and even worse, the band announces they are taking a break.

The lead singer hands the microphone to a perky young woman with a long auburn ponytail. She announces with an indeterminable accent—Australian maybe—that it is now time for pool games, and the first activity will be a belly flop contest. A rash of middle-aged men with protruding abdomens shuffle toward her to sign up, including the neighbor to my right, whose chest is now an abstract mosaic of hairy patches and sunburnt splotches. That event is not something I care to witness. My cue to leave.

I gather my items and head to the interior promenade. Aimlessly, I stroll past the stores and small restaurants that line the area until an English pub catches my eye. I slide onto a stool at one of the high-top tables set up outside the restaurant.

As I'm scanning the menu, a waitress approaches. "What can I get ya, luv."

I'm momentarily distracted by her amazing accent, then focus. "What's good?"

"Fish 'n chips is a must."

"Sold."

"Comin' right up, dear."

She walks away, leaving me to ponder if her accent is authentic. Do they only hire Brits to work at this pub? Or are employees required to watch a slew of British shows to perfect their dialect?

"Hello, dear." I turn to see a little old lady in a sailor dress standing next to my table. She's so tiny her chin barely makes it above the tall table.

I'm thinking she's mistaken me for someone else, then it hits me, I have met this petite grandma before. Even though she looks a little different without her saucer-sized sunglasses, it's most definitely my new friend from the bon voyage event. "Oh, hi. How are you?"

"I'm wonderful. It's such a beautiful day. I'm surprised to find you inside."

"I was at the pool all morning. Thought I'd take a break from the sun for lunch. Would you like to join me?" The question is out before I think about it. What if she accepts my invitation? That will require more of the dreaded small talk.

She shakes her head. "That sounds lovely, dear, but I am off to the ballroom dancing lessons. You should join me. I'm Midge, by the way."

Cute name for a cute little lady. "I'm Liz. Thanks for the offer, Midge. I do enjoy dancing, but I think I'll pass."

She pats my hand. "Well, there are several lessons scheduled throughout the cruise. Maybe you can join me on a different day."

I smile at my little pixie friend. "I'll keep that in mind."

With her hand still on mine, she squeezes. "Good. I could use a friend. Couldn't we all." She then turns and walks away.

Wise words. I watch her diminutive form as she threads a path through groups of passengers. More happy families. Sure, they might have moments of frustration and exhaustion after being together for so many days, but overall, you can just tell that special memories are forming. Memories that over time will focus only on the good while the bad wisps away like a cloud of smoke.

I've spent hours looking through the scrapbooks my mom made of our family vacations before the divorce, or what I like to call D-day. Our smiles all look genuine, but I was pretty little and don't remember the feelings. Did we just plaster on smiles for the camera, or were we truly having a wonderful time?

I quickly shove my thoughts to the recesses of my mind as a familiar face approaches. Cole. The turquoise blue of his shirt against his dark skin offers a striking combination of colors.

"Eliza! How are you?" He settles onto the stool across from me.

"In case you forgot, the name's Liz." I turn and smile at the waitress as she sets my lunch in front of me.

"Would you like anything?" she asks Cole.

"No, thanks. I'll just share with her." He reaches over and snags a French fry from my plate.

"Well, if you change your mind, luv, let me know." She flashes me a quick smile before heading to the next table.

Cole finishes chewing. "I didn't forget, but Liz is short for Elizabeth, I'm assuming?"

"Brilliant deduction." I squirt ketchup over my fries. Maybe that will keep him at bay.

"Well, Eliza could be short for your given name as well. And since you remind me of the silver-screen Eliza Doolittle, I think it fits."

I take a bite of the crunchy fish to give myself time to think before countering his well-thought-out defense. I've never once thought of Eliza being short for Elizabeth. Maybe he's onto something. A new name, a new identity, a new start.

Placing his elbow on the table, Cole rests his chin on his fist. "I'd love to know what goes on in that brain of yours."

I reach for a ketchup-coated fry. "I'm afraid it would probably disappoint you."

"I doubt that." He grins. "So, what excursion are you and your dad participating in tomorrow?"

I freeze, the fry inches from my mouth. "Excursion?"

He throws his head back with a laugh. "Do you not know how this cruise thing works? At each island we stop at, people disembark and go on excursions."

I pop the fry in my mouth and chew for a few moments, gathering my thoughts. "Of course, I know that. I just didn't realize we get to choose what we want to do." Maybe I should have read a little more of the information Dad sent me.

His smile widens, turning him into a toothpaste model, showing off his perfectly straight, white teeth. "Well, you're in luck because tomorrow's stop is Haiti. It's the cruise ship's private beach area, so all the excursions are in one spot."

"Okay, Mr. Tour Guide, I'll look into it."

"Just watching out for you. I wouldn't want you to get stuck with the lame tour bus excursion with all the old folks." He reaches over and grabs two more fries, gives me a devilishly cute grin, then leaves me alone with my food.

While I eat, I contemplate the plan for the afternoon and remember that I haven't prayed my novena today. I find it in my bag and silently recite the prayers. Today, I focus on the lines about being *compassionate, merciful, and forgiving as we struggle with the difficulties of our lives*. Sounds good in theory—like a greeting card sentiment, pretty words that don't match reality. Oh, Josie, the things I do for you.

After finishing the prayers, I slip the brochure back in my bag. Now what? Search for Dad? Nah, I'm not that bored yet. Find

Cole again? No—don't want to seem desperate. Shop? Seems better to save my money for souvenirs at our ports of call. Wander the ship? Curl up somewhere with my book?

Finally, a winner is chosen—walk around the deck, then return to the pool area. With another frozen concoction in hand, I circle the two levels of chairs in search of a place to sit, but each chair I pass is filled with a body or towels and bags. I'm about to give up the search when I notice someone waving at me.

It takes a moment to recognize the woman with the enormous hat and dark sunglasses—my buddy, Mrs. Tex Mex.

I walk toward her. "Hi, Linda."

She pats the end of her lounge chair, indicating I should sit. "It gets busy here. I was just leaving. You can take my chair."

"Are you sure?"

"Absolutely." She stuffs a book into her bag. "I was just heading in. Although, your drink looks awfully refreshing; I may need to stop and get one of those first."

"I highly recommend it—a Miami Vice." I suck on the straw.

She grabs her towel and stands. "Have you been to the Starlight lounge yet? I stumbled across it this morning and thought of you. They have all kinds of music-related events. I'm heading there now to check out the music trivia game. Want to join me?"

Hmm…I glance around. Lots of noisy kids, no live music, and an animated movie playing on the big screen behind the pool. Without my phone, I have no music to escape with. This plan of mine is sounding less appealing by the moment.

"Sure, why not." I return my bag to my shoulder.

"Great!"

"Although, my music knowledge is a little limited. If there are a lot of 80s references, you're on your own."

She wraps her arm around mine. "We'll make a good team then."

~

The trivia game is surprisingly not the lamest thing I've ever done. The entertainment staff could probably make anything fun. The game consists of a series of rounds, each representing a different era of music. I assumed they would just play the beginnings of songs and have people name the tune, but the staff livens it up by changing clothes between each round, donning the garb of each decade represented. The patrons divide themselves into teams, and whichever team waves the flag at their table and answers correctly gets a point.

Team Linda and Liz, aka the L & L Connection, tanks during the first round. Apparently, neither of us has ever paid much attention to big band swing music. Only the older folks in the crowd do well.

The next round, the 50s, is an improvement. Thanks to all the 50s music Josie and I listened to during *Bye Bye Birdie*, I provide some needed competition to the senior crowd. Josie will be so proud to know that our attempt at method acting finally paid off.

Linda keeps our team afloat during the 60s and 70s segments and totally knocks it out of the park during the 80s rock round. With each song, the tensions rise as Linda and some of dad's classmates at the next table keep raising their flag so fast and furiously it's almost impossible to know who answers first.

Linda's brows furrow in concentration as a new song begins. Her hand shoots up at the same time the guy next to us blurts out the answer. Since the dude didn't follow the game's rules, Linda is deemed the 80s winner. I reach out my hand to high-five my partner.

"Hey, sweetheart," the obnoxious fellow next to us yells. He points a shiny gold pen at the staff member. "You deaf? I said the answer first."

The cute game-show host gives a coy little grin. "Maybe it's you who's having trouble hearing since I clearly stated the rule that answers can't be blurted out, but flags must be raised for the guess to count." Clearly, she is used to dealing with unruly passengers.

The guy's friends start laughing.

One of his buddies nudges him. "She sounds just like your wife."

Mr. Obnoxious clenches his jaw. He begins furiously tapping his pen on the table—must be hardy since it doesn't shatter during the assault.

The game continues, although the staff nearly lose control of the crowd as we all begin singing at the top of our lungs. But come

on, you can't play Bon Jovi's *Livin' on a Prayer* and not expect some
rowdiness.

Some of the parents with younger kids easily win the 90s section. But, not to brag or anything, I am the clear winner of the
modern round.

As the staff tabulates the score, I pick up a flyer on the table
listing all the activities held in this lounge during the cruise. The
movie trivia sounds like a must-do but what really catches my eye
is an ongoing singing competition, Siren of the Sea. It begins tomorrow night with karaoke.

I'm still contemplating the event when Linda starts squealing.
She squeezes my arm. "Liz! We won!"

"Awesome! I guess our joint knowledge paid off."

"We make a great team." She holds up her hand for a high-
five.

One of the staff members waves us to the small stage up front.
"Congratulations! You have won free massages at the spa! Come
on down to claim your prize!"

I stand, and the annoying guy next to us reaches out with his
meaty paw and grabs my arm. "Lucky win, sweetheart. It should
have been our team who won. But I won't complain since I don't
care about a spa day."

I narrow my eyes and lean closer. "Too bad. A facial might
help those pores of yours."

I shake off his hand as his friends roar with laughter.

While Linda and I take our bows on stage, I make eye contact
with the annoying sore loser and blow him a kiss. He pushes away
his seat and storms off toward the bar. As we graciously accept
our prize, I spot Cole leaning against the door at the back of the
room. When our eyes meet, he grins. He uncrosses his arms and
joins in the feeble applause.

Chapter 3

I'm just finishing up my makeup when Dad raps on our adjoining door. After one last scan of approval, I let him in. He looks rather handsome in his navy sport coat and light blue shirt. The unbuttoned collar gives the stylish ensemble a bit of vacation casualness.

"You look lovely tonight." He pulls me in for an awkward half-hug. His cologne has a crisp, woodsy scent.

"Thanks." I look down at the pale blue dress. "And thank you for all the new outfits."

"Anything for my princess. Ready for dinner?"

I grab my room card and my crossbody purse, then head out of the cabin.

Dad leads the way down the narrow hallway toward the elevator. He glances at me over his shoulder. "So, what did you do all day?"

"Mostly just hung out at the pool. What about you?"

"It's been fun catching up with a few old friends. I tried my hand at blackjack at the little casino, too."

"Any luck?"

One shoulder rises in a shrug. "Broke even."

When we reach the bank of elevators, he pushes the up arrow.

"Hey, do we have any excursions lined up for tomorrow's stop?" The doors of one of the elevators slide open, and we enter.

"Tomorrow is Labadee, Haiti. Since it's the cruise line's private island, it's more of a relaxing day. Ziplining, boating, beach time, a water park—that sort of thing. What do you feel like doing?"

"Beach time, for sure, and ziplining sounds fun."

"Sounds good to me."

The elevator stops moving, and the doors slide open. The noisy din of the dining room welcomes us. The first person I see is one of the elderly couples from the afternoon trivia game.

The older gentleman points at me. "There she is! I still can't believe you beat me in the 50s round."

I smile remembering the fun afternoon. "I was just lucky with the songs they chose."

His wife tucks her arm around her husband's. "Well, it was an impressive win. Congratulations."

"Thanks!" I wave goodbye, then continue toward the dining room, ignoring Dad's raised eyebrows. Let him wonder.

Linda, her husband—whatever his name is, and Mr. and Mrs. High School Sweethearts are already seated at the table. The men stand when we approach. I slide into the seat next to Linda.

I lean toward her, then point to the empty two chairs at the table. "Think they're both done with us already?"

Linda nods. "Most definitely. We ran into Will earlier today, and he told us his wife prefers dining in the more upscale restaurants onboard."

Her eyeroll makes me giggle.

"Hey, Phil. Good to see you." Dad stands to shake the hand of a man who approaches our table. The heavyset man with the bad combover is one of the know-it-alls who sat next to us at the trivia game.

Phil's gaze shifts from me to Linda. "Wade, is this your wife and daughter?"

Dad places his hand on my shoulder. "This is my daughter, Liz."

Linda reaches out her hand. "I'm Linda, Matt's wife."

Matt! That's his name.

Mr. Combover shakes his hand. "Well, you two make a formidable team. Although, you did really win by default. Tank and I clearly answered first to some of those questions."

His arrogance reminds me of some of the jerks back at school who always have to be right. "Well, you might have beaten us if you had actually answered the first question instead of arguing with your buddy about which Madonna music video was the hottest."

Linda extends her hand toward me, which I high-five.

The big oaf grimaces. "Whatever. But when you're getting your massages, think of us."

A shiver runs down my spine. Ugh. No thank you.

The sore loser walks away, leaving our tablemates to stare at us.

"What was that about?" Mrs. High School Sweetheart asks.

Linda and I take our time sharing about the afternoon's activity. We exaggerate just a bit to make the story even more entertaining. Dad's approving smile warms my insides. I don't often see it.

Dad leans back in his chair. "Well, you couldn't have skunked a more deserving pair. Phil and Tank were the stars of the football team and always so arrogant. Tank was the one person I hoped wouldn't be on this cruise."

The arrogant part is easy to believe, but football stars? Hard to picture those overweight men as super-athletes.

Matt's head bobs in agreement. "Remember that time when our homecoming float won first place during the parade, but somehow before the big game, it was trashed? I'm still convinced Tank and Phil were behind that."

Mr. High School Sweetheart throws his head back. "Oh, man. I forgot about that. All that work we'd put into the float. But at least we got our picture on the front page of the paper."

"And below our photo was a picture of Tank and Phil and the story of the embarrassing loss by the football team." Amusement tinges Dad's words.

The adults all laugh. Amazing how times never change. Some of their stories sound just like what happens at my school. For the first time, I'm not dreading an evening of their reminiscing.

"Sounds like I'm missing all the fun." A female voice stops the laughter.

I look up to see a woman standing behind the empty chair next to Dad. Her shoulder-length, blond hair forms waves of beachy curls around her pretty face. The black cocktail dress shows off her thin figure.

Dad jumps to his feet. "Glad you could make it." He pulls out a chair for her.

Recognition creeps over me. This is the woman he was chatting with at the pool bar.

She settles into the seat, then Dad makes the introductions. "Gwen, you remember Matt, Paul, and Monica? This is Linda, Matt's wife."

Gwen smiles and nods at them all.

"And this is my daughter, Liz." He shifts his attention from blondie to me. "Since we lost some of our table mates, I asked Gwen to join us." Dad places his hand on my shoulder. I resist the urge to shake it off.

It's bad enough that he's been flirting with one of his old classmates, but now he's asked her to join us? This is *our* trip. How dare he.

~

I make it through dinner, although my earlier good mood has vanished as fast as a shooting star. Linda tries to engage me in conversation as the other classmates laugh and joke, but I'm unable to move past my anger at Dad for inviting some woman to sit at our table. I knew this trip was a bad idea—just like over the summer.

Last spring, when he insisted I spend my entire summer break in Chicago with him instead of my usual week, I reluctantly agreed. I hadn't even been in the Windy City for more than an hour before the forecast changed and the storm descended when he surprised me with Cassie—his much younger girlfriend. Dad had dated women off and on since the divorce, but Cassie was the start of something different. His hair, his clothing, his attitude—it all changed. He suddenly was acting like someone I didn't know. Cassie may be long gone, but his mid-life-crisis attitude, obviously, is not.

I watch as he leans intently toward Gwen as she tells a story, absorbing her words.

Those summer trips to Chicago used to be an anticipated adventure. At first, he'd take off work, and we'd fill our days with fun trips to the zoo, the lake, the museums. As I got older, he started working part of the week but still managed to take me shopping along the Miracle Mile, and we'd squeeze in at least one tourist attraction. Then even those excursions dwindled away, leaving me to fend for myself most days alone at his apartment complex. His priorities became apparent. So, his suggestion for me to visit for the whole summer came completely out of the blue. I often wondered if it had been Cassie's idea.

After the remnants of our dinner are cleared away, I tag along with the group to the evening show in the large theater, hoping the entertainment will make me feel better about being the seventh wheel in our group.

The variety show of singers, dancers, and a ventriloquist nudges away my anger for a short while but mostly makes me wish I were on stage and not stuck in the audience. The evening's entertainment ends with the cruise director, Miles, telling a few jokes, then sharing some information about our first stop—Labadee, Haiti. At least a beach day is something to look forward to.

When the lights turn on, the aisles immediately fill with people anxious to get to their next fun activity. Our group of seven lingers. The men stand while the ladies remain in the comfy theater chairs.

"That was a great show." Linda turns to look at me. "What did you think?"

While the performances were quite entertaining, they hadn't improved my ruined mood. I force a smile. "Yeah, they were really talented."

"Anyone up for a nightcap in one of the lounges?" Mr. High School Sweetheart asks.

While some of the group readily agrees, Linda and Dad both turn their eyes toward me.

"Please, go do what you want. I think I'll…" I'm about to say, "turn in," but it's probably only like 8:30. "Maybe I'll check out the teen activities." There is no possible way I'm going to the dumb teen lounge, but they don't need to know that.

I've seen the groups of teens swarming the ship. I don't know if they all knew each other before the trip or not, but I have no interest in spending my vacation trying to fit in with the cool kids. I've been snubbed by the so-called in-crowd for three years back at home. Why would I want to subject myself to more of it while on vacation? Especially going in solo. If I had a sibling or a friend, then maybe—but alone? No possible way.

"Well, if you're sure," Dad says.

I stand. "Yep, I'm sure. You all have a great evening."

Linda squeezes my hand. I smile at her gesture of solidarity, then join the migrating crowd heading out to do who knows what.

Once I'm free from the claustrophobic confines of the crowd, I head for the first door leading outside. Strolling along the deck, I stare out into the inky darkness. When I reach the front of the ship, I rest my forearms against the railing, admiring the moonlight shimmering off the ocean. A thin veil of clouds drifts away, in perfect dramatic fashion, to reveal a backdrop of twinkling stars. The celestial masterpiece is breathtaking. If only I had someone to share the moment with.

The thousands of stars remind me of when I was little and used to wish on stars. It's tempting to indulge my inner child, but I have no idea what I'd wish for. Really, something, anything, more than my life is now.

As I continue my stroll, all the canoodling couples become apparent. So much for an evening walk—the over-abundance of happiness is a little nauseating.

After a lap around the outside of the ship, I wander through the crowded pool deck where families are camped out watching a superhero movie on the giant screen. I head back inside, past a lounge that is now a makeshift dance club playing 80s and 90s tunes, no doubt in honor of the reunion. I pick up my pace. The bright lights of the casino reveal a room full of people. Their overly exaggerated mannerisms and loud laughter make it appear that they've had a little too much to drink. The center of the promenade is much quieter, full of tables stacked with jewelry, handbags, and other merchandise, while the shops that line the space look as neglected as a stood-up prom date.

Music draws me toward the end of the promenade to a small nook where a pianist is taking song requests from the crowd that packs the space. I recognize him as the entertainer from last night's reunion welcome event. Tonight, he's playing for a more appreciative audience. Finally, a place I wouldn't mind staying, but sadly, every inch is packed with nowhere to sit, so I keep on moving.

Everywhere I go, the smiling faces of the passengers make my solitary aloneness even more apparent. Why can't I be back at home? But would it be any different? As great as Josie is about making time for me, she now has Ryan. It's just not like it used to be. We no longer spend "every waking moment together," as her dad used to joke. Is this the way the next year and a half will be? Do I have to continue treading water until I head off to college and start a new chapter of my life?

Frustrated, I finally give up and head back to my room. I can enjoy the ocean view there as well as anywhere. I try not to dwell on the eerie quiet of the long narrow hallway as everyone else is upstairs having fun.

Well, almost everyone. The door on the far side of Dad's room opens, and Dad's nemesis, Tank—the obnoxious man from the trivia game—emerges. What luck, he and Dad are in neighboring rooms.

His wife's shrill voice shatters the silence. "Get over it!"

Tank slams the door shut, then staggers down the hall, luckily in the opposite direction of me—another encounter with him would not be enjoyable. From the looks of it, he'd be better off staying put and sleeping off his binge drinking instead of heading out presumably for another round. Well, the raging hangover he'll most likely wake up to couldn't happen to a more deserving guy.

When I swing the door open, the lights in my room are on, and my gaze is immediately drawn to a dog made from white towels, sitting on my bed. My sunglasses are perched on his little towel head. Aww… Finally, something worthy of a photo. I've got to share this with Mom and Josie. I grab the pre-paid phone from the desk where it's been sitting since Dad gave it to me. There, I used the phone. That should make him happy.

I plop the phone back on the desk then grab the bag I took with me to the pool this morning. Time to pack up for our excursion tomorrow. As I remove the unneeded items, my fingers brush a piece of paper. The task at hand flits out of my mind as I pull out a folded note. Curious, I open it.

A quiet place to be contemplative or to be swept away by a thousand adventures. The Islands we visit may hold the Treasure you seek.

The hand-printed words stare blankly at me. I turn the paper for any clues. The backside shows the mysterious words were written on one of the ship's notepads.

I read it again, trying to decipher the meaning. It sounds like a clue, reminding me of the Easter riddles Mom used to write. In order to make Easter morning a little more exciting, Mom used to hide my basket and create these elaborate scavenger hunts. Am I supposed to search for something?

I sink onto the bed next to my little towel friend. Is this note even for me? How did it get there? Maybe someone slipped it into the wrong bag.

My mind replays the day. I had the bag with me at the pool. Before the guy dripped water all over me, I was asleep, and my bag was sitting next to me. Lunch was spent at the pub in the promenade. The bag sat on the chair next to me. Several people stopped and talked to me there: that little old lady, the waitress, and Cole. Then I spent the afternoon with Linda and the crowd of people at the trivia game where my bag hung from the back of my chair. So basically, anyone could have stuck this note in there. But why?

There's only one way to find out—solve the riddle.

Chapter 4

"Smile!" commands the abundantly cheerful male photographer who's snapping photos of passengers as we make our way down the dock for our beach day. The ship, in all its magnificence, is the backdrop of this photo op.

Dad pulls me closer while I force a smile, afraid to disobey the overly energetic crew member. Years from now when I come across this photo, what feelings will it invoke? Sadness—remembering another failed father/daughter event? Anger—because I missed out on the most epic holiday season back in Minnesota? Fondness—as it was the first time I met my future stepmom, Gwen? Thankfulness—for discovering my unknown desire to be a cruise ship entertainer? Confusion—as I still wonder why Dad wanted me to take this trip with him. Only time will tell.

As we make our way down the long dock, I scan the fellow passengers around us. Could one of these people be the mysterious note writer?

"So, how do you want to spend the day?" Dad interrupts my pondering.

"Let's start at the beach so we can stake out beach chairs in the front row." Priorities.

"Okay."

I glance at him as we walk. He's looking very nautical today with his designer shades and jaunty captain's hat. "So, who's that Gwen person? You seemed rather friendly."

His focus doesn't veer from our destination, but the corner of his mouth twitches up into a grin. "Yeah, it was fun to run into her."

I allow the silence to linger for a moment, hoping he'll keep talking.

He rubs his stubbly face as if he's trying to wipe away the smile. "She and I actually dated for a while during our senior year."

Ah…Old flames reignited. Gross. "How long did you date?"

His head tilts and peers at me above the rim of his sunglasses. "We were part of a group that did a lot together that winter. It was brutally cold that year, so we had a lot of game and movie nights." His jaw twitches before he again turns his attention straight ahead. "Somewhere along the way, we became more than friends."

When we reach the end of the wooden boardwalk, I slip off my shoes and let the sand sift through my toes. The warmth of the soft, fine grains makes me smile as I picture Josie back in Minnesota pulling on her snow boots. Suddenly, I'm missing home a little less. "So, what happened between you two?"

He leads the way to the rows of brightly colored beach chairs and umbrellas enticingly set in front of the crystal-blue water that laps onto the shore. His eyes squint, whether from the morning sunbeams shining off the ocean or from deep thought, one can only guess. "We went out a few times and had some laughs. But since we were soon graduating, it wasn't the time to start anything serious."

As I avoid the tiny crab skittering sideways across the sand, I try to picture the younger versions of Dad and Gwen. I've seen a few photos of him from high school. He was athletic and fit. She probably had the big hair that was popular way back when. She looks good for her age now, so she was probably thin and cute. They would've made one of those nauseatingly pretty couples—an 80s version of Ken and Barbie.

As we approach the line of chairs, a man motions for us to come to him. His beaming white smile matches his pleated white shorts and white polo shirt, emphasizes his ebony skin. Instead of speaking, he motions to a set of chairs and an umbrella, his eyebrows raised.

Dad turns to me with the identical look of query.

"Yes, thank you. This will be perfect."

Dad's expectant expression relaxes while the man's smile widens even more. He sprints to a nearby shack, returning just as quickly with an armload of towels. As I arrange them on the chairs, he adjusts the umbrella so the tops of our lounge chairs are shaded. What service. Dad thanks him, then hands him a folded-up bill. The man bows in gratitude, then scurries off to assist another family.

I pull off my coverup and nestle into my chair. "I thought Haiti was super poor. I've seen pictures of run-down towns and overcrowded villages. Think they're near here?"

Dad leans back in his chair. "I haven't looked at a map, but I assume those areas are on the other side of the island."

I'm struck by a strange twinge of annoyance as I watch our fellow tourists with their fancy beach bags, designer sunglasses, and fashionable sandals migrate onto the beach. "Do you think the Haitian people are helped by all the tourists that come here?"

He rolls his head toward me. "I hope so. I don't know anything about their government, but you often hear how corrupt officials pocket tourism money, and the natives never see any."

"That's horrible." The beautiful new clothes I received for the trip flash into my mind.

Dad must read my thoughts. "But tourism does help. Think of all the workers on the cruise ship. They come from all over the world. Because of people who can afford to take vacations, they are able to have jobs and send money back home to their families."

"Yeah, I suppose." His words ease my guilt—slightly.

"Hey. The cruise director said there are some shops run by locals away from the beach. Why don't we walk over there this afternoon and buy some of the handcrafted items?"

"Really? Thanks, that would be great." There's not much I can do to help, but I can shop. Hopefully, that will give a few people a little extra money for their families.

One of Dad's classmates stops to chat with Dad on his way to the water, his two sons in tow. The young boys squirm through the standard introductions. Once the torturous pleasantries finish, the brothers race toward the ocean, splashing into the water. Dad and his friend end their brief conversation with some odd salute before the man scurries after his progeny.

Well, there's one benefit to this trip—witnessing a whole new side to my dad. Not sure it will help our relationship, but at least it's entertaining. "Is it strange seeing all your high school friends after so many years?"

He settles back in this chair. "Yeah. I've kept in touch with a few buddies. But I do have to say, it's a little odd seeing everyone again."

That I can believe. "Are you glad you came?"

"Yeah, it's fun." He cocks his head to the side, then turns to look at me. "What's really strange is realizing that the last time I saw most of these people was when I was about your age. Seeing them all brings back a lot of memories that don't feel like they happened all that long ago."

I lean back and watch the people splashing in the ocean, not sure I'll ever want to attend a high school reunion. Living it the first time has been less than pleasant. Why would I ever want to relive it?

"I assumed everyone would have changed over the years," he continues. "And maybe they have, but it seems like people revert back to their old ways." He lets out a little laugh. "That's why it was so great that you skunked Tank in that music trivia game. That guy was always such a pompous jerk who knew everything. Having him fail at something is oddly satisfying."

"Well, glad to help you out and put him in his place." I grin at the memory.

Dad pulls a tube of sunscreen out of his bag and begins lathering himself up. "I didn't know you were such a music aficionado."

I lower my sunglasses to look at him. Is he serious?

He raises one hand, white with lotion, in protest. "I know you love musical theater, but it sounds like you knew all the tunes from the 50s and 80s."

I settle back. "Well, Linda knew most of the 80s songs. Of course, I knew some of the classics. As for the 50s, that's all Josie and I listened to during *Bye Bye Birdie*."

"Sounds like it was a fun trivia game." He offers me the sunscreen.

I take the tube, then reach over to rub his shoulder until the streaks of white lotion disappear.

He laughs. "Thanks, kid."

"I have my dignity. I can't be seen with a splotchy, sunburnt dad." I squeeze a dab onto my hand.

He leans back, then starts patting the seat around his body in search of something. "Have you seen…"

"They're on your head."

He reaches up and feels his sunglasses. "What would I do without you?"

I honestly don't know how the man functions sometimes. "Hey, there are a bunch of fun activities scheduled at that lounge. You should join me at one of them."

His face turns all goofy puppy doggish. "Deal. Next one—I'm there."

A tiny spark of joy shoots through me. It would be nice to be like all the other families and do a few things on the ship together. "So, tell me some stories from your high school days."

He adjusts the brim of his hat. "Well, I do have a few good ones."

—

Returning from our shopping spree at the makeshift shopping district, an out-of-control volleyball bounces across our path.

A man sporting a torn Van Halen t-shirt jogs after it. He stops in front of us, bent over, his hands on his thighs.

Dad pats the man on the back. "Having fun, Greg?"

Greg grimaces but offers a thumbs up. "We could use another player or two," he manages to utter between gulps of air.

Dad turns to me. "How about it? Up for some volleyball?"

My head immediately begins swaying back and forth. "Nope. You know that sports and I don't get along so well. But go ahead. I'd like to work on my tan a bit more." Coming back from winter break with a killer tan is about the only perk for missing all the winter fun back home. Of course, with my pale skin, it's highly doubtful, but a girl can dream.

His head tilts. "You sure?"

I flick him away. "Go have fun."

"Okay. Want to text when you're ready to head back to the ship?"

"Um…sorry. I don't have the phone with me. Let's just meet back at the beach chairs."

He nods, then follows his friend toward the beach. "Don't hurt yourself, old man!"

"Ha-ha," he calls over his shoulder as his buddy punches his arm.

I shift my bulging bag from one shoulder to the next.

"Eliza!"

I turn toward Cole's familiar voice.

He's standing with a boy and a girl who both have that unsure-of-themselves middle school look. I wave, then walk over.

Cole nods toward my stuffed-to-the-max bag. "You come well prepared for a day at the beach."

I slide the bag off my aching shoulder and set it at my feet. "Dad and I were just doing a little souvenir shopping."

Cole's dark eyebrow raises. "A little?"

"Just trying to help the local economy one hand-crafted item at a time." I hadn't planned on buying so much, but it was nearly impossible to say no to all the men selling goods from their ramshackle huts. Each desperate plea for us to look at their merchandise tugged at my heart as I pictured hungry children back in Port-au-Prince. So now I am the proud owner of several woven shoulder bags, multiple rope and seashell bracelets, a cute pair of sandals, a hand-carved wooden nativity set for mom, two sun hats, a rosary for Josie, a hand-crafted harmonica for Ryan, and a toy sword whittled from a piece of driftwood for Josie's little brother. My best friend's two main fellas are the lucky beneficiaries of my inability to say no to the native vendors.

"Hey, have you met Mia and Connor?" The beautiful Asian girl ducks her head as she gives a shy smile. Connor nods in greeting, causing a strand of pale blond hair to slip down his forehead, covering one eye.

Cole is certainly a man of mystery. How many teens would befriend his father's classmates' middle school kids? But witnessing his welcoming friendliness causes a small stab of remorse as a flash of a memory zips through me.

Josie and I were about eight and hanging out at the park. I convinced her to help me round up all the random kids at the playground to join us in an impromptu game of capture the flag. What happened to that outgoing little girl who wanted to make sure no one was ever excluded? Not a hard question to answer. She went to high school and was bullied into self-submission. It didn't take long to learn that if you wanted to stay out of the line of fire, you kept your head low and worried only about yourself.

I offer a smile to the two innocent middle schoolers. "Nice to meet you. I'm Liz."

Mia exchanges a look with Connor, probably wondering about my real name since Cole insists on calling me Eliza. She then turns her dark-brown eyes toward me. "We are going up to the zipline. Want to join us?" Mia's voice is airy and light, exactly how you'd expect an angel to sound.

I glance up at the large hill. My stomach flips as I watch one of the zipliners soar down the wire toward the ocean.

"And then we're going to the water park," Connor adds.

The blowup slides and bouncing items bobbing in the water did look rather fun.

Cole nods. "Whaddya say?"

"Yeah, absolutely." What better way to spend the afternoon? The tan can wait.

～

"Liz, you look lovely this evening," Linda tells me. Her husband and Mr. High School Sweetheart stand again as we arrive at the table.

"Thanks." Tonight is one of the two designated formal evenings in the dining room, so I took extra care getting ready. The pale aqua-green dress with halter straps and matching shawl seemed perfect for the evening and my mood. Today's fun had exceeded my expectations.

I settle in next to Linda as usual. Dad takes a moment as he decides where to sit. Since our other tablemates seem to have permanently ditched us, the two empty chairs make for awkward conversation. He's most likely trying to decide if he should sit next to me or closer to his buddies and not have to yell across the table.

"I saw you out enjoying the water playground," Mrs. High School Sweetheart says in greeting. "I was tempted to join, but all that bouncing sounded a little too jarring on my back."

"Yep. Playing is for the young." Dad winces as he settles into the chair next to me. His volleyball game ended with a twisted ankle and sore back. Although, knowing Dad, he was probably trying to prove he's still as athletic as his eighteen-year-old self.

"You didn't have to go diving for all the balls, ya know." Matt confirms my suspicions.

"I wasn't about to let Moody and Fraley win. The pain is nothing compared to the agony of defeat."

The men all raise their glasses in salute of Dad's nonsensical words.

"At least Tank didn't join in and ruin the game," Mr. High School Sweetheart adds.

His wife reaches for her drink. "You needn't worry about that. I ran into his wife, Renee, earlier, and she told me they rarely leave the ship when they take a cruise. Sometimes they might go ashore to shop, but usually while us peasants run off on our silly excursions, they reap the benefits of any empty ship, being treated like royalty, and pampered all day."

Dad raises his glass again. "Well, here's to us peasants. And to beating Moody and Fraley."

"Here, here!" his cohorts cheer.

Mrs. High School Sweetheart shakes her head. "You three haven't changed a bit." Which gets them talking about another "classic" time their posse went up against Moody and Fraley.

While they're enthralled with the tale, after about ten seconds, I'm bored, so turn to Linda with the quandary that's been bouncing around my head all day. So much for the let-your-mind-subliminally-work-on-it system. I haven't been able to get the mysterious note out of my head. "Hey, what comes to mind when you hear the phrase, 'a quiet place to be contemplative or to be swept away by a thousand adventures?'"

Her face scrunches a bit as she ponders the words. "A quiet place full of adventures makes me think of a library."

I nod in agreement. "Right? But it has something to do with this ship. And it's not like there's a library on board." I reach for my water glass.

"Sure there is."

My eyes widen. "Seriously? There's a library? Where?"

She taps her index finger against her chin. "I think maybe deck seven or eight? It's not a huge library, more of a reading room. But there are shelves of books and cozy chairs."

"Thanks, I'll have to check it out tomorrow since we have another day of cruising."

"Glad I could help." She turns her attention to her menu.

I study her profile. Could it have been Linda who snuck the note into my bag? She didn't seem all that curious as to why I was deciphering a random saying. Maybe she knows I'm bored and is trying to add some excitement to the trip.

After the six of us place our dinner orders, the conversation shifts to the evening's festivities. There's another show in the theater, a blackjack tournament in the casino, a movie being shown poolside, the karaoke night in the Starlight lounge, some kind of a couples' gameshow event, as well as the usual lounges with their various live music.

"After the show, I think we're going to the newlywed game show. We'll see how well my bride knows me." Mr. High School Sweetheart winks at his wife.

Dad pats his friend's shoulder. "Sounds like a bad idea. You'll never live it down if you don't get every answer right. I wish I could come watch, but I'm heading to the dance club."

I sit up. "But Dad, you promised you'd go with me to the Starlight lounge."

Four sets of eyes dart between the two of us as uncomfortable silence descends.

Dad glances at his friends, then at me. "I didn't know you meant tonight. I figured the games were all during the day on our days at sea, like yesterday."

My fists clench the hem of my skirt. "No. Tonight is the start of the karaoke event."

Our tablemates shift in their seats and look away. Who could blame them? I also wish I could be anywhere else at the moment.

"Oh. Sorry, hon. I'd already made plans with Gwen."

The burning anger scorches my insides. Gwen. Of course. I just nod my reply, positive my words would come out in a blast of bitterness. Why am I even bothering with this stupid novena?

Nothing ever changes. The ensuing silence doesn't last long, as our meals are delivered, and new topics are discussed.

Dad changes seats and moves closer to his buddies, leaving a void between us that is much larger than the two empty chairs that separate us.

Chapter 5

Dragging along like a zombie, I slip into the Starlight lounge and make my way to an open chair against the wall. Who cares that I'll have a lousy view of the stage? It will give me the privacy to be alone in my misery. The hot Hispanic-looking guys from the pool deck band entertain the crowd with a medley of Latin pop songs. I close my eyes and let the music sweep over me.

Why did I think Dad would come with me tonight? It's stupid to care so much. But after the great day we'd had together on the beach, the sting of being rejected for Gwen cut me to the core.

I'm such an idiot. I know better. Raising my hopes always ends in disaster. After my parents' divorce, I discovered that the pain was more bearable if I turned off my feelings. I often pictured myself shoving my emotions into a box and hiding it deep inside my heart. Mom was so distraught by the whole ordeal that she seemed relieved by how well I was dealing with the destruction of our family. Only Josie knew my true feelings. She was the one who let me huddle in her room and cry for hours.

But over time, worried that Josie would tire of me too, I plastered on a brave face and acted like I was over it. That burying of emotions came in handy once we started high school. Our enthusiasm for the new adventures of high school quickly ended when Josie and I realized what a horrible place it really was. The popular upperclassmen ruled the place. They deemed who was worthy of

being accepted. The rest of us were fair game for ridicule and har-
assment. After years of practice, it wasn't hard for me to shut myself off and become invisible, but poor, accident-prone, free-
spirited Josie struggled to stay under the radar.

Thankfully, I haven't felt that desperate need to protect myself
over the last few months. I assume it's because we're now upperclassmen, so no longer preyed upon, but could Ryan and Josie's
safe place plan actually be changing the culture at the school?
Whatever the reason, losing that protective shell was a big mis-
take. Because at dinner, it all came crashing down on me again.

I squeeze my eyes shut, refusing to let the threatening tears
out. Why can't I just get over it? Tons of people have divorced
parents. What is wrong with me?

"Miss? Miss?"

So caught up in my thoughts, it takes me a moment to realize
someone is speaking to me. My eyes pop open to see a waitress
standing in front of me.

"Oh! Sorry. Just lost in my thoughts."

She smiles. "I was just wondering if I could get you something
to drink?"

"Sure, could I get a Shirley Temple?" Maybe the feel-good
drink from my childhood will improve my mood.

She jots down my order. "One ginger ale with cherry juice
coming up." She places a pencil and two squares of paper on my
table. "By the way, anyone can decide to join the karaoke competition. You just have to jot down your name and the song you'd
like to sing on this paper and hold it up. One of the staff will come
by and grab it."

"Oh, thanks, but I'm just here to enjoy the performances."

When the band finishes their set, I join in the applause as the
cruise director, Miles, takes to the stage. He shakes hands with the
band's lead singer and takes over the microphone.

"Let's hear it for The Mambo Boys. Aren't they fantastic?
They will be sticking around during our karaoke night, so if you
feel like buying them a drink, I'm sure they wouldn't say no." The
audience chuckles. "But the possibility of free drinks is not the
only reason they will be watching tonight's performances. Tonight
starts our Siren of the Sea competition. This evening will be your
typical karaoke competition where contestants will sing along with

the tracks of music. Those singers who get enough votes will be singing again in a few days, accompanied by The Mambo Boys!" He motions toward the band, who wave at the crowd. The announcement is met with more applause and some high-pitched whistles.

"Then finally, on our final night of the cruise, the finalists will perform on the main stage with our house orchestra, where the Siren of the Sea will be crowned!" He pauses again for the raucous applause. "So here are the rules. Your servers placed a few pieces of paper and a pencil on your tables. As the evening progresses, keep track of your favorite singers. You can vote for up to eight individuals to move on to the next part of the competition. At the end of the night, turn in your list, and we will compile the answers. The eight singers with the most votes will perform here in the Starlight lounge on New Year's Eve, after our stop in Curacao. The other piece of paper is in case you want to join the fun and choose a song to sing tonight. And the last rule is a reminder that we are all here to have a good time, so no matter how dreadful someone is"—he makes a distasteful face—"we will all be supportive." The audience laughs. "All right. Who's ready to get started?"

More clapping and catcalls.

"Excellent. Okay, so our first contestant is Millie Medved!"

Two tables loudly cheer as an elderly woman makes her way to the stage.

The cruise director welcomes her. "Wow, Millie. Sounds like you brought your own fan club."

"Yes, Miles, that's my husband, my children, and my grandchildren." She waves at the rowdy bunch.

"All right, well, do them proud!"

He steps away, and she grasps the microphone, then stares at the monitor in front of her. The lights dim as the opening notes to "White Christmas" fill the room.

Millie starts a little timid, but as the song continues, her confidence increases. Soon the whole lounge is singing along with her. Grandma Millie does a great job. She's followed by a few folks—some good, some horrific, but all entertaining. And then it happens.

I should have known that sitting still and simply listening would be impossible. The urge to sing overwhelms me. Only one song comes to mind. I jot it down. Even though the chances of them having this musical theater song in their karaoke machine are slim, I don't want to risk the news of my performance getting back to my dad, so I use an alias, writing down the first name that comes to mind.

I hold my paper in the air, and one of the staff members collects it. People around the room also raise their hands. There probably won't be enough time for all the want-to-be-performers to participate. As more contestants sing, I keep track of those I'll vote for to move on to the next round.

After a cringe-worthy duet, Miles walks to the microphone. "Well, folks. We are running out of time." He pauses as the boos fill the air. We only have time for one final performance."

I hold my breath while the crowd settles down, not sure if I actually want to perform or not, after all.

"Please welcome, Josie DelRio!"

It takes a moment to realize—it's me! Of course, I had to use my bestie's name. She's known for diving right in without weighing all the possible outcomes—like I just did. I stand and make my way to the front of the stage while the audience politely claps.

"Josie will be singing 'On My Own' from the musical *Les Misérables*."

I perch myself on the stool, smoothing my skirt down around me, I glance around the room, but the stage lights blind me. Since I've been in so many shows, they don't bother me; instead, they empower me. And since I don't know anyone in this lounge, my nerves remain calm.

My eyes close, and I'm instantly transported back in time. At the end of my freshman year, I chose this song for my voice teacher's end-of-the-year recital. I was so excited because Dad was driving in from Chicago for the event. He hadn't been able to make it to any of the shows I'd been in that year. I'd repeatedly told myself that it was no big deal since I'd just been in the chorus, but this recital was different. I knew that I sang this song well and couldn't wait for Dad to see how much I'd improved. But an hour before Mom and I were to leave for the recital, we got the phone call. Dad was not in his car driving from Chicago to Minnesota like he was supposed to be. He was still in a meeting in his office and wouldn't make it.

The beautiful strains of the song begin. I take a breath and begin singing. Just like during that recital, I pour my heart into the song.

The lyrics of the love song once again take on new meaning in my mind. Instead of singing about an unattainable love, the longing for a father's attention fills the song with tangible sentiment.

The passion of the song continues to build with each line until the final crescendo.

All that pent-up frustration causes my voice to crack in the final, soft, heartfelt words of the song.

I squeeze my eyes shut to keep the tears from escaping.

The eruption of applause nearly knocks me off the stool. I was so into the song that I forgot where I was. I blink away the tears and smile. Through the blinding lights, I see a mass of standing bodies. A standing ovation? My gaze falls on a woman in the front row dabbing her eyes with her cocktail napkin. Did I just bring someone besides myself to tears? I bite my bottom lip to keep my emotions from bursting forth in a humiliating ugly cry.

Miles comes near and leans so close I breathe in his musky cologne. "Wow. That was amazing."

I nod my thanks, not trusting myself to speak. Before heading back to my seat, I take a little bow, knowing the simple gesture could never express my overwhelming gratitude.

As I pass tables, people tell me how much they enjoyed the song. Geez, if I only put more emotion into my auditions, I might have been getting better roles over the past few years.

Miles explains the tabulation process, then bids everyone goodnight. People begin to filter out of the lounge, a few wander over to me to let me know they voted for me.

One little girl drags her parents over to give me a hug. "You're the prettiest." Her big blue eyes shine up at me.

"Thanks. But I think you're the prettiest."

She giggles, then happily skips away, her parents following along.

Soon the lounge has cleared out except for one family playing cards, a couple who seems to be having a very intense conversation, staff cleaning off the table, and the hot Latin band sitting at a table on the other side of the room. I shift in my chair as I notice their intense eyes focused on me. Awkward. I give a small smile. Instead of returning the friendly expression, they stand and swagger across the stage toward me. They probably want to discuss the next round in the competition. Do I want to move on? I hadn't planned on singing, but it was awfully fun.

The quartet of smoldering masculinity rearranges the chairs around me, creating a barrier of Spanish manliness. One thing's for sure, with this much testosterone, nothing dorky could possibly break through.

While they may be exceedingly handsome, they seem to be lacking basic conversation skills. Their intense brown eyes bore right through me. Maybe it's a language barrier thing. Might as well initiate it. "Hi."

The lead singer nods, his chiseled jaw clenches. "Is your name really Josie DelRio?"

How to answer. Am I in trouble? Was it wrong to make up a name? Did they search the passenger manifest? I go with the truth. "Um…No. My name's Liz."

The drummer leans forward, his thick eyebrows furrowing as he rests his forearms on his knees. "Do you know Josie DelRio?"

I can't think of any good reason to answer that question. Best to reply with a query of my own. "Why?"

The lead singer's broad shoulders relax just a bit. "Forgive our manners. We just know a Josie DelRio and thought it odd that you used that name."

"That is odd, but I doubt you know my best friend."

He tilts his head, his eyes narrowing. "Is she from Minnesota?"

"Long light-brown hair?" queries the so-far-silent guitarist.

The fourth man crosses his arms. "Obsessed with musical theater?"

The drummer's hands clench. "Unusually clumsy?"

My eyes widen. They do know Josie.

The lead singer nods, recognizing my acknowledgment. "We met her last summer. My name's Valentine Consuelos, Val, and these are my cousins, Carlos, Marco, and Juan.

Realization finally strikes. "Oh! You're Niko's cousins." Niko was someone Josie dated briefly last summer when she spent a few months at her aunt's South Carolina beach house. In the far recesses of my mind, it does seem to ring a bell that his cousins, who were in a band on the island, worked on a cruise ship the other nine months of the year. "Wow. What a small world. I'm glad you said something. She'll be so surprised that we were on the same ship."

The conversation seems to have reached its natural conclusion, but they don't make a move to leave.

Valentine runs his hand through his thick, dark hair. "We need to get ready for our second show, but can we talk to you again tomorrow?"

"Ah...sure." They'll be wanting an answer about this competition. I have a lot to ponder.

"Can you meet us here tomorrow morning at eleven?" Carlos asks.

"Sure. See you then." How will I decide by then?

The guys answer with curt nods, looking as grim as ever. I watch them return to the stage—what an intense bunch. I stand, ready to finally leave, when a lone figure catches my eye. Leaning against the archway to the lounge is Cole. As I walk toward him, he starts clapping.

I offer a curtsy. "I take it you caught my performance?"

He grins. "You were amazing."

"Aww...you just say that to all the cruise ship karaoke singers."

His eyes widen with sincerity. "No, I'm serious. It was sensational. I didn't even know you could sing, or that your alias is Josie DelRio."

I laugh. "That's my best friend's name. I just wanted to sing for fun. I'm not sure I want to join the competition."

"Well, if you'd hoped to go incognito, that performance wasn't helpful." He glances toward the band. "Are they your new groupies?"

"Nah." I watch the cousins huddle together. Still hard to believe they know Josie.

"Good. 'Cause I want the job."

His warm smile turns my insides to goo. Leave it to me to find a great guy who lives ten states away from me.

"Want to stop by the ice cream shop to celebrate your roaring success? I'll even treat."

"Isn't the ice cream free?"

"Totally beside the point." He offers his bent arm to me. I wrap my arm around his.

~

After Cole receives his towering double-decker cookies and cream cone and I'm handed my single scoop of mint chocolate chip, we head to the nearest door to stroll around the deck of the ship.

He holds the door open for me. "So, since you didn't give your real name, what happens when your adoring crowd's votes don't count? I think people will be quite disappointed. You might single-handedly be the cause of the first cruise ship mutiny in maritime history."

"Wow. I would hate to be the cause of such social unrest." I take the first lick of my dessert. Yum!

"Seriously, though. I think maybe you should reconsider. You were fantastic."

As we walk, I turn my gaze to the vast, dark ocean. "We'll see. I'm just not sure I want to risk moving on and performing in front of everyone in the big theater."

"Why? It certainly didn't seem like you get stage fright."

I glance at him. "No, not usually. I don't know. I really sang it more for myself tonight."

His face softens. "That song has a lot of meaning to you, doesn't it?"

The sweetness in his voice causes my eyes to well up. Darn it. I turn the other way, blinking away the tears. "Yeah, kinda."

When we round the back of the ship, he veers toward the railing. I breathe in the salty sea air, listening to the gentle lapping of water against the boat.

He leans against the iron bars keeping his focus out toward the water. "Does it have something to do with your parents?"

I take another bite of my ice cream instead of answering. He's easy to talk to, but it's probably safer to keep it all bottled inside of me.

"I'm sure it's tough going through a divorce." I sense his gaze on my face. "Especially as an only child."

I lift one shoulder in a shrug. "Lots of people's parents are divorced." Am I the only one who can't move on?

"That doesn't mean it wasn't hard on you."

"It was hard, but it was a long time ago. That song just brought back a lot of memories." I turn to look at him. "Was it that obvious?" So much for bottling up my feelings.

He grins. "Sort of. But I've also noticed a wee bit of tension between you and your dad."

My eyebrows rise. "A *wee* bit?"

"Yep." He holds his thumb and forefinger close together. "Not that you need to take advice from me, but you obviously love singing. I think you should reveal your real name and join the competition."

My gaze shifts back to the vast expanse of water. What's stopping me?

I turn to look at him. "Well, if I step out of my comfort zone and do this, I think it's only fair if you do the same."

One of his dark eyebrows arches. "I'm pretty sure performing on stage is not out of your comfort zone, but since I'm requesting you do something you're not sure you want to do, I guess it's only fair to reciprocate. What are you challenging me to do?"

I lick my ice cream, contemplating the perfect thing. One thought slides into my mind. I waggle my eyebrows. "I hear the dancers onboard offer ballroom dancing lessons."

He closes his eyes and shakes his head. Just when I'm about to suggest something else, his eyes pop open.

"Fine. But ballroom dancing requires a partner, so unless you have someone in mind, you'll need to join me." He pops the last of his ice cream in his mouth.

Little does he know that I love to dance. Although, musical theater dancing has probably not prepared me for the waltz or the rumba, but why not.

I extend my hand. "You've got yourself a deal."

"Excellent." His warm hand slips into mine, sending a quiver down my spine.

Chapter 6

You'd think a day at sea with nothing going on would be extremely relaxing, but my day is suddenly surprisingly full. Besides
deciphering the odd clue, I'm supposed to meet with the Consuelos cousins, and now I've also committed to ballroom dancing
lessons. So much for my original plan of lounging by the pool all
day.

Only to fulfill my promise to Josie, the first item on my busy
agenda is to pray the novena. At least I'll be able to tell her I tried,
although I'm pretty sure it's a useless endeavor. After that is
crossed off my internal to-do list, I grab my bag, check to make
sure it's packed with all I'll need for the day, then head off to find
the library. I don't know who the note is from or if it's even for
me, but it certainly has piqued my curiosity, and added some excitement to this cruise.

After scanning the ship's directory, I find it on deck 9. The
interior room, painted an inviting shade of blue, is lined with dark
wood bookshelves, and offers several comfy seating areas. The
top half of the shelves hold books and nautical decorations, while
the bottom shelves are packed with games, puzzles, and movies.
As inviting as the space is, I'm the only one there. My enthusiasm
drops at the realization that there is no apparent organization to
the hundreds of books. Oh well, it probably doesn't matter. I have
a suspicion of a book title that I may be searching for, but without

internet access, there's no way to find the author—a painstaking quest.

The note mentioned the words *island* and *treasure*, and I'm pretty sure there's a famous book titled *Treasure Island*. There's only one way to find out if my hunch is correct.

So, with an audible sigh, I get to work scanning each book's spine. My systematic search begins with the bookshelf to the left of the entrance, starting with the top shelf and working my way down. The task is tedious, and I keep losing focus. When my vision blurs, or I realize I haven't been paying attention, I backtrack and repeat a few shelves. Finally, when I'm about halfway around the room, my gaze zeros in on what I'm looking for—*Treasure Island* by Robert Louis Stevenson.

With the hardcover book in hand, I curl up on the nearest couch. A quick flip through the musty tome releases a piece of paper which flutters out from between the pages. A burst of excitement surges through me. I smooth out the creases of the folded note and lay it on my lap to reveal a short message printed in block letters.

G24 THE BEST VIEW ON THIS SHIP

I reread the words trying to reveal any secret message. How can there be one best view? *Stop being so literal—it's a clue.* Okay— think. Where would there be a good view? From someone's room? No. There are no letters in the stateroom numbers. On the deck? Yes! The lifeboats are marked with letters and numbers. I pull out my room card, which lists my lifeboat number. C12. Now to find G24.

I glance at the clock on the wall. Darn—that search will have to wait. It's just about time to meet up with the Consuelos boys. My disappointment quickly shifts to curiosity. Why were they insistent that we meet? Could they be the ones behind this mysterious scavenger hunt? Time to find out. I replace the book and stuff the note in my bag before heading out the door.

Even though I arrive at the Starlight Lounge a few minutes early, the Latin hotties are already waiting for me. Their broad shoulders nearly touch as they lean in toward the center of the table where they're sitting. Low voices, creased brows, and set jaws slow my steps not wanting to interrupt their family powwow. As soon as one set of dark eyes spots me, the cousins quickly stand. I try to remember all their names. The tall intense lead singer is Val. The drummer with the curlier hair is Marco. The slightly shorter guitarist with broad shoulders is Carlos, and the quiet keyboardist is Juan.

"Thanks for meeting us." Not a surprise that Val is the first to speak. He gestures to an open seat.

I sit, and in unison, they also sink into their chairs.

Juan clenches his hands. "We weren't sure you'd show up."

"Well, here I am." The four sets of dark eyes watching me cause me to squirm in my seat. "So, we're here to talk about the singing competition?"

Val lets out a deep breath. "No. Did Josie tell you much about her summer?"

They want to talk about Josie again? "A little." During my brief journey from the library, I scanned the far recesses of my brain, trying to remember anything Josie had said about these men. She'd been quite taken with their cousin Niko, at first. She gushed about him in her letters. Then, of course, there was the whole sticky situation involving the police that she helped them with.

Marco leans forward—his voice barely above a whisper. "Josie kinda did a little detective work last summer when she was on the island."

"Yeah, I heard a little about that. But I don't remember the details." Honestly, I was so shocked with her new relationship status that I didn't pay attention to any other part of her amazing tale.

"Do you do that kind of thing too?" Carlos asks.

My forehead crinkles. What's he talking about? "You mean like solve crimes?"

He nods, his gaze never leaving my face.

I shift in my seat again, not enjoying this odd interrogation. "Not really. Why?"

Silence follows my quite reasonable question.

Spokesman Val is again the first to speak. "We have a bit of a situation that we need help with. He tilts his head toward Juan. "The woman Juan dates is in a bit of trouble, and we want to help her."

I glance at the four men. Obviously, I'm missing something. "I don't understand. How could I possibly assist you?"

Juan squeezes his hands together, causing his veins to swell. "We don't know, but we need help."

His desperation stirs my compassion. "Well, what's going on?"

He focuses on his hands for a moment, then lifts his gaze to look me in the eye. "Rosaline has been accused of theft."

"She's one of the room attendants," Marco explains.

Juan leans toward me causing me to lean back as he invades my personal bubble. "But she didn't steal anything. She wouldn't."

I pull my bag against my chest, like a safety shield from the radiating intensity. How does this involve me? The lightbulb turns on. "Wait. You want me to prove her innocence?"

All four guys nod their answer.

How would I possibly do that? Just because Josie helped them once, why would they think I could do anything? I'm about to ask them but their pleading eyes stop me. I guess it doesn't hurt to ask a few more questions before turning them down. "How long has she worked for the cruise line?"

"For two years," Juan answers.

"When did the trouble begin?"

Val shakes his head. "She'd never had any complaints until our last trip. After the passengers departed, a couple filed a report that a valuable piece of jewelry was missing."

Juan finally leans back, giving me more space to breathe. "Rosaline is so distraught. She needs this job. She's the only member of her family working."

Marco squeezes his cousin's shoulder. "She's from Haiti and was lucky to get this job, but it means she's away for long periods of time. She has two children who have to stay with her sister."

I picture the poor people I saw at our stop in Haiti—how thin they were, the pleading in their eyes, how anxious they were for us to purchase their handcrafted items. My heart goes out to this woman I haven't even met. "How horrible. You say she doesn't get to see her children very often?"

"No, only every few weeks for the hours when we are in port," Carlos answers. "Her sister drives across the island to bring the whole family closer."

Juan drops his head to his hands. "Yesterday was supposed to be one of the days she could visit them, but because of the accusation, she's not allowed off the boat or to do her job while they investigate." His voice cracks. "She was so heartbroken not to see her children."

Poor woman. "I'm so sorry, but I don't know how I can help."

Val rubs his jawline. "We don't know either, but we've got to think of something, and when Miles announced your name—well, Josie's—we thought maybe it was a sign that you could help somehow."

The four faces in front of me come into focus—their desperation tugs at my heart. There's no way I can turn these guys down. I squelch the inner voice telling me that this is not my problem, and I should just walk away. "I'll try to think of something, but I can't guarantee anything."

"Thanks for trying." Juan offers a weak smile.

"Do you think I could talk with Rosaline?" Might as well go all in.

The guys silently communicate through their exchange of looks.

Val nods. "We'll figure something out. Staff is supposed to limit their interaction with the guests, and she's pretty much confined to the staff quarters while they investigate, making it even more complicated. But we'll see what we can do and be in touch."

"Okay. I'll wait to hear from you." I stand to leave.

"Wait." Marco reaches out his hand but stops short of touching my arm. "We told Miles that we'd find out your real name."

"Yeah, you had the most votes." Carlos smiles like this is good news. "The staff was freaking out when they realized there was no Josie DelRio on the passenger manifest."

Even serious, leader-of-the-pack Val offers a grin. "You did great last night, and your fans would not be happy if you didn't participate in the next part of the competition."

My cheeks color at their kind words. "I wasn't planning on being part of the competition. I just had a moment of weakness."

Their smiles fall, like they don't want to be the ones to break the news to Miles that I won't participate.

"But," I continue, hoping to ease their worry, "I promised a friend that I would sing again if I had enough votes." Speaking of that friend—I glance at the clock on the wall. I hitch my bag on my shoulder and stand. "So, I guess I'll participate under my real name, Liz Kennedy. I've got to run, but I'll try to think of a way to help you out."

⁓

In the few minutes that remain before I need to leave for the large theater for the dance lessons, I swing by the sandwich shop. I carry my grilled turkey panini to one of the high-top tables next to a window. My teeth sink into my lunch, and I gaze out at the endless blue ocean.

How the heck am I supposed to help Rosaline? Why do they think I can do anything?

Despite the gorgeous view in front of me, there are a few images I can't get out of my brain: The worry lines etched into Juan's handsome face. The gaunt faces of the Haitian people selling their crafts with welcoming smiles despite some missing teeth. And one image from my imagination—two young children crying when they found out they couldn't see their mother this week. I have no idea how I can possibly help, but one thing is for sure—I've got to try.

Chapter 7

En route to the afternoon dance lesson, I detour along the boat's deck, scanning the lifeboat numbers, hoping to get an idea of where G24 would be located. It soon becomes apparent that the number on the lifeboat corresponds to the deck on which it can be found. And too bad for me—there is no twenty-fourth floor on this boat. Back to square one since that was my only idea.

I pull open the heavy door to the auditorium, and instantly, my frustration ebbs away like an outgoing tide. The cavernous room feels completely different without the bright lights that highlight the stage and the crowds of passengers. As always, the site of a theater brightens my mood.

Cole waves at me from the stage where he stands with a handful of people. I recognize several couples from Dad's reunion group. There are also a few elderly folks. One white-haired couple's hands are clasped together—adorable! Cole continues his conversation with a rather dashing older gentleman who, in his white pants and navy jacket, looks like he just strolled off his yacht. There is no doubt about it—we are the youngest participants.

"Oh, Liz!" I turn around to see Midge, my petite friend who told me about this event, walking down the aisle behind me. "I'm so glad you are joining us!" She wraps her thin arm around mine.

"You will just love Svetlana and Ivan. They are such amazing instructors."

She clings to me for support as we climb the steps to the stage. "Have you met Harold?" She guides me across the wooden stage toward Cole and the yacht-dude.

Taking a wild guess, I reach out my hand. "Hi, Harold. I'm Liz."

He grasps my outstretched hand, gently turns it palm down, then bows to kiss the back of my hand. "A pleasure to meet you, Liz." He next leans toward Midge and kisses her cheek.

I take a step closer to my dance partner. "And this is my friend Cole."

A clapping of hands draws our attention stage left. Two of the dancers from the evening shows glide onto the stage. Presumably, the tall, thin, graceful redhead in a flowing red dress is Svetlana, and her dark-haired, black-fitted-shirt-and-slacks partner is Ivan.

"Thank you all for joining us this afternoon." Svetlana welcomes us with a wave of her long arm.

"In a few hours, you will all be experts, no?" Ivan winks at one of Dad's classmates. The woman blushes, and the rest of the group chuckles.

As much as I love to dance, I'd be content just listening to our instructors' Russian accents all afternoon. I've never before realized how harsh and unsophisticated our American dialect sounds.

"Today, we will be teaching you the tango," Svetlana announces.

Our small group murmurs in response.

Cole's eyebrows shoot up, and he leans toward me. "There's still time to make a break for it."

I clamp onto his arm to keep him from escaping. "Nope. You're not going anywhere, that is if you want me to sing in the competition."

He grimaces. "The things I do for you."

"Let's get started," Svetlana purrs. "Each couple, find your space."

Cole and I take a few steps back. All other couples dutifully spread apart as well.

"Very good." Ivan nods his approval. "You all excelled at the first step."

Everyone chuckles again.

Ivan, with his perfect posture, takes a few steps to his left. "Each couple now must decide who will be the lead partner."

More chuckles.

"Once you have determined that major decision, that person will follow my steps."

All the men shift to be on the same side as Ivan.

Svetlana takes a step closer to Ivan. "Ladies, that means you are to give control to your partner. I know how difficult that might be, but in dancing, it is imperative to let your partner lead, or your tango will become more of a tangle."

Cue the polite laughs.

"Men," Svetlana continues, "the way you lead your partner is through your handhold. With gentle yet firm pressure from your hands, you will guide your partner."

For the next few minutes, Ivan shows the men their part. After they practice the eight basic steps, it is the ladies' turn. I recite the words in my mind as I imitate Svetlana's movement—forward, right, back, back, cross feet, back, left, close.

"Perfect!" Ivan encourages us after a few minutes. "Now for the fun part. Let's try it as a couple. Gentleman"—Ivan turns to look at Svetlana—"place your right hand on your partner's back. Ladies, place your left hand on your leading man's shoulder. Your free hands will meet at shoulder level, like this." He and Svetlana meld together. "Okay, now your turn."

I turn to look at Cole. He moves closer and places his hand on my back. His touch sends a ripple through my body. *Oh, dear.* What did I get myself into? I follow the instruction and place my left hand on his shoulder. We clasp our free hands.

"Wonderful," Svetlana tells us. "Now remember the Tango is a game of seduction. If you keep your gaze on each other, your bodies will become one."

A blush spreads through my entire body, but I force myself to look into Cole's eyes.

He bites his lip. Out of amusement or because he's equally uncomfortable, I'm not sure.

"All right," Ivan says, "let's try this together. Cue music."

We all watch Ivan and Svetlana, and when Ivan gives an exaggerated nod, we begin. I move forward like I'm supposed to, but instead of stepping backward, Cole also goes forward, and we crash into each other, my nose smashing into his chin.

A fit of giggles bubbles out of my mouth.

Cole drops my hand. "Sorry. But in all fairness, I warned you this was not a good idea."

I take his left hand with my right and place my left hand on his shoulder. "We are not giving up yet."

He grimaces but places his hand on my back. We are ready to try again.

After a few more mishaps, I begin reciting his steps for him while doing my own.

"Um, thanks, but how are you able to do that—saying the opposite movement of what you're doing?" Cole asks.

I shrug. "A hidden talent, I guess."

"Well, I'm impressed." He steps backward instead of moving forward.

"Don't talk; just concentrate," I scold.

He smirks. "Yes, ma'am."

While the students continue to practice the basic eight, our instructors mingle among us to offer suggestions. Out of the corner of my eye, I notice Svetlana watching us.

After everyone successfully completes the eight steps, she claps. "Very nice. Now, raise your eyes and look at one another instead of your feet."

Again, my cheeks warm as I look into those pools of chocolate brown. *Focus!* The gentle push of Cole's hand on my back leads me forward. Our gaze remains locked, and we move as one, perfectly gliding through the basic eight steps.

"Excellent!" Svetlana says to Cole and me. "You make a beautiful couple, on and off the dance floor."

My eyes drop to the floor, unable to look at Cole, but luckily, Ivan saves the day by announcing that it's time to move on to the next set of moves, the eight swivel steps, otherwise known as the *ocho* step.

Our feet tangle a few more times as we practice the swivel steps, but by the end of the lesson, we've got it down.

"Wonderful job, everyone. Make sure you keep practicing," Ivan tells the class.

I turn to Cole. "We did it!"

He shakes his head. "Only thanks to you and your patience. Hopefully, I didn't injure your toes."

"The bruises won't show if I wear close-toed shoes from here on out," I tease.

"You two were fabulous." Midge appears at my side. "I kept watching you and was so impressed."

"Thanks for mentioning the class. It was a lot of fun."

Cole takes a step closer. "Ah, so you are the one I have to thank for this."

She lets out a hearty laugh that seems more appropriate for a bulky sailor than a petite older woman. "You don't fool me. You were having a wonderful time."

His head tilts to the side. "Well, I'll admit it was more fun than I thought it would be, but I think Liz deserves a much more graceful partner."

"Nonsense," I tell him. "Dancing with you just makes me look even better."

He bows. "Glad to be of service."

Midge's eyes sparkle with glee as she squeezes my hand. "I will see you later." She turns and walks toward Howard, who is deep in conversation with Ivan.

Cole and I make our way down the side staircase of the stage, then continue up the slope of the auditorium aisle.

"Well, I did my part. Now you will do yours, right?" Cole nudges me with his shoulder.

I nudge him back. "Yes, I'll participate in the next phase of Siren of the Sea."

He stops walking and turns back to look at the stage. "Just think, in a few nights, you'll be here singing on that very stage."

"Don't get ahead of yourself. I still have to make it through the next part of the process." I stare at the stage, trying not to get my hopes up, but it would be fun to be up there singing in front of a packed house.

"That's just a minor detail."

Cole continues talking, but I don't hear any of the words. As I turn to walk up the aisle, my eyes lock onto the little brass plate on the arm of the row of theater chairs I'm walking past. The letter N indicates the row. It hits me. G24. Could that be a seat in this room? A ripple of excitement courses through me.

"Liz?" Cole touches my arm. "Are you all right?"

I glance at him. "Oh. Yeah. I'm fine. Hang on. Can you wait just a minute?"

Not waiting for his reply, I scurry off, heading back toward the stage until I find row G. Each seat is folded up against the backrest, brass plaques with the seat numbers aim toward the towering ceiling. With growing excitement, I continue toward the center of the row until I reach seat 24. I turn and look at the stage. This is the center seat of the row—the perfect view.

I quickly search around the comfy seat. Is there another clue here somewhere? My hand feels around the velvety material, and on the backside of the cushion, where the material tucks into the metal rim, I spy a white slip of paper. I pinch it between my nails and slide it out. Cole stands in the aisle, his hands in his pockets, watching me. I give him a little finger wave. Should I share this search with him? While it would be fun to uncover these clues together, something inside me wants to keep this little mystery to myself. I discretely slip the paper into my bag.

"Sorry," I say when I reach him. "Just checking on something."

His eyebrows raise. "Okay. Need any help?"

"Nope. I'm good." With one last backward glance, I head toward the exit of the auditorium.

"Well, I think we did pretty well, overall." Cole pulls open the auditorium door for me.

"What? Oh. Yes, now we just need to find someplace where we can show off our new skills."

"I don't know about your hometown, but the tango is all the rage where I live." His teasing tone makes me smile.

I love this guy's sense of humor. And his amazing smile. Heck, his whole face is pretty nice to look at. My emotions swirl like they're being stirred together in a pot. Why couldn't he live closer?

When we reach the door to the deck, he holds it open for me. "So, are you going to the pizza party on the pool deck since there's that dinner thing tonight?"

I stop and stare at him. He may as well have spoken a foreign language because I'm unable to comprehend his words.

A little chuckle escapes from his forming grin. "Your dad didn't tell you?"

Oh. Dad's involved. That explains a lot. I walk out onto the deck. "My dad doesn't tell me anything. So, there's no dinner in the dining room as usual?"

"There is an adult-only dinner and slideshow tonight for the reunion group and a pizza and movie night for the kids."

I take in a deep breath. The clean ocean air fills my lungs. "Well, I guess pizza and a movie it is."

"Hey, look, I found our next activity."

I follow him toward the painted triangle on the deck. "Shuffleboard? Isn't that for the retired crowd?"

He opens the doors of a cupboard that is bolted to the ship. "No, it's for the cruising crowd, and that is us." He hands me a stick with a metal moon shape at the end and several red discs.

My first attempt at pushing the disc ends with said disc sliding only halfway to the intended target. I try again. But this time, the extra force sends it soaring far past the area of play. A quick-thinking gentleman stops my out-of-control puck with his foot.

"Sorry!" The man grins as I rush over to retrieve it. "This game is harder than it looks." He nods in agreement before continuing his stroll.

Cole slides his disc onto the triangle. Show off.

"Let me guess; you are a shuffleboard champion back at your high school."

He pats himself on the shoulder. "Well, I don't usually brag, but…"

I can't stop the eye roll.

He laughs. "Nah, my siblings and I were playing yesterday."

"Ahh…" I set down my runaway disc.

He leans against the railing as I send the disc sliding along with the stick. "So, what's the deal with your dad?"

The disc slows, unable to reach the intended target. "Oh. Well, it's complicated, I guess."

"Seems like it." He watches as I make another attempt.

"It's hard to get over how he destroyed our family." The disc slides onto the board. I glance at Cole to share my sporting achievement. His sad smile reveals the harshness of my words.

Logically, it makes sense to give Dad a break. It's not like he's a horrible father, but I hate constantly feeling like I come second to his social life. Shouldn't his only child be a little more important than the string of women he's dated over the years?

Cole takes a shot, making it look easy. "It probably was especially tough dealing with their divorce on your own."

If he only knew how many times I wished for a sibling to complain to or travel with when I went to Dad's place.

Thankfully, Cole seems to recognize my desire to end this topic, and our game continues with less personal conversations.

~

After the intense shuffleboard game, I head down to my stateroom to freshen up before the pizza party. As I exit the elevator, I hear raised voices. Charming Tank duking it out with his wife perhaps? I round the corner to the hallway and find two of the room stewards in a heated discussion. The moment they see me, the petite, wavy-haired female ducks into one of the rooms while the mocha-skinned male pushes his cart further down the hall. Feeling bad I interrupted whatever was going on, I push open my door.

An oblong white envelope someone must have slid under my door rests on the dark carpet, looking like a lone ship on a vast blue ocean. I take the note to the balcony, tossing my bag on the bed as I pass. Sinking into the deck chair, I pull out three sheets of paper. The first is a typed form detailing the singing competition, followed by two sheets listing song titles. I scan the information. Those contestants moving on to the next level will be meeting with the band sometime during the next two days. My practice time is scheduled for two days from now, right before dinner. Sometime before then, I'm supposed to contact the entertainment office with my song choice from the provided list. Below the typed information is a hand-written note.

Liz,
Please meet us tonight at midnight at the back of the ship on deck
9.
Val

I lean back and stare out at the endless blue ocean in front of me. How the heck am I supposed to help this Rosaline chick?

"Hey, there."

Dad's deep voice makes me jump. I shove the papers under my leg and turn to see his head peering around the door frame.

"Oh, hey."

He steps out onto the balcony. "What ya got there?"

"Oh, nothing. You look nice." I scan his dress pants and a crisp white shirt.

He fiddles with the collar of his shirt. "Thanks. Gwen and I are going together to the dinner tonight."

Gwen—his newest love interest. "You mean the dinner that you neglected to tell me that I'm not invited to?"

He flinches. "Oh. I'm sorry. I guess I forgot. Although, it is on the reunion itinerary I'd given you before the cruise."

I picture the sheets of paper he handed me before we left Chicago. The ones I hadn't looked at before stuffing in my suitcase.

"Oh. I'll have to look for that."

"I could text you the day's itinerary." He looks inside my room toward the little desk where the phone rests. "Although, that might not help much."

"That's okay. I'll look for the schedule you gave me."

"So, how was your day? Around lunch time, I looked for you on the pool deck but didn't see you." He shifts positions and stuffs one hand in his pocket. "Hopefully, you found a way to keep busy."

Dancing in Cole's arms flashes into my mind, warming my insides. "It was a pretty great day. What did you do?"

As he rambles about a poker tournament that kept him busy all day, my mind wanders to the piece of paper I found in the auditorium. How could I have forgotten my mystery? Suddenly, I'm anxious for Daddy Dearest to make his exit so I can study the next clue.

"I did pretty well," Dad continues, unaware that I zoned out for most of his story. "I was just glad Tank got out quickly."

Dad's old nemesis' arrogant face comes to mind. "Do you think people never really change, or do you fall back into old ways when they're reunited?"

With one finger, he tugs at his shirt collar again. "Good question. It is hard to ignore all those emotions. They just seem to erupt. I know I should get over my feelings about him; it's pretty irrational after all these years, but it's hard to move past the old wounds."

I stare at him. It's not like Dad to make an analogous point, but his words almost sound like a personal message to me. Are my feelings irrational? Do I need to move past the old hurts? Probably, but how do I do that?

He glances at his watch. "Welp, I should get going. I told Gwen I'd swing by her room to pick her up."

"So, your old flame is being rekindled?"

"I wouldn't go that far. It's just nice to have a single companion to do things with amid all the married couples." He bites his lower lip before continuing. "Hey, sorry I didn't mention there's no dinner as usual tonight. I heard there's a pizza and movie night on the pool deck for the kids."

"Cole already told me."

His left eyebrow arches. "Cole? Tad's kid? Have you been spending a lot of time with him?"

"Well, unless you haven't noticed, I don't know anyone else on board. Besides, he's a nice guy." Dad's face scrunches in concern. "Don't worry—we're just friends." What else could we ever be since we live in different states?

I read his furrowed brow as being unconvinced, but luckily, he abandons the topic. "Um…okay. Hey, tomorrow's stop is Aruba. I signed us up for the submarine excursion?" His voice rises at the end, turning the statement into a question.

"A submarine? That sounds cool."

His face relaxes with relief. "Great. Well, I should head out. Have fun."

"Yeah, you too. Be on your best behavior, and don't be out too late."

"Yes, ma'am." He salutes, then leaves.

The moment he's out of my room, I flop onto my bed and dig through my bag. My fingers grasp the scrap of paper, and I carefully unfold it. Today, the words are written in bold blocky letters.

Within containment, I still may grow,
Yet if I'm dead, I'm just for show.

I dwell on the words for a few moments but remain bewildered as no ideas come to mind. I shove the clue back into my bag. Best to just let my mind contemplate it while I find the right outfit for a pizza party.

Chapter 8

A few minutes before midnight, I force myself to bid farewell to Cole in order to make my scheduled rendezvous with Rosaline and the Consuelos guys. Leaving the crowd and the bright lights, the night air cools considerably. Luckily, I'd come prepared and pull a sweater from my bag. As I walk the deck, I hum the song that's been stuck in my head for the last hour, remembering the wonderful evening.

The pizza party and movie night were a blast. They showed a sing-along version of *Grease*. Right up my alley! The entire crowd joined in on all the songs—even Cole, who proved that he doesn't have a bad voice. Not suggesting musical theater is something he should pursue, but his singing definitely wasn't cringe-worthy. After the movie, the entertainment staff encouraged the crowd to participate in a series of games. From blindfolded Pictionary to super-sized Jenga. Cole and I teamed up with Mia and Connor, the kids we'd hung out with during our Haiti stop.

This ship is so much fun. *Whoa*. The realization startles me—never thought I'd feel that way. But it's true; everyone's just having a good time. I don't have to worry about what anyone thinks about me. I can just be myself instead of trying to fit into a persona that is deemed acceptable by the popular crowd. It's so refreshing.

I run my hand along the stair railing as I head down an outdoor flight of stairs. Every time Josie tries to convince me to attend her new youth group, she says something similar—that the kids have fun and don't worry about what others think. I doubted her—it seemed too hard to believe. I figured she enjoyed it because she attended with her popular boyfriend, Ryan. Could their youth group possibly be like it was tonight, non-judgmental and accepting of everyone? Maybe I'll finally give in and go with them sometime and find out for myself.

Reaching the bottom step, my sandal smacks on the deck, emphasizing the quiet of the night. People must be heading to their rooms for the night or enjoying the nightlife in the casino or various lounges because I seem to be alone on my midnight stroll around the deck. The solitude offers more peacefulness than eeriness, but I still welcome the faint sounds of laughter and music as I round the stern of the boat.

Accompanying the jovial tones is a faint glow that illuminates the deck. With each step, the sound and light increase. Finally, I come upon the source. A staircase leads down to an unseen lit room. A gate at the top of the stairs keeps me from exploring any further. Curious, I lean over the rail, trying to peer into the open door at the bottom of the steps.

"Liz?"

The male voice behind me causes me to jump. I spin around to face a figure standing in the shadows of the deck. Juan steps into the light. At his side is a dark-skinned woman with short hair. Her large eyes remind me of the deer we often see while driving through the woods near our home—fearful and ready to bolt at the first sign of danger.

"You must be Rosaline?" Hopefully, my smile puts her at ease. "I'm Liz."

Her nervous expression transforms as she graces me with the most beautiful, heart-warming smile. "Thank you for helping me."

Juan motions for me to follow them deeper into a shadowy nook on the deck. He must have purposefully chosen the darkest corner of the ship for this meeting. Would they really get in trouble for interacting with guests? As my eyes adjust to the darkness, I notice they have settled into a pair of deck chairs. I sink into one opposite of them while Juan scooches his chair closer to Rosaline's so he can hold her hand. His devotion is touching.

"Juan tells me you have a beautiful voice," the lovely Rosaline tells me.

I wave away the compliment. "There are a few songs I sing pretty well."

Juan shakes his head. "She's being modest. She stole the show the other night. Did you choose a new song yet?"

"Actually, I wanted to talk to you about that. I wasn't feeling any of the choices."

"Do you have something else in mind?"

"As a matter of fact, I do." I dig a piece of paper out of my pocket and hand it to him.

Unable to read it in the dark, he pockets my request. "I'll chat with the guys."

"Thanks. I included my cell number if you have any questions." I don't think it's a particularly challenging tune to accompany, so I'm fairly certain they will agree. But now is the time to get to the business at hand. I turn to Rosaline. "I don't want to get your hopes up. I honestly don't know how to help you."

"I understand." Her soft voice is layered in sadness. "We just don't know what else to do."

"The guys told me that you've been accused of stealing from a passenger?"

The whites of her eyes increase. "Yes, but I would never do that. I am an honest woman and believe stealing is wrong. And besides, I need this job to support my family. I would never jeopardize it."

How could anyone not believe this woman? She exudes sincerity. "So, this supposedly happened on last week's trip?"

She sucks in a breath. "Yes. Mr. and Mrs. Brummel were an older couple. She was a very sweet woman who loved to chat. She asked me all kinds of questions about my life and my family. This was a bit unusual because we don't often have interactions with guests besides the occasional friendly wave."

I think about my own cabin steward. His name is on the little card he always leaves next to the towel animal he creates. Vincent? Victor? It never dawned on me to ask him about his life.

Rosaline continues. "I think she suffers from some memory issues. She often told me the same stories, but I pretended I'd never heard them before. She also misplaced a few items during the trip, but they would eventually turn up, except apparently for one item. I remember that piece of jewelry because as she was getting ready one evening, she asked me to help her with the clasp. She had quite a tremor and couldn't get it to hook. As I helped her, I complimented her on the beautiful piece. That was the last time I saw the item. When they were packing at the end of the trip, they couldn't find it. Mr. Brummel reported it missing."

Juan squeezes Rosaline's hand. "When something is reported lost, it automatically is connected with the room stewards that work in that block, as a precautionary measure."

"Block?" I ask.

Rosaline's nod is barely perceptible. "The room stewards work in groups. Each block of rooms has three stewards and one supervisor assigned to them. Each member of the team has access to all the rooms in the block. This way, we can assist each other and take a day off during the week."

My steward must work with that couple I saw arguing. "Are the other members in your team under suspicion as well?"

Rosaline's head moves back and forth. "No, because when Mr. Brummel reported the jewelry missing, he mentioned how much I had admired it. Actually, no one pursued the incident at the time. But this week a recorder and an expensive mirror have gone missing and were thought to have last been seen in two of the staterooms that I am assigned to. Now they are refocusing on the Brummel necklace."

My mind spins as my gaze locks on her pleading eyes. "Maybe the items were misplaced and will show up in the staterooms or in a Lost and Found."

Her voice cracks. "At this point, I'm not sure it would help. It could seem like I panicked and got rid of the items to save my job."

"I think management is making an example of her, showing they will not tolerate any theft," Juan grumbles.

I pull my bag against my chest as a shiver runs down my spine, the unfairness of the situation further chilling the night air.

"But that's understandable," she quickly adds. "The company needs to make sure all their employees are trustworthy. Guests won't come on our cruise if there are worries about theft."

"I suppose, but it's not right." A thought comes to mind. "Do you know where this Mr. and Mrs. Brummel live? Maybe we could contact them and see if it ever reappeared."

She reaches into a pocket. "They gave me their email address in case I happened to find the piece when I was cleaning after they left the ship."

I take the folded note from her. "Did you ever contact them? Maybe they found it and didn't bother to tell the cruise line."

Her eyes widen. "Oh, no. My roommate, Janie, thought I should, but that would not be appropriate and might cause more trouble."

Juan squeezes her hand. "Contacting guests is not permitted. If they tried to contact her, though, that would be another story."

So many rules. I glance at the email address in my hands. "Too bad we don't have internet access." I hate waiting until we get back to Miami.

"Once we dock in the morning, we'll have internet service," Juan answers.

"Perfect." The computers at the little library come to mind. "I'll send them a message first thing tomorrow. That will be our first step."

"Thank you." Before I know it, Rosaline wraps me in a hug.

I pat her back, hoping I'm able to help her.

Chapter 9

Dad's rhythmical knocking on our adjoining door echoes through my stateroom to the tiny bathroom where I'm finishing my hair and makeup.

"Come in!" Through the mirror, I take note of his disheveled hair, wrinkled t-shirt, and athletic shorts. Overall, not a bad look on him. "Did you just wake up?" Strange for the normal early riser.

His face contorts with a yawn. "Yeah. It was a late night." He leans against the door frame. "A bunch of us got to reminiscing, and the hours flew by. You're up rather early."

"Couldn't sleep." A text from Val woke me, and the subsequent back-and-forth messages confirming my song choice kept me from falling back asleep.

He rubs his stubbly jaw. "Give me fifteen minutes, and I'll be ready for a quick breakfast before we need to head to shore."

Satisfied that the mirror reveals no drastic flaws in my appearance, I turn to face him. "Why don't I meet you in the cafeteria. I've got something I need to take care of."

"Sounds like a plan." He pulls the door shut behind him.

I stuff all needed items for a day in Aruba into my bag, grab the note Rosaline gave me, then leave for the library.

Right outside my door stands my room steward, sorting through his cart of towels and cleaning supplies.

"Good morning, Vincent." My eyes dart to his nametag. Whew, got it right. Typed neatly below his name is his country of origin—the Philippines.

He looks up from his task and smiles brightly. "Good morning, miss. Is there something I can do for you?"

I shake my head. "No." Now, what do I say? *Hey, just wanted to talk to you so you know I see you as a person and not just my room steward.* Don't think so. "Um…I adore the folded towel shark you left last night. It's always such a nice surprise to come back to the room and be greeted by something so sweet."

Creases form around his eyes as he beams. "You are very welcome. I'm glad you enjoy them."

"Are you able to spend some time in Aruba today?"

"No, not today. Tomorrow is my day to go ashore."

I remember what Rosaline told me about the stewards working in groups. "Oh, nice. I heard that stewards work together so you can take days off."

He nods. "Yes, miss. Jamal and Janie are my co-workers, and our supervisor is Rafael. If you ever need anything, any of us can be of service."

"Oh, is that the Janie that is Rosaline's roommate?" Janie and Jamal must be the couple I saw arguing, since the supervisors wear different colored vests.

His smile loses its genuineness, becoming tight and forced. "Um, yes, miss."

"I've been working with the Consuelos guys for this competition thing. Juan told me about Rosaline."

His eyes dart down the hall, looking like Josie's little brother when we catch him snooping. Maybe chatting with passengers is frowned upon as well?

Well, when no other discussion topics to fill the awkward silence come to mind it's time to bid farewell and put the poor man out of his misery. "Well, have a good day."

He visibly relaxes. "You as well, miss. Aruba is beautiful. I'm sure you will have a wonderful day."

Poor guy, does no one ever just chat with him? While I walk toward the library, faces of the various people I come into contact with on a daily basis and pretty much ignore sift through my thoughts. Have I ever stopped to converse with the lunch ladies at school? What about the barista when I stop for coffee? Since I don't have a New Year's resolution yet, that would be a good one. Be a friendly face and offer kind words to everyone.

While certainly not crowded, the library is not as desolate as my last visit. One older woman scans a bookshelf while a middle-aged man pecks away at a computer keyboard. Eager to test out my new resolution, I'm ready with a smile and friendly wave to my fellow library visitors, but neither look my way. Oh, well. It's the thought that counts, right? After settling in at one of the work-stations, it takes a few moments to figure out how to log in. With no sign stating the internet usage fee, there's no way of knowing how expensive this communication attempt will be. But whatever the cost, Rosaline is worth it.

I enter the email address for the Brummels and type a quick message of introduction and inquire if they possibly found their missing jewelry. A quick prayer accompanies the sent email. Hopefully, they will provide good news for Rosaline. Before logging out, I compose one more quick message.

Josie,

What's the scene, jelly bean?

I bet you're surprised to hear from me, but I thought I'd send a quick update of the good and bad.

I'm having a lot of fun. **However**, Daddio pulled another father-of-the-year move by hooking up with an old flame.

I've been spending time with a super sweet guy—Cole. **However**, he lives in Virginia.

A karaoke competition, scavenger hunt, and helping to save someone's job is keeping me busy. **However**, that doesn't leave me much time to work on my tan.

Oh, and you'll never believe who I met on board—fans of yours. The Consuelos cousins send their best.

I hope you and Ryan are having fun!

Miss you~

Liz

There. That should be enough to intrigue her. I glance at the clock on the wall—Aruba time.

~

Dad waits until we're walking toward the tour bus that will ferry us to the submarine excursion, to break the news.

"Hey, I hope it's all right if Gwen joins us." He peers at me over the top of his Ray-Bans.

"You invited Gwen?" Stupid me for not seeing this coming. Man, my guard has been way down this trip.

He shoves his hands into the pockets of his shorts, looking a bit like a little kid sheepishly trying to explain his way out of trouble. "Well, she mentioned she didn't have an excursion scheduled for today, and she seemed interested in this one, so I said she could join us."

Before an appropriate reply shoots its way out of my mouth, his gaze shifts, and he waves at someone behind me. Taking a step back, I'm able to observe his reaction to Gwen's approach. A dorky grin crosses his face as he watches her sashay toward us. She does look rather stunning in a pale-yellow sundress, the same shade as her enviously naturally wavy hair. Her giant sun hat and dark glasses hide most of her face except for the bright red lipstick that matches her sandals and the ribbon circling her hat.

She kisses Dad's cheek, somehow not leaving a bright red lip print, then sends a smile my way. "Thank you, Liz, for sharing your day with me. I don't know what I was thinking coming on this cruise by myself. It was silly of me to think that more of my classmates would come alone on this holiday reunion."

"Hey, the more the merrier. It's not like we were planning a special father-daughter day or anything." With a sharp pivot, I climb on the bus.

Seat selection on a bus can be a strategic move, but today I just aim for an open row, slide close to the window, and place my bag on the seat next to me. While some may find my action rude, I prefer to think of it as helpful by alleviating any contemplation on Dad's part as to which of his female companions he is obliged to sit beside.

Once loaded, the bus rolls through town. The talented driver not only maneuvers the big rig but also plays the part of our tour guide. Occasional chuckles from the passengers must mean that his stories I'm ignoring are entertaining. They can't possibly be as interesting as the interaction between Dad and Gwen, who chose to sit directly in front of me.

Completely comfortable with one another, they chat and laugh, also not paying attention to our driver's prepared speech. She reaches out and touches his shoulder. His eyes crinkle as he smiles at her. Somewhere along our drive, my annoyance shifts to thoughts of Cole and wondering what he's doing today.

Once we reach our destination, a long dock not far out of town, we dutifully file out of the tour bus and down the long pier like a line of ducklings. Gwen's numerous bracelets clink softly together as she wraps her arm around Dad's.

Only the white top of our underwater transportation can be seen from the dock. One by one, the captain welcomes us and offers a hand as we step from the dock onto the sub. Once onboard, I cling to the metal handrail, then follow the person in front of me down the narrow steps into the bowels of the vessel.

The tourists are ushered into a large seating area with rows of benches angled toward portholes on either side. The deep blue water outside the porthole near where I sit stirs as a school of tiny yellow fish swims past. So cool.

This time, Dad sits next to me with Gwen on his other side. As soon as the last passenger finds their seat, the large top hatch closes. The heavy clank sends a flicker of unease rippling through me.

A thin lady with long blond braids snaking out from beneath her sailor cap moves to the front of our observation room. "Welcome to the Atlantis Submarine Excursion!"

The whirr of the motor and the darkening of the water are the only indications that we are moving.

After our tour guide commences with the usual questions—where are you all from, are you having a wonderful vacation, is this your first time in Aruba—she explains the excursion.

"Today, we'll be diving to a depth of 130 feet. We'll travel past colorful coral fields, a gorgeous sponge garden, and a shipwreck. As we move, you'll most likely see many schools of tropical fish and maybe even an unusual, larger sea creature or two. If anyone does see something exciting, please let the rest of the group know so we can all catch a glimpse."

An unusual sea creature? What did I get myself into?

The captain and his blond first-mate entertain us with funny stories and interesting facts. As all the other tourists snap lots of pictures, I'm regretting my boycott and leaving the new cell phone in my cabin. At least Dad takes a few. By the time we head back to the dock, realization hits that I've been having such a good time that I forgot to be annoyed at Dad for inviting Gwen.

During the return trip, the bus driver's sightseeing spiel makes its way to my brain—who knew Aruba was part of the Netherlands? Once we're back near the cruise ship dock, Dad asks Gwen and me if we'd like to find a restaurant for lunch.

Considering that it's too early to head back to the ship for my rehearsal time, I acquiesce.

Gwen again slides her arm around Dad's, and the two of them stroll down the sidewalk. "I'd love to explore some of these shops. This place is so sweet."

Quaint was the word that came to my mind to describe the Dutch influence on the architecture, but *sweet* works as well.

"Well, we have time after lunch. Liz, want to join us?" Dad looks my way.

"While that sounds like a tremendous amount of fun, I have a scheduled appointment back on the ship this afternoon."

Dad's eyebrows shoot up, but I don't bother explaining.

"That's too bad." Gwen's words sound sweet enough, but a trained ear such as my own can detect the lack of conviction. Her red sandals stop moving. "How about this café?"

Wrought-iron tables and chairs line the front of the little restaurant. Colorful umbrellas and flowerboxes add even more charm.

As much as I don't want to enjoy lunch with Dad and his new paramour, hearing details of their high school romance is surprisingly entertaining.

"We were in a group that was spending every weekend together," Dad explains when, in a desperate attempt to think of something to talk about, I politely ask how they met.

Gwen's manicured fingers rest on Dad's arm. "Remember all those games of round the world ping pong we played?"

"And how much pizza we ordered." He grins.

"Jimmy's mom was a saint, letting us hang out there so much."

He lets out a loud half-laugh. "That was the only way she could keep an eye on him."

After taking a sip of his drink, he smiles sweetly at Gwen. "Then, one day, we all decided to go sledding."

Gwen nods, keeping her gaze on his. "We were riding together on a sled and, at the end of the run, slipped off and landed in a heap of snow."

Dad's cheeks color. "That's when I knew I wanted to be more than friends."

Her eyes get all doe-y. "I think the rest of the group was a little surprised."

He places his free hand on top of hers. "That was one of the most memorable winters of my life. So many great memories."

She tilts her head. "Like the bowling tournament?"

He leans forward. "And snowshoeing."

Her voice drops. "Hours spent watching MTV in your family room."

Good grief. "Sounds fun," I interject, afraid if they continue their walk down memory lane, they might start making out or something.

Dad clears his throat and readjusts his chair. "It was."

"I think that was the only year I was sad to see the endless Minnesota winter end." Gwen reaches for her sparkling wine.

While curious about what happened between them, the story may contain details I don't want to know about, so I keep my mouth shut. After the tasty lunch, I leave the star-crossed lovers to browse the shops of Aruba alone while I head back to the ship for my rehearsal.

~

Late for dinner, I hurry into the dining room as fast as my heels will allow. Rehearsal took longer than expected due to a contestant earlier in the day who had scrapped their song halfway through their scheduled rehearsal time—and chose a new selection, which put everyone behind schedule.

And, of course, before heading to my room to change for dinner, I swung by the library to see if the Brummels had answered my email. No such luck.

Expertly winding my way through the maze of tables in the grand dining room, I grimace at the sight in front of me. Gwen will apparently be joining us once again. Would they care, or even notice, if I just skipped dinner? Before I can sneak away undetected, Linda spots me and waves. The men all acknowledge my appearance by standing.

"Sorry I'm late," I murmur and slide into my seat.

"We were just telling them about the submarine excursion," Gwen says. Tonight, her soft curls are swept up in an elegant updo. The soft blue of her dress matching her eyes. Dad's tie complements her dress. Yuck.

Linda sets down her menu. "It sounds like such a great experience. I would've been game, but Matt gets a little claustrophobic."

I tuck a wayward strand of hair behind my ear. "It was pretty cool."

Linda's gaze shifts to my left. Everyone's eyes follow her lead. I turn to see what has captured their attention. Dad's nemesis, Tank, and his wife are standing next to our table.

"Tank," Dad sneers.

"Wade," Tank says through a snarl.

Glad to see they are capable of acting like mature adults.

"Having a nice evening?" Linda asks while all the other adults at our table revert back to bratty teenagers watching the couple through suspicious stares.

"Yes," Tank's wife answers. "It's charming." She reaches up her hand to brush a strand of her overly colored hair from her face. Her diamond bracelet shimmers from the light of the overhead chandelier.

"Your bracelet is so beautiful," Linda says—apparently the only adult capable of making polite conversation.

Tank's wife touches the piece of jewelry with her perfectly manicured finger. "Thank you. My darling just gave it to me this evening. It's our anniversary, and he surprised me with this gift and two dozen red roses."

Linda glances at her husband and his friends, who are all still warily scrutinizing the couple in front of us. "Well, happy anniversary. What a wonderful place to celebrate."

Throughout the conversation, I've been amused by the unspoken battle raging between Tank and Dad of who will be the first to break eye contact.

"We stopped by to ask you something." After a lengthy pause, Mrs. Tank glances at her husband. Seeing that he's not paying any attention to what she's saying, she huffs, then elbows him, effectively ending the ridiculously uncomfortable stare-down.

"What?" Tank glances at his wife's angry face. "Oh, yeah. We are having a little anniversary cocktail party tonight in the portside whisky bar, and Renee wanted you to come."

Dad and his buddies glance at one another, but no one answers. Finally, Linda breaks the silence.

"That's very nice of you. Thank you for the invitation. We will make sure to stop by."

"Excellent." Renee shoots a satisfied smirk toward her husband, then turns and walks back to their table.

Tank hovers for another moment, then follows his wife.

"What was that about?" Matt looks as confused as I feel. "Why would they invite us?"

Mr. High School Sweetheart reaches for his drink. "Two nights ago, Aaron and Kristie Zimmerman had an anniversary party that people have been buzzing about. Tank could never let anyone else get the glory. I bet they want to try and throw their own bash that people will be talking about."

"But why invite us?" Linda asks.

Dad cocks an eyebrow. "They're probably only concerned with the number of attendees. That was his MO back in high school. He had to have the biggest party. Some things never change."

I shiver. That is for sure. "Are you going to go?"

Dad glances at Gwen. "I'm not sure. I'll have to think about it." Dad shifts his attention toward me. "So, how was your *appointment?*"

"Fine." Fantastic, in fact. The Consuelos guys knew just what I was thinking. The bluesy twist to the classic song should be a hit.

"Appointment?" Linda reaches for her wine glass. "I hope you didn't go use our spa certificates without me."

"Of course not." I scan the menu hoping the subject will drop. Where are all the boring tales of old when you need them? "This was just something else I needed to take care of."

"I have a feeling I know what this mysterious appointment was about." Mrs. High School Sweetheart adds, a teasing lilt to her voice.

Everyone's gaze shifts from her to me. Suddenly, it feels like a crime to keep my private life private. Not sure why my schedule is suddenly a mystery, but I am slightly curious as to what she could possibly be suggesting. "It's nothing. Why don't we hear about everyone else's day?"

Mrs. High School Sweetheart waves away my suggestion. "We already covered that before you arrived." She keeps her eyes on me but slightly tilts her head toward Dad. "Wade, I don't know if you are aware of this, but your daughter put on quite the show the other night."

Oh, no. Why didn't I sneak away when I had the chance?

Dad's forehead creases. His head snaps my way. "A show?"

Oh, well. It was bound to come out sooner or later. "It's no big deal."

"That's not what I hear."

Mrs. Sweetheart was much more likable when she completely ignored me and only wanted to relive the past.

The woman reaches for her wine glass, looking a little too proud of herself. "Maggie Donovan told me that Liz here participated in a karaoke competition the other night and pretty much stole the show." She grins. "Despite attempting to hide her identity, Maggie recognized her."

Linda turns to me and touches my arm. "Is that true?"

The narrowed eyes and tilted heads reflect my tablemates' curiosity.

Time to fess up before I have to hear Maggie Donovan's version of the evening. "Yes. I sang a song from *Les Mis*, and the audience seemed to like it."

Mrs. Sweetheart jumps in again. "They not only liked it; they gave her a standing ovation, and she's moving on to the next part of the competition tomorrow night."

Her words drip with former-high-school-mean-girl smugness.

"That's so exciting." Linda pats my hand in her motherly way.

Dad leans forward. "Why didn't you tell me?"

His intense interest causes me to squirm in my seat. "It's just a silly cruise ship game to pass the time. It's no big deal."

"Nonsense," Linda says. "We'll all be there to watch you perform."

"Absolutely!" Dad raises his wine glass. "To Liz!"

All the adults raise their glasses in a toast. "To Liz!"

My focus remains on Dad's beaming smile, savoring that proud look that I haven't experienced very often.

Chapter 10

Our little group of seven meanders to the theater after dinner. I make sure to keep my distance from Mrs. Sweetheart. She's going to have to earn back my trust. The night's entertainment is a variety show with acrobats, jugglers, and dueling pianists—all exceedingly talented. My favorite act by far though is provided by the ship's dancers. They perform a medley of dances through the years. Watching the dancers, especially Ivan and Svetlana, my mind drifts to Cole and our tango lesson. Which then makes me think about the note I found here in the auditorium. Why can't I decipher that clue? Maybe it's time to seek some help. And I know just who to ask.

As we're shuffling out of the theater, I spot Cole at the top of the aisle. Is he waiting for me? He grins as I approach, causing a flood of warmth to flow through me. Get a grip, girl.

"I was hoping I'd run into you," I say in greeting.

"Well, that's good to hear." He leads us away from the stream of passengers eager to get to their next activity of the night. We move to a quieter nook with two chairs and a coffee table. "Were you in need of a tango partner, or did you just miss my engaging personality?"

In short supply of witty comebacks, I just shake my head. "Neither. I need your mind."

He sinks into a club chair and pats himself on the shoulder. "Brains and beauty, all in one place."

He may be joking, but I couldn't agree more with the description.

I dust crumbs off my chair, then sit across from him. "Remember when I said I'd dropped something in the theater and went searching the seats?"

He gives a cockeyed grin. "Yes, that rings a bell."

"Well, that wasn't exactly the truth."

One dark eyebrow arches.

As I try to explain about the note I found in my bag, the search in the library, and discovering the message in the auditorium, his light-hearted expression slowly slips away.

By the time I'm finished with my tale, he's leaning forward, his forearms perched on his thighs, gazing intently at my face.

He lets out a breath. "Wow. Do you have any idea who the notes are from?"

I pull out the newest note. "No. But I'm having trouble deciphering the latest clue. Maybe you could help? Unless you've got plans for the evening." Puzzles are usually my thing, but it's been difficult to concentrate with so many distractions on my plate— my upcoming performance, Rosaline's troubles, and Cole's deep brown eyes.

"Nothing sounds more intriguing than spending the evening with you." A flash of mischief in his eyes, he reaches for the folded scrap of paper.

I swallow the lump that has somehow lodged in my throat. Why can't there be a guy like this back home?

Seriousness settles in as he scans the note, his strong jawline set in determination. "Okay, let's figure this out. *Within containment, I still may grow, yet if I'm dead, I'm just for show.* Hmm."

"Okay, time to see if you're as brainy as you claim."

His eyes squint as he bites his bottom lip. He probably has no idea how cute he is when he concentrates.

"Well," He leans back, looking toward the ceiling. "What grows?" His hand rakes through his thick, dark hair.

"Hair!" blurts from my mouth.

"Hair?"

"Yeah, maybe we're supposed to go to the salon?" Seems like a reasonable suggestion, but his raised eyebrows reveal his doubts.

"But what about the second line? Once you cut the hair, it's dead, I guess. But how is that for show?" he logically queries.

"What about a wig? Cut hair can be made into a wig."

"Maybe. But I haven't come across any on-ship wig shops."

I glance toward the auditorium. "What about backstage? There must be wigs in the costume room."

He bites his lower lip again as he ponders the thought. "I suppose, but if you're meant to follow these clues, that doesn't seem like a likely spot. I'm pretty sure we wouldn't be allowed back there."

I hate to admit that his logic makes sense. "Well, what else is alive?"

"Animals? Although, there's not a lot of those on board."

"Fish! There's that enormous aquarium in the dining room."

His head bobs back and forth like he's weighing my newest suggestion. "*Yet if I'm dead, I'm just for show.*"

"Well, so much for that. The only dead fish around are the ones we eat." While their presentations on the plate are practically works of art, they really aren't just for show.

He sits up a little straighter. "There's a huge, mounted swordfish in that piano bar lounge."

"Really?" A shiver of excitement quivers down my spine. "Think we need to wait until tomorrow when the lounge isn't so crowded?" That pianist is like a rockstar on this ship, with groupies surrounding him whenever he plays.

"He's always got the whole place singing along. Trust me. No one will be watching us." He stands and extends his hand to me.

~

As we near, the singing draws us closer to the lounge, if that's the right word for the area. It's standing room only in the jampacked space which is really just a large open balcony above the main atrium. A grand piano sits at one end of the space, while club chairs and small tables fill the area. Every single person happily sings along to Billy Joel's *Piano Man*.

Cole nods to the wall opposite of the piano. Perched above a love seat hangs the giant swordfish. He confidently wanders closer, then asks the entwined couple occupying the love seat if they'd mind if he took a closer look at the fish.

They nod their agreement while continuing to sing with the crowd.

"Careful," I tell him. "Don't get your hand stuck in the mouth."

His eyes widen in fake indignation. "I'm offended that you think so little of my sleuthing skills."

I push him toward the fish as the crowd belts out the second verse. "Don't say I didn't warn you if you have to spend the rest of the evening with a giant fish attached to your arm."

He shines the light of his phone in the open mouth and peers in. His hand slowly enters the giant fish. When the forward progress stops, he looks at me, and winks.

My eyes widen, trying to convey my question. *Is there really something in there?*

His eyebrows arch in reply, giving me a moment of hope before he shakes his head, a grin slowly forming at my dismay.

The guy is incorrigible.

Raising up on his tiptoes, he carefully scans the top of the fish, then thoroughly checks all sides before joining me.

He leans close to be heard over the loud singing. "Either that is not the right guess, or someone else found the note."

I pull him out of the makeshift lounge as the crowd erupts in applause. "Darn. Well, let's wander. Maybe something will come to us."

"Okay, but it's tough working on an empty stomach. I think some ice cream would help us concentrate."

A man after my own heart. "To encourage creativity."

"Exactly." He motions for me to lead the way down the spiral staircase to the main corridor.

I glance over my shoulder as I descend to the shops and cafes. "What did you and your family do today in Aruba?"

"The Hidden Gems tour."

"Sounds intriguing." At the bottom of the steps, I veer toward the ice cream shop.

He brushes against my arm as he walks alongside me. "It was cool. We visited these coral cliffs and a bunch of caves."

Reaching our destination, I settle in line behind a family whose children are having a tough time making their culinary decisions.

As we wait, he continues. "The best part was the stop at the Lourdes Grotto, this amazing shrine to Mary. We stayed there awhile. My mom talked half the tour group into joining us in a rosary."

I move forward a few inches as one of the children ahead of us finally makes their choice. "You're Catholic?"

He nods. "You?"

"Not exactly."

His forehead creases. "Seems like you either are or you aren't."

Oh, if it were only that easy. "Well, my mom always attended a non-denominational church. My dad grew up as a Protestant but never really attended church with Mom and I, except on holidays or when we visited my grandmother. After the divorce, Mom had a tough time, and we stopped going. My friend Josie's parents offered to take me with them, so I started attending Mass with them."

"Miss?" I look up to see that I'm at the front of the line.

"Rocky road in a chocolate-dipped waffle cone with sprinkles."

Cole nods his approval at my unusual choice. "Make that two."

With the confectionary masterpieces in hand, we sit at one of the tables.

"But you never became Catholic?" he asks just as I take too big of a bite.

I squeeze my eyes shut and wait for the brain freeze to subside. "No. Josie's mom asked me a few times. When Josie was going through confirmation, I thought about it but never followed through."

"Ah." He wipes the corner of his mouth with a napkin. "Do you still go with her?"

"Yeah, it just doesn't feel right if I don't go." I wipe my mouth as well, just in case his action was a subtle hint that I was the one with ice cream smeared across my face. "Although, she started doing a lot with the youth group at a different parish with her boyfriend and loves it. They keep inviting me, but so far, I haven't gone with them."

"Why not?"

Another good question. "I'm not sure. I don't want to be the third wheel, I guess." Does the excuse sound as lame to him as it does to me? Because when it comes to Ryan and Josie, while I'm often a tag-along, they always make me feel comfortable. The truth is, Josie's faith has grown, and mine has stayed lukewarm. She keeps trying to include me, but part of me just wants to stay in the bitter, complaining stage. In some ways, it's easier.

Cole clears his throat. "I think a lot of people turn away from faith when they're going through tough times. But really that's the time you should be embracing it."

I look up at those eyes, the same shade as my delicious choc-olatey dessert. "Yeah, I know. Lately, I've been thinking about going with them."

"Maybe this is the year you'll join the church that has been in existence since Christ." He grins. "The one that literally sits upon Peter—the rock on which the Church is built."

The confusion must show on my face.

"You haven't heard this?" His face lights up. "It's kinda mind-blowing. You know the Bible verse where Jesus changes Simon's name to Peter?"

I nod, curious about his excitement.

"The name *Peter* means *rock*. Jesus goes on to say, 'Upon this rock, I will build my church.'" Satisfied, he takes a bite of ice cream.

Still not sure what is so astonishing. "Yeah, Peter and the dis-ciples started the first churches."

"Not only that. Peter becomes the first pope." His eyes widen. "And do you know where the Vatican, the home of the Pope, is built?"

"Rome?" Seems obvious.

"Of course." His enthusiasm is practically palpable. "But it ac-tually is built on the land where Peter was buried—directly above Peter's tomb." His hand reaches out in emphasis. "Meaning that Peter is the actual rock on which the Church Christ founded is built."

His words sink in. *Whoa.* "Really? I've never heard that be-fore."

He leans back. "I know. It blew me away when I first learned about it."

"Well, becoming Catholic would certainly make Josie happy. For the last few years, after the Easter Vigil, when new members join the Church, she's offered to be my sponsor. Maybe one of these days."

"Well, a new year begins in two days. Maybe it's time for a fresh start." His eyebrow cocks as if in a dare.

"Here's to fresh starts." I hold up my ice cream cone.

He taps his against mine. "To fresh starts."

Why have I been holding back from joining the church that has begun to feel like my safe harbor? I glance off in the distance, contemplating all that we talked about, when something behind him shifts into focus. I suck in a sharp breath.

"What?" He turns to look over his shoulder.

"Look! Potted plants."

He turns back to me with a grin. "Uh, yeah, they're pretty, but they're fake."

"Exactly! Come on, Mr. Brains and Beauty, did a sugar high slow you down? *Within containment, I still may grow.* Plants can grow in containers such as pots."

His eyes light up. "*Yet if I'm dead, I'm just for show.* The only purpose of fake flowers is for decoration."

My gaze takes in the long interior hall. Every single store, restaurant, and lounge has two large pots sitting outside their doors. Identical small pines wrapped with Christmas lights fill each container. My heart sinks as I stare at the dozens of possible hiding spots.

Cole chuckles. "See, I knew we'd need to keep our strength up. Let the hunt commence." He pops the rest of his cone into his mouth.

And so begins the tricky search through the potted artificial plants. What seems like a simple, yet time-consuming process becomes encumbered by the watchful eyes of the ship's crew. No sooner does one of us have our hand at the base of the mini-Christmas tree, blindly feeling around for a scrap of paper than a store clerk starts scrutinizing our actions. The task turns laboriously slow as we're forced to take turns searching and being a human shield for prying eyes.

Halfway down one side of the Grand Promenade, even Cole's enthusiasm wanes. The two candy wrappers, a crunched-up soda can, and hairbrush we've discovered do little to endear us to our fellow passengers. Seriously, people, there are trash cans about every ten yards. You have to throw your trash into the plants? At the next stop, a little general store, we each purchase hand sanitizer.

While the mouthwatering aroma emanating from the neighboring establishment makes my mouth water, the site of the Italian Bistro makes me groan. The hallway seating area lined with fake plants makes an inviting patio but the numerous artificial flowers and vines that offer the authentic look also have suddenly increased our workload.

"Now what?" Please say it's time to throw in the towel for the evening.

But Cole is not a man who is easily dissuaded.

He points to an empty table for two next to a long faux marble container with a wooden latticework that is draped with grapevines. "The perfect spot for our reconnaissance mission."

We claim the seats. While Cole keeps watch, I stealthily slide my hand into my side of the long narrow container, my fingers probing plastic stems and crumbly moss.

"Nope." I pull out my hand sanitizer and squeeze out a dollop. "Your turn." As Cole continues the search, a waitress walks by, delivering a scrumptious-looking tiramisu to a table across the way. Her gaze stays on us a moment longer than usual.

"Na-da." He reaches for his liquid cleanser.

"How are we going to check all of these?" The weight of our undertaking dampens my spirit.

"Very carefully." Cole grins. "The table behind you just opened up. Let's move and check out the next grapevine."

When we shift to the next table, the curious waitress changes direction and heads our way.

"Can I get you something?" Her Italian accent practically turns the simple sentence into poetry.

"Not yet. We're still deciding where to sit," I lamely respond.

She glances between us, then turns and makes her way into the restaurant.

I lean closer to Cole. "She's on to us."

"Well, then we'd better get to work before she returns."

We repeat our strategy but, besides a crinkled gum wrapper, come up empty-handed once again. I notice the suspicious waitress whispering to one of her co-workers and pointing toward us.

"Um, Cole." I reach out and touch his arm. "I think we've caused enough of a scene here for one night. Why don't we continue on with the Christmas tree planters? If none of them yield our next clue, then we can come back here tomorrow when new staff will hopefully be working."

He brushes off his hands. "Sounds like a deal."

As we walk away from the bistro and the suspicious gaze of the Italian waitress, Cole nudges me with his shoulder. "I must say, this evening will definitely be one of the most memorable of the trip."

"I couldn't agree more." Not because we made fools of ourselves in this ridiculous search, but because of this handsome boy.

Chapter 11

Touring Curacao has me suddenly believing in fairytales. What a kaleidoscope for the senses. Each colorful building more vibrant than the next. The bright yellows, reds, pinks, and every shade of blue makes me smile. I long to explore each enticing shop we pass, but Dad shoos me to the bus that will take us to all the stops on our excursion.

The charm of the island continues at our visit to an ostrich farm where tiny, fuzzy babies capture my heart. And the natural wonderland of the Hato caves makes me feel like I've been transported to another world. The meandering pathways through the underground world of stalactites and stalagmites, past pools of water reflecting the uniquely shaped spires of coral limestone—simply breathtaking.

In this magical world, I genuinely feel like the princess about ready to attend the ball, because tonight, on this final day of the year, is my next performance, followed by a New Year's Eve party on the pool deck. And if dreams do come true, maybe I can ring in the new year with Cole at my side.

The expression of having to pinch yourself never made sense to me—until now. Because that is precisely how I feel; everything feels so right. Perfect. And that is a feeling I haven't experienced in a long time.

As Dad and I are about to reboard the ship, I smile realizing how much fun we had together. I turn around to take in the magic of Curacao one last time. I hate to leave this amazing place, but at the same time, I can't wait for this evening and the promise it holds. The perfect ending to a glorious day.

Following Dad through security, I place my purchases on the conveyor belt, then walk through the metal detector to reboard the ship. Over the attendant's shoulder, the image of my purchases slides across the x-ray machine's screen. Shopping in Curacao was as perfect as the rest of the day. Mom's going to love the colorful scarf I bought her. I couldn't resist the bright floral pattern against the aqua background, which reminded me so much of the unique island. Once I saw it, there was no leaving it behind.

Then I'd found a beautiful cross necklace made from shells that I instantly knew Josie would adore. Sure, I'd already bought them both those handcrafted items in Haiti, but when you find such perfect gifts, you can't pass them by. And when Dad insisted I find something for myself, I dutifully obeyed and bought a small watercolor painting of the island.

"We have about two hours before dinner." Dad grabs the bag of souvenirs when it makes its way through the machine, easily passing inspection. "I may go back to the room and relax a bit before the busy evening."

"And recovering from a late night?" I tease as I grab his phone that he neglected to remove from the dish after it passed through the metal detector.

He takes it and laughs. "Thanks. Well, it was a late night, but we only stayed at the anniversary party for a little while. Watching Tank lavish his wife with gifts was too much to handle on a full stomach."

"She must have been happy with all the attention."

His head sways back and forth. "You'd think. Monica told me he's been giving her gifts every day of this trip. But apparently, it's not enough. When I got back to my room, I could hear her screaming at him. It almost made me pity the man."

"Sounds like she might be the perfect match for him. I'm not heading back to the room right now. I have a couple of things to do first before I get ready for tonight."

"All right. I'll knock on your door when it's time to leave for dinner. Oh, before I forget, some friends invited me to play in a golf tournament tomorrow during our stop at Bonaire. I told them I'd let them know. I didn't know what you wanted to do on our last stop."

His final two words fill me with an unexpected sadness. How can tomorrow already be the last stop of the trip? At least we still have a few days of cruising before we reach Miami.

"No, that's fine. I actually wouldn't mind some beach time before heading back to the frigid cold of Minnesota."

"Okay. I'll let them know." He pulls me close and kisses the top of my head. "It was a fun day, kiddo."

"Yeah, it was." Especially since Gwen didn't tag along. "Thanks for bringing me on this trip. It's been a lot more fun than I thought it would be." If I'd had my way and stayed home, I'd never have experienced the wonders of this island. Or met Cole.

Dad's smile spreads across his face as he disappears down the hall.

Things with Dad are better than they've ever been—maybe there is something to this novena that I've been diligently praying each day.

A twinge of guilt suddenly turns my stomach. How could I be so self-centered? The day had been so great that I'd nearly forgotten about Rosaline. I was out having fun, while her life is falling apart. I glance at the clock on the wall behind the security guard's desk—just enough time to check my email before meeting Cole and continuing our madcap search for the next note.

As I ride the elevator, I think about last night. I thought for sure someone would come up and question our antics. We were inundated with questioning looks and wary gazes, but no one ever asked what we were doing. But honestly, they should be thanking us. Our thorough search in every potted pine tree was a public service because despite coming up empty-handed for a clue, we retrieved a surprising amount of trash.

When I reach the library, I'm not surprised to find I have it to myself. Who would come to this inner room with no windows when the beauty of Curacao is right outside the ship?

It takes me just a few moments to log in and pull up my email. My heart sags when no message from the Brummels appears in my inbox. I'd been counting on a reply from them to clear Rosaline's name. Well, maybe tomorrow. Half-heartedly, I click on Josie's response.

How's the cruise, my theater muse?

I literally fell out of my seat when I read your email. Okay, I was perched on the back of my couch and threw my head back in surprise, which caused the rest of me to follow the downward trajectory. As you well know, gravity is not my friend.

The Consuelos boys are on your ship?!?!?! What are the chances? Please give them my best. I think of them often. They, however, probably had wished to erase me from their minds! Haha!

And you are performing! PLEASE have someone record you! I would love to see it.

Happy New Year! I can't wait to see you in a few days and hear every detail about the trip and Cole!!

Love you!

Josie

I send a quick reply. Time to head down to meet Cole. My heart flutters with the thought of spending some time with him. We should have almost an hour to continue our search before I need to start getting ready for the evening. This princess does not have a fairy godmother so needs plenty of time to make sure her hair, makeup, and outfit are perfect for the ball.

Cole's waiting for me just outside the bistro. He smiles as I approach. "Hey, how was your day?"

"Amazing! How was yours?"

"Great. We had such a blast kayaking through these cool caves."

"Oh! That sounds fun. What I wouldn't give to stay here longer."

He slows as we near our destination. "Yep, the one bad part of a cruise—you only get a little taste of each stop."

We choose to sit at a new table to resume our search when someone approaches.

Uh-oh. The waitress from last night. And she does not look happy—no mandatory crew-member smile today.

"Can I help you with something?"

Busted. I glance at Cole, who bites his lip. I try to think of a plausible excuse for us digging around in their décor but decide any fib would make less sense than the truth.

"Sorry. I know our actions seem strange. We're actually on a bit of a scavenger hunt."

Cole and I take turns describing the notes and our assumptions. The woman in front of us remains completely expressionless as we tell our tale.

When we finish, she blinks twice, then turns and walks away.

I lean toward my cohort. "Think she's going to get her supervisor?"

He rubs his chin. "Or she's giving her consent. I don't think we're technically doing anything wrong. We might as well continue until we're told to stop."

I giggle.

His eyebrows furrow. "What?"

"I have a feeling you're a by-the-rules kind of guy and this sneaking around is new to you."

He lets out a little chuckle. "I guess you're just a bad influence on me."

A quick glance back into the restaurant reveals our waitress friend has resumed her job of filling salt and pepper shakers. Guess he's right, and she doesn't care what we're up to. When I turn back, he's on his knees, already searching one of the faux marble containers.

"You excited for the show tonight?" he asks.

I join in the search, focusing on the flower box. "I actually am."

"What will you be singing?"

"You'll just have to show up to find out." I dust off my hands. No luck. I move on to the container next to where he's working—kneeling on the hard wood.

He sits back on his heels. "I wouldn't miss it."

"Oh, hey, would you do me a favor and record it with my phone? I want to show my mom and Josie."

He moves to the planter on my other side. "Absolutely. By the way, I recorded your first performance as well, so I can just use my phone and send them both to you later."

I stop and turn to him. "You did?"

He leans in, extending his hand further into the planter. "Of course, I did."

Wow.

He glances at me with a grin. "I figured if you were terrible, I could use it as blackmail."

I grab one of the loose artificial leaves in front of me and throw it at him. But the feathery light leaf just gently floats through the air.

He snatches it and hands it back to me. "Just kidding. I figured you wouldn't volunteer unless you were good. And I was right. You were phenomenal."

He turns back to his task, but I continue watching his handsome profile, taking in his dark hair, warm complexion, strong jaw, and long eyelashes.

"Hey!" His hand emerges from amid the fake grapevines, grasping a folded note.

"You found it!" I fling my arms around him, my face burying into his neck. The energy radiating between us seems to slow the space-time continuum, like nothing else exists in that moment. The warmth of his hand on my back shifts me back to reality and I pull away. "Umm…let's see what it says."

He clears his throat, then hands it to me. "You must do the honors."

We dust off our knees and move to a table. Cole pulls out his little bottle of hand sanitizer and squirts out a dab into each of our hands. I thoroughly rub in the cleanser, taking the moment to control my emotions. Then, I carefully unfold the paper. The words in this note slant to the left. Whoever is writing these notes is certainly trying to disguise their writing.

A trusted friend on whom the lost depend will be your guide for this journey's end.

Cole stares off to the left. "Hmm…Any thoughts?"

I continue to stare at the words. "Nope. Not a clue." A trusted friend? Obviously, Josie comes to mind, but whoever created this game wouldn't know her. Right? Of course, I still don't even know if these notes are even intended for me. I could be enjoying someone else's scavenger hunt.

Cole's forehead creases. "Maybe something will come to us eventually."

"Well, at least we found it." I fold it back up. "I'd better go get ready for the evening."

He reaches out and touches my arm, sending a new wave of electrical current pulsing through my body. "Hey, tonight is New Year's Eve." He glances at his hand, then back to my face. "After your performance, there's a party on the pool deck. Are you planning on going?"

I look into those deep velvety eyes of his. "I thought I'd make an appearance."

He smiles. "Good." His hand lifts. "If I don't see you before your performance, good luck. Your biggest fan will be cheering you on."

A blush spreads across my entire body.

~

My spastic nerves make it difficult to enjoy the scrumptious dinner set before me. The meal looks and smells delicious, but a jittery tummy and food is never a good combination. Mom always fussed at me to eat before a show, but usually, a milkshake was all I could stomach.

"Are you nervous?" Linda asks as I swirl my spoon through my lobster bisque.

"Not exactly nervous, more like anxious."

"Well, I know you'll do just fine," she assures me.

"We'll all be right there cheering you on." Dad squeezes my shoulder.

His encouragement is sweet. More of this while growing up would've been nice, but as they say, better late than never.

"Yes, your own little fan club," Gwen adds.

Yippee. Gwen will be there too. A flash of guilt washes through me. Gwen has been nothing but nice. It's not her fault that Dad can't seem to live life without someone pretty by his side. And there it is, the question that's haunted me all my life. Why weren't mom and I enough to fulfill that desire?

"You know," Linda says, "before I give a presentation before a large group, I always say a prayer. I pray for God to calm my nerves and use my excitement in a positive way. I also pray that the Holy Spirit guides my words and that He can use me to reach someone."

Excellent advice from my pseudo-mom for the week. "Thanks. I love that." While I do usually pray before a performance, it's more of a desperate plea that I don't screw up or make a fool of myself. Touching someone through my singing is a much better request.

Another look at my practically untouched meal, and my stomach turns. Nope, not happening. I place my napkin on the table. "I think I'm going to take a little stroll around the deck before I need to get to the lounge."

I push my chair back, and before I can stand, the three men at the table are on their feet. A girl could get used to this chivalrousness.

"And, Liz, you look absolutely stunning," Mrs. Sweetheart tells me.

"Thank you." I shoot her a grateful smile despite still being a little wary of the former popular girl—do they really ever change? Whether or not her comment is sincere, this outfit does give my self-confidence a boost. When I saw this gold dress at the store, I figured the shimmery material would be perfect for New Year's Eve. I love the vintage style, cinched at the waist with a fuller skirt that ends mid-shin. I also added some curls to my usually straight hair and just a touch of makeup, so my pale skin doesn't make me look like a ghost under the bright spotlights in the lounge.

Heading outside to the deck, I lean my forearms against the ship's railing. Taking a deep breath, I savor the salty sea air. The setting sun glimmers off the ocean, the golden rays creating a halo of warmth.

Have I ever truly appreciated all the beauty of this world? God is amazing.

Thank you, Lord, for all the incredible things you created for us. Thank you for the new friends I've made on this trip. Please be with me tonight. Help my song and words to touch those who need it. Amen.

Chapter 12

By the time I arrive at the lounge, the other contestants are already there. A single microphone has been placed at the front of the small stage. The Consuelos cousins are set up off to the side, warming up their instruments. Since Val won't be singing, he'll be the lead guitarist while Carlos plays the bass guitar. The Mambo Boys' Hawaiian shirt color choice of the evening is a muted blue.

Miles, looking spiffy as usual in his cruise director uniform, welcomes the contestants and gives us a few last-minute instructions. We all sit together on the left side of the stage. As I watch passengers file into the lounge, I concentrate on my breathing. Dad and the rest of our tablemates arrive early and claim a table in the very first row. Dad waves and points me out to his friends as if they couldn't spot me on their own.

Before long, the lounge fills to capacity. People continue to flow in, lining the perimeter of the lounge. What a crowd. Without a regular show in the theater, this is the evening's entertainment, but still, that many people want to watch amateurs perform?

The lights dim, and Miles takes to the stage. "Welcome! Thank you for joining us this evening for the next round of Siren of the Sea. I hope you all had a fabulous day on the beautiful island of Curacao. And tonight is New Year's Eve!"

The audience whoops and hollers.

"The party on the pool deck to ring in the new year will be one you'll never forget, so please make sure you join us." He pauses for a moment, taking in the crowd. "I hope you all have been enjoying the shows brought to you by our fabulously talented entertainment staff."

The audience shows their appreciation with loud cheers and whistles.

Miles nods his agreement. "Yes, they are great, aren't they? They work extremely hard to provide top-notch shows. But sometimes, they need a break as well, so what better way than to make our guests provide the entertainment for an evening."

The audience politely laughs.

"This competition is always one of my favorite parts of the cruise. Discovering the hidden talent among you is quite special." He looks our way, acknowledging us with a dazzling smile. "So, let me explain how this evening will proceed. There will be eight singers who are lucky enough to be accompanied by our incredible Mambo Boys."

A shrill whistle and catcall are followed by laughter from the crowd.

Miles cocks his head toward the band. "Marco, I didn't know your mother was on board this week."

The crowd laughs, and Marco sheepishly shrugs.

"Okay, back to the rules," Miles continues. "Three of tonight's singers will move on to the final round of our competition, which will be held on the last night of our trip."

Someone in the crowd calls out, "No!"

Everyone starts laughing again. Geez, these people are lively tonight. Hopefully, they will remain quiet during the songs.

Miles points in the direction of the heckler. "Well, you'll just have to book your next cruise right away."

More laughter.

My foot begins to tap. *Come on.* The anticipation is driving me crazy.

Miles expertly takes control of the room once again. "You will each find slips of paper and pencils on your tables. For those of you standing, a server will bring them to you. You can write down three names. We will tabulate the results, and the three contestants with the most votes will get a chance to perform on the large theater stage with our fabulous main theater band!"

Another round of raucous cheering.

"Now, let's begin. Our first contestant this evening was actually our first contestant of the whole event. This spunky woman is here with her husband, children, and grandchildren. This clan is joining us from the great state of Arkansas. Please welcome Grandma Millie!"

And so, it begins. Five contestants perform while I continue my deep breathing. After each song, the person is asked a few getting-to-know-you questions, but my mind is so focused on my song that I don't pay much attention to what is happening on stage, until the guy next to me nudges me with his elbow.

I glance up to see Miles looking my way. Oh! My turn.

With one final soothing breath, I walk on stage. It has been set up just the way I requested, with a stool behind the microphone. Val is perched on another stool off to the side, his guitar resting on his knee.

Val winks at me. I nod. This is going to be great.

I carefully sit on the stool and look out into the audience. But only the first two rows are visible due to the bright stage lights. Dad gives me a thumbs up. Beyond him, I notice Cole, who holds up his phone, letting me know he will record the performance. The lights then dim, except for two spotlights. One focused on me, and a dimmer one on Val, who will start out the song before the rest of his cousins join in.

Val begins strumming. The room turns hauntingly quiet. Those beautiful opening notes instantly calm my nerves, and I begin singing my bluesy rendition of *Somewhere Over the Rainbow*. The melancholy song was one I'd listened to repeatedly after my parents' divorce. My eyes close and I pour my soul into the slow, emotional version of the song. In that moment, I'm swept away with those raw childhood memories and lose myself to the music, the crescendo capturing all the hope and despair of a little girl feeling utterly alone in the world.

Too soon, the slow final line flows through me.

I hold the last note for an extra beat.

Then savor the silence.

The crowd suddenly bursts into feverish applause. My eyes open to take in the exuberant ovation. Dad beams and leans sideways to the people at the next table. Reading his lips is not difficult—*that's my daughter.*

Miles strides over to me as the applause dies down. "Wow, young lady. That was beautiful."

My gaze sweeps the room. "Thank you."

"It seems like this song really meant something to you. Can you tell us about that?"

I freeze for a moment, not sure how to answer. I hadn't prepared anything to say. But then the words just spill out. "I used to listen to that song after my parents divorced. I felt such a connection to Dorothy and totally understood what she was feeling. She felt so alone—that no one understood her or even wanted her around. She wished for a place that was different, one where dreams come true. That was what I longed for as well."

Amid the polite applause, my gaze lands on Dad. His proud smile has disappeared. He's looking down at the table, his right hand covering his mouth.

Oh. I avert my eyes from his crushed appearance. If only I could take back my response, but it's too late.

"Well," Miles continues talking, unaware of the cosmic shift in the atmosphere, "that was truly beautiful. Let's hear it one more time for Liz!"

He offers his hand to help me gracefully get off the stool. I curtsy to the warm applause, then turn around and mouth a thank you to the Consuelos cousins.

The final two performances continue, but all I can think about is the look on Dad's face. He'd been so happy and proud, and I destroyed it. All the progress we made this week is gone. Maybe it was all an illusion like Dorothy found in Oz.

As the show ends, I'm determined to find Dad and talk to him. Despite having no idea what to say, I feel an urge to try and explain. But before I can leave, one of the entertainment staff asks the contestants to stick around for a few moments. We're all thanked and congratulated on our performances, then given a rundown on what will happen next. By the time they are finished with us, the lounge has pretty much cleared out. So much for any reconciliation.

I walk back on stage where the Consuelos cousins are putting away their instruments. They look up as I approach.

"That was even better than rehearsal. Great job," Val tells me.

"Well, thank you for agreeing to that song. I wouldn't have done nearly as well if I'd had to choose one from the list."

Juan's serious expression seems out of place. "Is everything okay with Rosaline? I sent an email to the Brummels, but they haven't responded yet."

Juan slowly shakes his head. "We appreciate you trying to help, but Rosaline was informed this afternoon that she will be dismissed when we get back to port."

I catch my breath at the crushing news. "No! That's not fair!"

Carlos offers his cousin a tight smile. "I doubt they necessarily want to let her go, but they can't afford any risks."

I reach out my hand and squeeze Juan's arm. "Don't give up hope. I think something will work out."

His shoulders sag in defeat. "It would take a miracle at this point."

"Maybe I'll hear from the Brummels tomorrow." I look around at the cousins and their grim expressions. I bite my lip to stop the threatening tears.

I turn around and freeze at the sight before me. Cole, looking oh so handsome in his dark button-down shirt and dark pants, once again leans against the doorway—waiting for me. A flutter of excitement stirs within me.

He grins and begins clapping as I near. "Another amazing performance."

"Thanks." Knowing I don't sound overly grateful, I try to add a little warmth to my voice. "And thanks for recording it for me."

His eyebrows furrow. "Is something wrong?"

"I'm just not sure my dad would agree with your assessment." Even saying the words causes a pang of sadness.

He tilts his head. "Are you kidding? He was the first one out of his seat for that standing ovation."

A sigh escapes my lips. "Yeah, but you should've seen his face when I answered that question about the song."

"Ah." He glances to the side, then back at me—his expression grim. "I can see how that might've upset him, but you were just telling the truth."

"I know. But the truth can hurt."

"Maybe he needed to hear how you felt." He stuffs his hands into the front pockets of his pants. "You guys do have a few unresolved issues between you."

I take a deep breath, composing myself. "Maybe, but I probably should have thought before I spoke. Dropping that truth bomb in front of everyone was a bit harsh." Although Cole's right. For years, Dad and I have been in need of a heart to heart, so maybe this was the only way.

"Still feel up to going to the party?" His deep brown eyes are pools of compassion.

It's New Year's Eve—today's troubles can wait a few more hours. I force a smile. "Absolutely."

He offers his arm, and I loop mine around it. Time for the princess to head off to the ball with her handsome prince.

"My family loved the performance. I'm sure they'll swarm you with congratulations as soon as they see us."

"They came? How sweet." I can't wait to meet them. Finally, my curiosity will be satisfied about what his mom and siblings look like. I've been picturing his mom as an exotic beauty of middle eastern descent—can't wait to see if I'm right.

When we reach the pool deck, the party is already underway. The deck has transformed into a fairyland with what must be hundreds of strands of lights. A carefree crowd dances to popular tunes that emanate from large speakers. Videos and pictures from the past six days flicker across the giant screen. Staff members circulate through the crowd carrying food and drink trays.

"Smile!" a staff photographer appears out of nowhere. She motions for Cole and me to get closer. My handsome escort puts his arm around me, and our heads tilt together. She snaps a few photos, then looks at the display on her camera. "Oh, you make a beautiful couple."

Although I have yet to stop by the photo gallery to check on any of the photos—wasn't that interested in the shots of Dad and me during the cruise—I will definitely be stopping by tomorrow to purchase this one.

But that's tomorrow. Tonight, I'll try to focus on the here and now. I turn to Cole. "It's so pretty up here tonight with all the lights." Who knew it was possible for this place to get any prettier. "I wish I could soak in all this beauty."

Cole's eyes soften and his mouth opens as if to say something but then his gaze shifts to something over my shoulder, causing the expression to disappear. "Oh, watch out. Here comes the family."

The moment I turn around, Mia, the girl we've been spending time with once in a while, wraps me in a hug. Her family must be hanging out with Cole's tonight. Makes sense since they seem to know each other well.

"You were amazing tonight, Liz."

"Thank you." I return the hug.

Connor stands behind her, nodding in agreement. Then my gaze flicks to Cole's dad. His arm draped across the shoulder of a woman—a very pale, blond woman with a beautiful, warm smile.

It suddenly hits me like a tidal wave. Connor and Mia aren't family friends. They are Cole's *siblings*. And these very light-skinned adults are their parents. Cole is adopted.

Please, God, help me pull off an even greater performance than my earlier stage appearance because I'm not sure I'm a good enough actress to hide my shocked realization.

"Liz, your song was beautiful." Cole's mom only says a few words, but somehow, they emit genuine kindness.

"Thank you. It's so nice to meet you." I flash back to all the complaining I've done to Cole about my father. Never once did I think that maybe Cole had his own situation and emotional baggage regarding his parents. Cole's adoptive parents seem like loving, caring people, but it would be only natural for him to have questions about his birth family. What a self-centered idiot I am. Here I am whining about my dad and my life, assuming I'm the only one with a complicated, hurtful past.

We chat for a few more minutes, then Mia insists we all head to the dance floor.

Thank goodness for cheesy dance music—the perfect excuse to hide my gamut of emotions.

The DJ keeps the dance floor filled, playing one great song after another. Eventually, I spot Dad leaning against the bar with a drink in hand. After so much dancing, I'm about ready for a breather anyway, so I tell Cole and Mia I'll be back in a few minutes.

I make my way through the crowd toward Dad when Tank suddenly blocks my path. "Loved the performance," he says with a crooked grin. "Such a heartwarming father-daughter moment."

I'm ready to push him out of the way when his scowling wife grabs his arm and yanks him back to her side. What a creep.

As I approach the bar, Dad smiles and raises his glass. "And there she is, the belle of the ball."

From the glassy look in his eyes, I can tell that is not his first cocktail of the evening. He leans in and kisses my cheek. I grimace at the bitter smell of alcohol.

The guy next to him and the woman he's with pose for a series of selfies. Their not-a-care-in-the-world smiles annoy me. What I wouldn't give to feel that way instead of knowing I've crushed any progress in the relationship that Dad and I have made over the last few days. The man carelessly tosses the disposable camera on the bar counter.

"Your song was wonderful."

My eyes turn to him, but his gaze drops to admire his drink.

"Thank you." I should say something more but am at a total loss.

Then he looks up, and our eyes lock. The moment balloons around us with so many unspoken words and feelings.

His hand moves toward my arm but then pulls back. "You did such an amazing job, kiddo."

Say something—now's your chance.

"Oh, Liz!"

I turn to see Midge approaching. She places my left hand between her wrinkling but bejeweled hands. Unlike Dad, she has no trouble touching me. "You did such a wonderful job tonight. You sing like an angel."

"Thanks, Midge."

Midge's head cranes upward to look at Dad. "You must be so proud."

He nods, then turns his focus on me. "Never been prouder."

I long to tear my gaze away from the sad look on his face. The one that I put there.

"Oh, Wade!" Gwen squeezes her way through the crowd and takes his hand. "It's almost midnight. We need to get our champagne."

Dad leans in and kisses my cheek. "Happy New Year. I have a feeling there's someone else here you'd rather celebrate with than me."

He disappears, letting Gwen pull him along through the crowd.

Midge squeezes my hand. "I think we'd better find our handsome men for the countdown." She winks at me, then makes her own vanishing act.

I stand there glancing around at all the couples and families huddled together, watching the giant screen where the countdown is ticking away. Frustration wells inside me. Three minutes until midnight. I wander toward the railing to stare out at the dark ocean. This is definitely not how I envisioned this evening.

"There you are." Cole emerges from the crowd.

"I thought you'd be celebrating with your family." I can't believe he came looking for me.

He holds up two glasses of sparkling cider. "I do that every year. I'd rather spend this one with you."

I take the glass he offers. "Thank you."

The crowd starts chanting. "Sixty! Fifty-nine!"

He leans closer. "I don't think I told you yet how amazing you look tonight."

"Fifty!"

I squirm under his intense gaze. "Are you making another *My Fair Lady* reference? An Eliza Doolittle transformation?"

He shakes his head. "No. I mean it."

"Thirty!"

"I'm so glad I met you," he continues. "You've made this vacation memorable."

"Twenty!"

I've dreamt all day of this moment and the possibility of celebrating with this incredible guy at midnight. And now I'm standing next to him, looking at his handsome face, moments away from my first New Year's Eve kiss.

"Ten!"

He reaches for my hand.

"Nine!"

My heart skips a beat.

"Eight!"

"Cole." His name comes out in a whisper.

"Seven!"

He takes a step closer.

"Six!"

Our eyes lock.

"Five!"

I force myself to breathe.

"Four!"

I try again. "Cole."

"Three!"

He smiles.

"Two!"

"I can't."

"One!"

"Sorry." I turn away from the greatest guy I've ever met and slip into the crowd.

"Happy New Year!"

I weave through hundreds of kissing, hugging, toasting passengers as fireworks explode above us, tears streaming down my cheeks.

Chapter 13

I burst into my room and shut the door behind me. Leaning against the door, I swipe at the tears coursing down my cheeks. Poor Cole. How could I have left him standing there all by himself? But there was no way I could let him kiss me. He's such an amazing guy and deserves so much more than a stupid vacation romance with someone completely undeserving of him.

With a deep breath, I walk to the closet and kneel to unzip my suitcase. I toss aside the sweaters I wore in Chicago at the beginning of this trip, to unbury my favorite purse. I unzip it and turn it upside down. Fresh tears blur my vision as items tumble onto the bottom of my suitcase. A romance novel, a small digital recorder, a handheld poker game, a silver pen, a bracelet, and a pair of sunglasses encircle the iPod and gold compact that started this whole mess.

I toss the disposable camera I swiped during the New Year's Eve party to the stash of items I've stolen from the unsuspecting vacationers, then lean against the closet door. How did things get so out of control? What a disaster.

It all started innocently enough—during the summer after fifth grade. Josie and I thought it would be fun to be part of the community theater production of *Oliver*. We were cast as orphans and had a blast with the choreography of *You've Got to Pick a Pocket or Two*. The man who played Fagin knew how bored us kids were during the long rehearsals, so he began sticking scarves and use-less prop pocket watches on his person. He'd give candy to any-one who could successfully "steal" one of the items. The game kept us entertained and helped make the choreography for that song a crowd favorite. It also started a new obsession for Josie and me.

All summer, we would sneakily take each other's belongings and see how long it took the other to notice. While the game soon died out, I discovered it was an excellent way to keep Dad's atten-tion. His missing keys meant he couldn't leave as early as he wanted to. His "misplaced" phone meant the office couldn't get ahold of him. Without his watch, he lost track of time and played cards a little longer.

But over time, as my anger with Dad grew, my newfound skill shifted from opportunities to spend more time with him to pun-ishment. When we came home early from the zoo so Dad could watch football, the lost remote control made him miss the game. When he didn't want to go on a bike ride because he had some work to do, his computer mouse somehow wasn't where he thought he'd left it. I always put the items under a cushion or in the pantry. With his propensity of misplacing items, he never sus-pected a thing. Even though I still didn't get my way, watching him search gave me a strange satisfaction.

I knew it was wrong, but it was like I couldn't control myself. Then when I started high school and the popular crowd made life unbearable, I used my sleight of hand as payback. When the homecoming queen forced some nerdy freshmen to vacate "her" table in the quad, her phone disappeared. I have no idea what was on that phone, but she went full freak out before someone found it at the next table. And there was the time one of the popular jocks berated his younger brother in front of the entire lunch-room. His lucky hat, the one that ensured he'd do well in that night's basketball game, somehow ended up in the lost and found. Like a modern-day Robin Hood, I doled out punishment to those who deserved it. Even though I felt justified, the guilt started gnawing at me, so I forced myself to stop.

That was until six days ago. Somehow, my dad-infused frus-tration always makes the irrational surface, and I reverted back to my old coping mechanisms. Watching that man at the bon voyage party so engrossed with listening to something on his iPod that he was completely missing the special moment just put me over the edge. And I wanted to shake the mom who was too busy reading that trashy romance novel to take a moment to witness just one of the flips into the pool her son was begging her to watch. And then that woman at our dinner table who thought she was so much better than the rest of us. Checking her reflection in her compact was more important than chatting with us.

Only what were the odds that two of those random people had rooms near each other with Rosaline as their room steward?

My plan had been to take the original three items to the concierge desk, but then the Consuelos guys told me about Rosaline's problem. I actually had the iPod, book, and compact in my bag as the handsome musicians pleaded for my assistance. Even if the items appeared then, I was pretty sure that wouldn't help the situation and Rosaline agreed that security would probably assume that she was trying to clear her name by returning the items.

I figured the best way to help was to contact the Brummels and hopefully discover that they had just misplaced the missing necklace. If it wasn't actually missing, then there would be no reason to suspect Rosaline. No answer from them led to plan B—taking more items to shift the focus away from the innocent woman. I never thought they'd actually fire her without any proof.

Then tonight, Juan told me the bad news, and I knew that my stupid idea hadn't worked. Rosaline will lose her job, and it's all my fault. Her poor kids, who rarely get to see their mom, are now even worse off without any income to support the family. Rosaline and Juan, who clearly adore each other, will now be separated. All because I have issues with my dad.

Dad. I bury my face in my hands. That moment in the lounge keeps replaying in my mind. My performance made him beam with enthusiasm. I'm not sure I've ever seen him so proud. Then that stupid question from Miles. The gutted, pained look on Dad's face refuses to vacate my brain. Why did I pick that moment to tell the truth?

I lean my head back against the wall. The irony is that's what I've always wanted—to cause him pain. For him to know how much I've been hurting all these years. So, now that it's happened, why do I feel so much worse?

Then there's sweet Cole. He probably hates me now. What a coward I am—running off and leaving him standing there alone at midnight. But I couldn't let him kiss me. Even though that's what I've dreamt of all day, I couldn't let it happen. He deserves so much better than a vacation romance with someone this flawed. He's a genuinely good guy, and I can't be the one to tarnish him in any way.

I push myself off the closet floor and move into my room. I freeze at the sight in front of me. On my bed is an array of towel animals. A swan is perched on my pillow, my bracelet creating a little tiara for its head. My barrel head hairbrush leans toward the princess swan like a microphone. The swan's audience, a turtle, a bunny, a pig, and a crab, sits in a line in the middle of the bed, watching her sing.

How did Vincent know I was performing this evening? Knowing how much extra time it must have taken for him to create this for me brings fresh tears streaming down my face.

⁓

When my eyes flutter open, sunlight streaming into the room reveals that I slept curled around the towel animals, still wearing my gold dress. I rub my temples, trying to stop the tear-induced headache. It's been years since I've cried myself to sleep. One look at myself in the mirror across the small room causes me to grimace. Just lovely. My matted hair clings to the side of my face. My pale cheeks are streaked with black mascara from my puffy eyes to my chin. Wow. Looking good.

Worse than my haggard appearance is the memory of last night's train wreck—when my life completely derailed. Certainly not the New Year's Eve of my daydreams. And to top it off, today is sadly our final island stop. Bonaire.

Time to get moving before Dad knocks on my door. I extricate myself from the protective nest of towel animals and am halfway to the bathroom to take a shower when I remember. Dad's golfing with his buddies today. I'm on my own.

My first thought is, *as usual* but then I stop myself. *Enough.* It's a new year and time for a new attitude. Who knows how I'll ever make things right with Dad, but the self-pity has to stop. I'm not the only one with family issues. Rosaline's kids barely know their mother. Cole and his siblings may never have even met their biological parents.

I veer into the small bathroom, then backtrack three steps and stare at two pieces of paper that someone slid under my door. A glimmer of hope that one may be from Cole quickly fades. The first is a note informing me that I'll be moving on to the next round of the competition. The news does nothing to brighten my mood. The second is the list of available activities for our day on Bonaire. Dad must have slid it under on his way out.

Not that I feel like sightseeing but staying cooped up on board all day is not an option. So, I scan the list. Tour activities can immediately be eliminated. The last thing I want to do today is be surrounded by happy families. That pretty much leaves the beach or a self-guided walking tour around town. I read the description of the sites I could walk to—an open-air market, some historical buildings, a botanical garden, and San Bernardo church.

San Bernardo? Saint Bernard? Was there actually a Saint Bernard? Are those adorable search dogs named after a person?

Wait. The paper slips out of my hand and flutters to the ground. I scan the desk area for the last cryptic note I found. Wasn't the clue something about a trusted friend who helps the lost? Isn't that what Saint Bernard dogs are known for? I frantically search through the accumulated papers until I find it.

A trusted friend on whom the lost depend will be your guide for this journey's end.

A glimmer of hope flickers. Could the clues be leading me to San Bernardo church? Well, only one way to find out.

~

Using the provided map for the self-guided tour, I beeline it for San Bernardo church. Brightly colored buildings line the streets of this Dutch colony, just like in Curaçao. But the beautiful day and charming buildings barely make an impression as I hurry along. What was the reason for this scavenger hunt? What could possibly be waiting for me at this church?

When I round the corner, I'm no longer in need of the map's assistance. A bright yellow clock tower and similarly painted A-frame church comes into view. The church is surprisingly simple except for the large, circular stained-glass window above the front doors and the white cross adorning the peak of the building. The beacon of faith lures me closer.

With a deep breath to calm my growing apprehension, I pull open the white wooden door. Cool, aromatic air greets me. A sense of calm fills me as I walk down the aisle between the rows of dark wooden pews—like I've made it home after a long journey. The white pointed arches draw my focus to the front of the altar, where a dark wooden crucifix stands in front of a stunningly beautiful stained-glass window.

With no idea where to begin my search for whatever brought me here, I silently slide into one of the pews. A wave of exhaustion overwhelms me. I'm suddenly so tired of being bogged down by the bitterness of my parents' divorce. Why am I hanging onto those old feelings? Why can't I move on?

I pull down the kneeler, practically collapsing into the familiar prayer position.

Lord, please help me. How do I move forward? How do Dad and I get past all this? Please show me the way.

Soft footsteps pull me out of my prayer. From the side of the church, an elderly, stern-faced priest walks toward me. Uh-oh. Am I not supposed to be here? But I can't leave now. I haven't discovered the answer to the riddle yet.

The sour-faced priest slowly shuffles closer. Each step increasing my dread.

He finally stops a row in front of me and stares at me.

Should I say something? Does he speak English?

He clears his throat. "My dear, is your name Liz?"

I slide back onto the bench, never so surprised to hear my name. "Um…yes."

His smile transforms his solemn face into a friendly, grandfatherly one. "Someone thinks you are very special." He reaches toward me, a folded piece of paper in his hand.

I reach out and grasp the corner of the note.

The priest's wrinkly fingers don't release their grip, so we are awkwardly both holding onto the paper. My gaze lifts from our hands to his watery eyes.

"I will be in the back if you need me." He finally lets go of the note and continues his slow trek down the aisle.

Well, that was unexpected. While I'm happy to have so easily found the note, I'm more confused than ever. The priest called me by name, so this hunt I've been on was definitely designed for me. But who could have set this up? Since I slept in, I suppose anyone could have gotten off the ship before me and come to this church and asked the priest to hand me this paper if I showed up. But whoever is behind this planned it days ago. How did they know the priest would help them? Maybe they didn't, and they were just lucky when he agreed. Perhaps he'll tell me more? I turn around to see where he went. My gaze scans the area near the entryway, but the marble baptismal font and wooden confessional are all I see. He's nowhere in sight. I'm once again alone in the sanctuary. Where'd he go?

I turn my attention back to the note—the sheet of paper wobbles in my shaking hand. Smoothing out the creases, I lay it on my lap.

The key to happiness is forgiveness.

That's it? After days of deciphering clues that lead me on a hunt all around the ship, this is it? Who would go through all the trouble to send me this message?

I crunch the note into a ball—what a waste of time.

A tear sneaks out of the corner of my eye and slides down my cheek. I take a few deep breathes to calm myself before leaving the peace of the church. There's still plenty of time to spend the rest of the day on the beach.

The key to happiness is forgiveness.

My clenched fist relaxes. Is that what I need to do? Forgive my dad? Hurting him with my actions and words certainly didn't make me feel any better and just made our relationship more tenuous.

But can I truly forgive him? It's so hard to let go of the pain he caused by not being there for me and for destroying our family. I just don't know if I can do it.

My gaze shifts to the crucifix and Jesus' battered and bloody body hanging from the cross. *Father, forgive them.* That's what our Lord prayed as he was dying. If He could forgive, why can't I?

I squeeze my eyes shut and breath in the sweet smell of incense. *Please, God, help me to forgive my dad. Help us to find a way to move our relationship forward.*

And then my mind shifts to all my actions that resulted from my pain and frustration. The rude behavior, snarky comments, stealing, causing Rosaline to lose her job. Is it possible to put that all behind me and move forward? Somehow, Josie has been able to do it. Maybe it's time to try out that new youth group with her and Ryan. Maybe I need to make a few changes during this new year. Maybe Dad's not the only one who needs forgiveness.

I focus on the crucifix. Maybe Cole's right, and it's time to join the church. *Lord, please forgive my actions. Help me to become a better person.*

Suddenly, I have a feeling as to where the priest disappeared to—the confessional. *Forgiveness is the key to happiness.* Anxiety twists my insides as I think of revealing my sins to someone—even if I'll never see him again. No, thank you.

I glance back at the confessional. Josie once explained to me that during the sacrament of reconciliation, the priest acts in the person of Christ. A chill runs down my spine.

I can't imagine how freeing it would be to share this burden. And I sure could use some advice on how to move forward—trying to handle it all on my own has always ended in failure. Maybe it's time to try something different. I let out a breath. What do I have to lose? But can non-Catholics even go to confession?

I stuff the note in my bag. Time to find out. Because no matter what—it's time to forgive myself.

Chapter 14

The first time I see Dad all day is when he sits down for dinner—his pink hue a telltale sign that he'd neglected his sunscreen while on the golf course.

He slides in his seat, giving me a cautious smile. "Hi, did you have a good day?"

Our tablemates suddenly seem overly interested in their menus. Is our father-daughter awkwardness that obvious? Stupid question. Of course, it is. They were all at the show, witnessing firsthand the devasting blow I delivered to dear old dad.

I try to reassure him with my return smile. "Yes, it was great." Life-changing, in fact. Bearing my soul in Confession felt amazing. Despite the difficult penance of needing to tell Dad everything, I felt free and ready to turn a new leaf. This must be how Josie felt when she returned from her summer in South Carolina. She'd tried to explain her life-altering change, but I didn't get it. Now I do.

Dad's eyebrows raise in surprise. "What did you do?"

Obviously, this is not the time or place to explain everything. "I explored the town a bit." Mostly just San Bernardo church. "Then spent some time on the beach." Not soaking up the sunshine but taking a long walk, praying, and contemplating my life. "Before coming back here to confer with the band about my next song choice." After once again striking out in the email-from-the-Brummels department.

Linda pushes away her menu, done pretending not to be eavesdropping on our conversation. "Congratulations on moving forward in the competition!"

Mrs. Sweetheart claps her hands. "How exciting!"

He fiddles with the napkin. "That's wonderful."

"Thank you."

"What song will you be singing?" Linda probes.

I wiggle my eyebrows up and down. "You'll just have to wait and find out." Truth be told, I'm a little conflicted about my song choice, despite being one of my favorites.

Our waiter comes to tell us about the evening's specials. Tonight, I'm famished and order the prime rib.

"Is Gwen joining us tonight?" Matt asks Dad after we all place our orders.

Dad shakes his head. "No. She said she has plans but that she'll meet up with us later."

I push away the snarky thought that first pops into my mind. *Remember—new leaf, Liz!*

Mr. Sweetheart nudges Dad. "Don't look now but Tank and Renee are making the rounds."

I watch as the least-likely-to-be-invited-to-dinner couple moves from one table to the next. Renee's fake laugh, like nails on a chalkboard. Tank's smug grin is no less grating.

Mrs. Sweetheart shakes her head. "Take a gander at her necklace. We got stuck riding the elevator with them this afternoon, and she had to tell us all about the newest anniversary gift Tank gave her."

As if on cue, Renee turns to wave at someone and the multicolored jewels around her neck glimmer in the light from the chandeliers.

"Wow," Linda mutters. "Think that will make finally make her happy?"

The men exchange looks and answer in unison. "No."

The table shares a laugh then before everyone can start their individual conversations, I make my move.

"I wanted to thank you all for coming to the lounge last night to cheer me on. To show my appreciation, I got you each a little something." I pull my bag out from under my seat.

"Oh, you didn't have to get us anything," Linda says. "We were excited to see you sing."

"Well, since we've left the dock, it's too late to return them now," I joke. I hand Dad and the two couples that have been our dinner companions all week little gift bags.

They open them together, revealing ornaments made of small coconut shells with hand-painted beach scenes.

"This is beautiful!" Mrs. Sweetheart's exclamation seems genuine—maybe I misjudged her previous actions.

"Thank you." Linda wraps her arm around my shoulder and pulls me in for a side hug.

"That was really thoughtful of you." Dad's eyes mist up. That and his slightly sunburned skin make him appear way too vulnerable.

Matt and Paul chime in with their thanks as well.

"Every year, when you hang it on your Christmas trees, you can think about this trip."

The dinner conversation then morphs into a discussion about everyone's favorite island. After reminiscing about all the fun excursions, the overall consensus is that it's just too hard to decide. The islands we visited have all been spectacular.

After dinner, our group migrates down to the theater for the evening show. Mr. and Mrs. Sweethearts lead the way and file into an open row, sitting close to the center. Matt and Linda enter next, and I follow, taking the seat next to Linda. Dad sits on my other side. Soon other passengers fill in the rest of the row.

While we wait for the show to begin, Dad and Matt lean around Linda and me, chatting about the day's golf tournament that lasted so long that it delayed our departure time.

Linda turns to me. "We still need to use our free spa coupons."

Still hard to believe we're on the last few days of the trip. "Yes, we can't let them go to waste."

She leans closer, keeping her distance from Matt's exaggerated hand gestures. "I'm thinking maybe the day of your big performance would be good, even though it's the last full day on the ship. We could get you all glammed up before the show."

"Thanks." A perfect way to end the trip.

As the lights dim, Dad and Matt settle back into their seats.

Miles once again takes the stage, and the audience applauds. "Good evening! I hope you all enjoyed your time on the beautiful island of Bonaire." He pauses for the audience's enthusiastic response. "Tonight, we have a great show for you. For those guests here for their class reunion, our incredible dancers and singers will be performing a tribute to your formative years—the 1980s. I hope those of you that are part of this reunion appreciate this because while it might bring back good memories for you, the rest of us will have to painfully relive the era."

The audience laughs.

"Speaking of the high school reunion folks, one of their own will also be performing tonight. A very talented comedienne, Gwen O'Riley!"

The audience claps, and like a row of dominos, our group turns to look at Dad. He returns our baffled looks with one of his own, then shrugs.

I lean closer to him. "You didn't know she was performing tonight?"

Dad shakes his head. "No. I didn't even know she was a comic."

Miles exits the stage, and all goes dark. Then begins the familiar strains of an 80s rock anthem. The stage lights flash on, revealing the singers and dancers decked out in 80s garb. My eyes immediately go to Svetlana and Ivan. I don't get it. Why would anyone want hair that big? Years from now, how will people remember this era? Are there certain fashions that will become iconic from my high school years? Probably, but it's hard to picture—today's style seems too normal.

After their high-energy tribute to the era of legwarmers and sequined gloves, the curtain closes. A booming voice comes through the speakers. "And now, please welcome Gwen O'Riley!"

The audience claps, and Gwen strolls out on stage carrying a microphone stand. She sets the stand in the middle of the stage. Her black pantsuit and high heels make her look particularly thin and sleek. The spotlight adds an extra shimmer to her pretty golden locks. She waves at everyone.

"Wow, thank you for the warm welcome. As you already heard, my name is Gwen, and I'm on this cruise celebrating my thirtieth high school reunion with my fellow classmates."

A few scattered cheers erupt around the crowded theater.

Her blond waves bob up and down as she nods. "Those enthusiastic classmates must be on the reunion committee, trying to convince us this trip was a good idea. Because the rest of us are still wondering why we agreed to spend ten days during the holidays with people we've spent the last thirty years trying to forget."

The audience laughs. My exact thoughts. I can't imagine wanting to spend a week with my classmates.

Gwen pulls the wireless microphone out of the stand and takes a few steps stage left. "You know, this week made one thing crystal clear. Our seventeen- and eighteen-year-old selves were horrible at predicting the future. For instance, the couple we voted Most Likely to Get Married didn't even stay together through the summer after we graduated."

She pauses for the chuckles and murmurs to die down.

"I guess we didn't do too bad with our Most Likely to Succeed. I mean, Cory Fields is the most successful used-car salesman in Crosby, Wyoming—population five hundred."

Ouch.

She slowly walks along the front of the stage, crossing to the other side. The enraptured crowd clinging to her every word. "It has been great to see people again. Like Tony Zanelli."

A bunch of women cheer.

"For those of you who don't know, Tony was Mr. Popular. Captain of the football team. Homecoming King. The guy every male wanted to be, and every female wanted to date. Every school seems to have one, right?"

People shout out their agreement.

"Tony had the best hair—thick and dark. You just wanted to run your fingers through it." She wiggles her fingers. "And those bulging muscles." With her free hand, she indicates massive biceps.

As people cheer, Mrs. Sweetheart leans in to share something with Linda and me. "He really was such a dish."

"Yep," Gwen continues, "it was great to see Tony again. But those muscles. Well, let's just say they migrated south a little bit."

Her hand lowers down and stops at her stomach. "Tony, that is one impressive beer gut you've got there."

That joke gets a huge response. One loud voice shouts something I can't understand.

Gwen shields her eyes to peer out into the audience. "Tank, is that you? If I were you, I wouldn't be so quick to laugh. Have you looked in a mirror lately?" She makes a face that receives another appreciative reaction.

I glance at Dad, who's grinning, thoroughly enjoying her diss on Tank.

The audience quiets down, and Gwen lifts the microphone again. "But you know what the best thing about a class reunion is?"

A man's voice yells out something indecipherable.

She turns and points in the direction of the heckler. "Is that you, Vinnie? You never could handle your liquor."

A burst of laughter erupts from Dad's classmates, who appreciate the inside joke.

"No. The best part is realizing that karma is a beautiful thing."

A few chuckles spread through the audience.

"Hey, I'm serious. Take Troy Wellan, for instance."

Out of the corner of my eye, I see Dad nodding.

"Talk about revenge of the nerds. That skinny little geek who was relentlessly razzed by the jocks started his own tech company and is now a bajillionaire. He probably owns a yacht the size of this boat."

Whistles and cheers. What a great thought—the kids at my school who are being picked on now may someday getting the last laugh.

Gwen walks back to center stage. "And then there's my personal reconnection."

As the audience provides a slew of catcalls, I sneak a glance at Dad, whose grin has widened.

"Yep. I reconnected with an old flame during this trip. Wade Kennedy." She points our way as the audience's approval explodes.

"You see, Wade and I had a thing for each other during the long winter of our senior year."

Aahs fill the room.

"I know, so sweet. We had a blast together—sledding, skating, snuggling together as we watched MTV."

While I cringe at the thought, the audience chuckles.

The spotlight highlights the wistful look on her face. "And I don't know if I'd ever been more excited as when he asked me to prom."

The audience continues with their oohing and aahing.

She lets out a little laugh and shakes her head. "I hadn't been to prom before, so worked extra shifts at my folk's restaurant to save money for a fancy new dress."

Her story commands everyone's rapt attention. Silence fills the auditorium as everyone anticipates the next part of the story. I settle back, anxious to hear about their prom date. The audience remains silent as they hang on to her every word. She expertly adds a few moments of anticipated silence as she walks a few steps, then stops.

She turns her face back to the waiting crowd. "But those extra shifts didn't pay off because a week before prom, I found out through the grapevine that Wade had asked someone else to be his date."

An audible gasp erupts from the crowd. I glance at Dad. His eyebrows furrow. Even in the dark, his cheeks color.

Gwen holds up a hand. "Don't worry. Don't worry. As I said, karma is a beautiful thing." A few whistles puncture the silence. "Seems like ole Wade and his cheating ways never changed. He's now divorced."

A slew of claps spread around us. I slump in my seat. Dad's fists clench.

She takes a few steps back toward center stage, then turns to face the audience. "His life has fallen apart so much that the only person he could find to bring on this trip is his teenage daughter, who hates him."

Mrs. Sweetheart gasps, and Linda grasps my arm. My mouth drops open. I sneak a peek at Dad—his jaw twitches in anger.

"But the most pathetic thing is that he thought our romance was reigniting, while I was just searching for material for this set. See, my friends, revenge can be a good thing."

The audience laughs and cheers. I sit there stunned. How could someone be so awful? I look at Dad and can practically see the humiliation oozing from him. He pushes himself out of his seat and storms out of the row.

I watch his retreating figure as he heads up the aisle toward the exit.

Thankfully, Gwen moves on to jokes about the cruise.

What do I do? Poor Dad. There's really only one thing to do—go after him. I squeeze my way past the people seated in our row, offering apologies as I step on toes on my way to the aisle. I have no idea where to search for him, but I at least need to try.

— ⁓ —

It turns out finding him isn't all that difficult. I just had to think like him. Where would Dad go if he were upset? Probably not outside like I would. He'd be more likely to hide out in the casino or a bar. And luckily, due to the relaxed rules while in international waters, I'm able to walk through both those areas.

After striking out in the casino, I locate him bellied up to a bar near the piano lounge. He's hunched over, staring at the glass of amber liquid in his hand. I take a deep breath, then hoist myself up on the stool next to him.

He glances at me. "Great vacation, huh?"

Again—such irony. For years, I wished something would happen to make him as miserable as I felt, but now seeing him like this breaks my heart. If only I possessed the ability to make him feel better.

He turns back to stare at his glass. "Sorry I drug you along on this trip."

"I'm not."

He smirks and shakes his head.

"No. I'm serious." Now would be the perfect time to open up and tell him how I'm feeling and all that I've done, but I falter. "Is what Gwen said true? About prom?"

He lifts one shoulder in a shrug, keeping his focus on the whiskey glass. "I'm not sure. That's not how I remember it, but maybe."

"Even if you did ask someone else, what she just did was wrong. Only a horrible person would lead you along all week, then do that. She's the pathetic one, never being able to move past something that happened to her so many years ago." *Kind of like not being able to move past things that happened in your childhood?* Okay, conscience, I get the message loud and clear.

Dad turns to look at me. "She was right, though. I didn't have anyone to bring on this trip except you. And don't try to make me feel better. I know you didn't want to come."

Unsure of how to respond, I stare at the defeated creases around his eyes.

He takes a swig of his drink, then continues. "And I didn't realize until last night when you answered that question on stage just how much I've screwed up—not only my life but yours as well."

I have no idea exactly what I'm going to say but know now is definitely the time to bring everything out into the open.

I slide off the stool. "Dad, will you come with me? I've got something to show you."

He grimaces like he's unsure but swigs the remainder of his drink, sets his glass down and stands. I grab his abandoned card key from the bar.

Neither of us says a word as I lead the way to my stateroom.

I open the door and smile at the towel monkey hanging from the reading light near my bed. The inanimate creature somehow boosts my confidence that things will be alright.

Dad sinks into the chair next to the bed. "What do you want to show me?"

In the closet, I once again throw my winter clothes on the floor, then scoop up the stolen items and walk toward the bed. With a watchful eye on his face, I let the pilfered items spill out of my arms and across the mattress, in front of the towel peacock perched upon my pillow.

Dad's eyes widen. "Wh-what's all this?"

I sink onto the bed next to all the items. "Things I've stolen."

He flinches, then his quivering hand moves toward his open mouth.

I start at the beginning and tell him every painful detail. As I share, he slumps back in his chair, tears welling in his eyes. My voice cracks at seeing him so visibly upset, but I continue, knowing he needs to hear everything.

I finish with the mysterious scavenger hunt and how I was led to San Bernardo church, my Confession, and my determination to start a new chapter by forgiving him and myself.

He leans forward, his elbows resting on his knees, his face buried in his hands.

Should I comfort him? Should I say something? Unsure how to respond, I silently wait for his reaction. Will he yell at me? Will he storm out? Will he break down and cry? Hopefully not the latter—that would be the hardest to deal with.

He finally straightens, rubs his eyes, and lets out a deep breath. "Wow. We are a messed-up pair, aren't we?"

"Like father, like daughter." Again, I speak before thinking. The comment was meant to lighten the mood, but too late, I realize it may make him feel even worse. I bite my lip, forcing myself to remain quiet.

He runs his hand across his face. "I've completely screwed up my life. I've been so selfish and only ever thought about what I wanted. And now I've messed up your life as well." His voice catches. "I missed so much. I don't know how I can ever make that up."

I slide off the bed and sit at his feet. "Today, I realized I can't blame you for the mistakes I make." Breathe. "Maybe we can move past this and start fresh somehow?"

He pulls me in for a hug. "I would love that."

His firm embrace wraps me in a blanket of safety and protection. Tears slide down my cheeks.

He kisses the top of my head, then releases me. He nods toward the bed and the stash of items. "But first, we need to do something about that."

Chapter 15

Dad's unsuccessful attempt at arranging a morning appointment with someone from the security office means we're free to enjoy a leisurely breakfast. While I definitely wasn't looking forward to the meeting, I had been anxious to finally clear Rosaline's name. That will now have to wait for a few more hours.

As I follow Dad toward the buffet, I can't help but smile. Praying the novena this morning was a completely different experience from the previous days. My faithful recitation of the prayer all week lacked any real conviction since I didn't truly believe anything could change the dynamics of my relationship with Dad. But today, I'm full of awe at the power of the prayer. *Thanks, Holy Family.*

I reach for a tray and scan the vast array of breakfast choices. "Now, what's your plan for the day? Another poker tournament?" Hopefully, he doesn't feel the need to keep an eye on me all day until our dreaded appointment.

"There is one scheduled at three, but I don't think I'll go." He scoops a large portion of diced potatoes onto his plate.

"You might as well. I have my dress rehearsal this afternoon anyway."

He reaches for the bacon. "I can't believe you're going to be performing in the large theater. I'm so proud of you for taking the risk and joining the competition."

"Yeah, I wasn't planning on doing it, but that first night, I couldn't stop myself." Ready-made omelets catch my eye.

"I wish I could've seen that first performance."

"Well, Cole has the video. He's supposed to send it to me." I snag a blueberry muffin. Then move on to the drink station.

"So…is there something I should know about you two?" Dad queries as he follows me.

Oh, how I wish there were. "We're just friends. It was fun having someone my age to hang with." I spot an open table and hurry toward it before someone else takes it.

Dad settles in across from me. "Hey, I noticed on today's schedule there's a movie trivia game starting in a half hour in the lounge. Would you maybe want to go? With me?" His cautiousness makes me smile.

"Well, we have watched a lot of movies together over the years." I choose to not dwell on the fact that watching movies was not necessarily a fun father/daughter activity but a way to keep me occupied while he worked on his computer. "I bet we'd make a pretty formidable team."

He smiles, then reaches for his fork. He stabs at a hunk of potato, then sets his utensil down and looks at me. "Hey, I just wanted to thank you for opening up to me. I know that had to have been extremely difficult. I hope we can move forward with our new and improved relationship."

"Me too." Hopefully, he realizes I have no further interest in mushy conversations about feelings though. "Speaking of working things out, are you going to talk to Gwen?"

His jaw twitches. "No. I have no desire to see her. Or really anyone. This ship can't return to port soon enough."

I set my muffin down. "Dad, don't let her win. You can't let the bullies get away with their behavior. I think you should just act like it doesn't bother you. Then she won't get the satisfaction of making you feel bad. Your classmates will either think you were in on the joke or that you don't care."

His eyes narrow. "When did you get so smart?"

"Two and a half years of dealing with my own set of high school drama." I pop a piece of muffin into my mouth.

He reaches for his fork once again, his head slightly nodding.

"Besides," I say, "I finally looked at the reunion itinerary and noticed there's a prom scheduled for tomorrow night. It sounds fun, but it'd be weird if I showed up by myself."

He glances at me, one eyebrow raised. "Really?"

"Sure. Ever since fifth grade, I've been looking forward to a father-daughter dance." Better late than never—my new motto when it comes to our relationship.

He grimaces, probably feeling guilty about missing the milestone, but then smiles. "I'd be honored."

"Great. It's a date." I turn back to my breakfast.

~

Turns out the movie trivia game is no ordinary game, but a set of skits performed by the entertainment staff. Donning wigs and costumes, they act out famous movie scenes. The rules are easy enough: the audience writes down their answers to the ten skits, and whichever team has the most correct answers wins.

As we take our seats, Tank plops down at the table next to us, a self-satisfied smirk residing on his face. "Surprised to see you here this morning, Wade. I figured you'd be nursing your wounds after Gwen's roast last night."

Tank's wife sends a smirk our way as she somehow manages to sit next to him without ripping the fabric of her skintight dress. She looks ready for a night out on the town instead of an afternoon trivia game in her black cocktail dress, jeweled necklace, diamond bracelet, and pendant earrings. Guess she needed to dress up to show off all her new gifts.

Hang tough—don't cower to bullies. I glance at Dad, trying to convey my advice.

Dad's gaze flicks toward his old nemesis. "At least she didn't comment on my physique." He turns away from Tank's scowl and winks at me.

I nod my approval. The priest at San Bernardo would most likely have preferred if Dad turned the other cheek, but I'm just glad he isn't still drowning his sorrows.

The entertainment staff soon has the audience laughing hysterically with their ridiculous reenactments. The majority of the scenes are ones most people know, such as the "I'm king of the world" boat scene from *Titanic* and scenes from other classic movies like *Forest Gump*, *Psycho*, and *Gone with the Wind*. Then the crew ups the ante and starts choosing a few more obscure films that not everyone is familiar with—*The Godfather*, *Freaky Friday*, *The Wedding Singer*, and *Die Hard*.

Unable to resist, I peek toward Tank. He shoots me a satisfied smirk. Only two more scenes—we've got to win this.

The next skit seems to stump most of the room, but I'm pretty sure the song and dance routine is one of the less famous musical numbers from *Singing in the Rain*. Josie's sure that will be our spring musical, so she insisted we watch it just a few weeks ago.

As I lean over to jot down my answer, I notice Tank craning his neck toward our table, trying to see my answer—what a cheat. Well, two can play at that game. I write *Some Like it Hot*. While Tank scribbles the answer on his sheet, I scratch out the bogus answer and add the correct one. Dad covers his mouth to hide his laugh.

Sadly, the final skit leaves both Dad and me stumped. Not admitting defeat, we agree on a wild guess.

As the titles are revealed, Dad and I cheer a bit louder with each correct answer. When the correct answer of *Singing in the Rain* is announced for the second to last skit, Dad and I high-five our movie knowledge.

Tank grunts his disgust and storms away. Not only a cheat but a sore loser. His wife shuffles after him.

But Dad and I are not the only movie buffs in the audience. An older couple gets all ten questions right and is crowned the winners.

"Oh, my. I haven't laughed that hard in a long time," Dad says as we leave the lounge.

"Yeah, we make a good team."

He grins. "We do, don't we?"

"That was a blast, but now I believe you have a poker tournament to join."

He holds up his hands. "Okay. I know when I'm no longer needed. I'll see you for our meeting with Quentin, the security person?"

"If we must."

"We must."

His head tilts. "You got your phone with you?"

"No, but I can get it. You got yours?"

He pats his pocket. "Yep. Bring yours for once in case there's a change in plans." He kisses the top of my head and departs.

~

With some time to waste, I stop by the photo gallery. Towers of displayed photos line the space, showcasing hundreds of pictures that the staff photographers have taken during the cruise. The images are organized by date to aid the search. All the faces start blending together, but I do locate one of Dad and me on the pier in Haiti—the giant cruise ship looming behind us. Not a horrible picture. I pull it off the tower and continue my search.

A few towers over, I spot several images of our dining table. I take one of the seven of us laughing at something for my collection. The final tower brims with pictures from New Year's Eve. My breath catches, for there, amid all the smiling faces, is one of Cole and me. I pull it out and stare at Cole's handsome face.

"You might have to fight me for that one."

The familiar voice behind me floods me with a happy warmth. Cole. I thought maybe he'd ignore me for the rest of the trip— and who could blame him after I ran off like Cinderella at the stroke of midnight.

I turn and wave the photo in his face. "Finders keepers."

His smile seems genuine, but it lacks the usual teasing quality that I've come to adore.

"Searching for photos, too?" I ask him.

He shakes his head. "Searching for you."

My heart leaps into my throat. "Let me pay for these. Then we can talk." I turn and walk toward the counter. As the staff member scans the photos and charges the purchases to my room, I think of what to say to Cole. Ever since I left him standing there alone on New Year's Eve, I've been hoping I could talk to him and somehow smooth things over, but how do I do that? Is it even possible? More likely, he's here to chew me out. I certainly deserve it.

The guy behind the counter hands me my bag of photos— time to face the music.

I turn toward Cole. "I have a little bit of time before my rehearsal. Can I tempt you with an ice cream?"

His hand covers his heart. "You've discovered my kryptonite."

I glance his way as we walk down the long corridor. "I didn't see you at all yesterday. Busy with your family?"

He nods, keeping his focus forward-facing. "Yep. We did a snorkeling excursion on Bonaire. Today we've mostly been hanging out on the sports deck. Connor is obsessed with the climbing wall, and Mia can't get enough of the mini zipline. I needed a break, but they're all still there. One can only play so many rounds of minigolf."

We reach the ice cream parlor and order our matching rocky roads. With our treats in hand, I lead the way out the doors to the deck. Cole leans on the railing and gazes out at the deep blue sea.

"Hey." We say in unison as we turn toward each other.

I giggle. "Cole, I wanted to tell you how sorry I am."

"Liz. Don't." His dark brown eyes imploring. "I'm the one who should apologize. I should never have tried to make a move on New Year's Eve."

My heart sinks a little. He regrets wanting to kiss me?

With a deep breath, he continues. "You were right to walk away. You deserve so much better than just a brief vacation romance. That was disrespectful of me."

I stare at him in amazement with a side of bewilderment. What teenage boy thinks like that? Not that there was any doubt, but he is genuinely a good guy. Time to say something. You can do this—new leaf. I swallow the lump in my throat. "You know, that's exactly what I've been thinking, but in reverse—that you deserve more than some dumb fling." I break my eye contact and shift my attention to my melting ice cream.

He takes a bite as well, then grins. "So, you're not wishing you could throw me overboard?"

I laugh. "Hardly. I'm wishing we didn't live in different states."

He reaches for my free hand. "Me too."

We turn to look out at the horizon, our fingers interlaced.

"Any luck with the last clue?" he finally asks.

"Oh!" I turn to look at him, our hands losing their connection. "Yes, I figured it out." I tell him all about the church, the note the priest handed me, and reconciling with Dad. I leave out the whole being a thief thing—no need for him to know the gory details.

His face lights up. "Wow, I'm glad you made up with your dad. That's fantastic."

Okay—time for the second confession of the day. "Cole, I feel so stupid for complaining non-stop about my dad…to you."

His forehead creases. "Why?"

"I didn't know you were adopted." I bite my lip.

The corners of his eyes crease in amusement. "I thought you looked a little surprised when I introduced you to my mom. You didn't know Conner and Mia were my siblings, did you?"

My cheeks burn with embarrassment. "No, I didn't." I focus on the dripping treat in my hand. Maybe the frozen dessert will cool my cheeks.

"Don't feel bad. We're not the most usual family. I just figured your dad had told you." He focuses on his ice cream for a moment then glances my way. "I'm glad you felt comfortable talking to me about your dad."

"It's just that I had no right complaining about my dad, who's in my life, when you…well…"

He cocks his head to the side. "You mean because I don't know my biological parents?"

I nod.

His gaze scans the vast ocean, then shifts back to me. "I've wondered about them over the years, but my folks are amazing, and I've realized that this is the life God chose for me, for whatever reason. You know, every family is unique. Some certainly have more issues than others. But our families, whether they are filled with hardships or blessings, help form us into the people God needs us to be in order to do His work."

Huh. Would I have started attending church with Josie if my family hadn't fallen apart? God really can use any situation for good. And the idea that I can use my past to help someone else is astounding. I turn my attention to the sparkling blue water, suddenly incredibly thankful for this trip.

"Speaking of your dad," Cole's voice takes on a tentative quality. "We were in the audience last night during Gwen's act. That was pretty harsh. How's he doing?"

Anger flashes through me at the memory of her *comedy*. "That was actually the catalyst for our heart to heart. I can't believe her. Who does that to someone?"

He shakes his head. "Honestly, I think it came off petty and made her look bad. Hard to imagine hanging onto all that anger for so many years."

I nod in agreement despite knowing that's exactly what I'd been doing. Thank goodness I recognized it. Who would want to turn into Gwen and spend their whole life dwelling on the past?

"Hey." Cole smiles. "My family wanted me to ask if you and your dad want to join us tonight in the Starlight lounge. That piano guy is performing in the larger space tonight. Mia and Mom love singing along with his songs. They figured you'd enjoy it too."

"Thanks, I'd love to." A chance to spend more time with him—what could be better? "I'll check with Dad."

His smile widens. "Good. Well, I'd better let you get to your rehearsal."

"Yeah. I have to stop at my room first." I need to pick up my phone and the stolen items in order to head straight to the security office after rehearsal.

"Can't wait for your performance tomorrow." He holds up his phone. "I'll make sure to record the award-winning song."

"You're getting a little ahead of yourself."

His head tilts. "Who would beat you? Grandma Millie?"

"She does have a built-in fanbase with that huge family of hers."

"But you have a whole high school reunion to cheer you on."

"And my own videographer." I nod to his phone.

"I prefer to think of myself as your number one fan."

Cue the warm gushy feeling that only Cole seems to induce in me.

~

I hustle down to my room to drop off the photos and retrieve the stolen items. Spending time with Cole was amazing, but if I don't hurry, I will be late for rehearsal. When I insert my key card and push the door open, a movement catches my eye. I gasp. For a moment I'm fearful that someone is in my room, then my eyes focus on the flutter by the sliding glass door—just the curtains blowing in the breeze.

With a deep breath to calm my racing heart, I turn to the task at hand. I grab the purse from my luggage where I've been storing all the stolen items. Purse in hand, I freeze. Something's not right—it's much too light. I flip it over, but nothing tumbles out. Frantic, I squeeze the material, then peer inside. Nothing.

A chill runs down my spine. How could it be empty? I rummage through all the sweaters and leggings. The items have got to be here somewhere.

Don't panic. Dad probably stopped by for them. Another deep breath helps keep the anxiety at bay. I lean to the side, and my gaze focuses on the billowing curtain. Did I leave the sliding glass door open? The morning's activities run through my brain. I don't remember going out there. Maybe Dad came in through our joint balcony to get the items.

I push myself up and creep toward the balcony. With a quick flick of the wrist, the curtain yanks open. I half expect to find Dad lounging on his half of the connecting balcony. But he's not there. His stateroom appears empty.

He must have assumed I'd run out of time between rehearsal and the meeting to come back here, so he grabbed the items himself. Should I text him and make sure? Nah, if he's in the middle of a game, he won't bother checking his phone. Besides, it's time for rehearsal. I glance at the clock on the wall. Make that—late for rehearsal. Darn it.

I scurry out the door and hurry to the theater.

⁓

Breezing into the auditorium, every single band member silently stares at me as I rush down the aisle. *Yikes.*

"I'm sorry I'm late." Not the way I wanted this to go.

"Well, let's get working." The conductor's voice matches the expressions of the band—cold.

I push all other thoughts out of my mind and focus on my song. The allotted half hour flies by. The rehearsal can't be categorized as awful, but it certainly isn't great.

"Okay. I think we got it. We'll see you tomorrow evening for the show." The conductor dismisses me with the wave of his hand.

Disappointed, I thank all the musicians. A few offer tight smiles. Turning to leave, I notice four men sitting in the empty theater—the Consuelos guys. I wave and make my way down the steps, thankful for their support. After the less than stellar rehearsal, I could use some friendly faces. As I near them, I can't help but notice the scowls transforming their usually handsome Latin features. What is with the musicians on this ship today?

"Hi." I glance at the stage to make sure none of the other musicians can hear me. But the band members have all scattered into the wings of the stage. "I sure wish you guys were accompanying me tomorrow. The song would be much better if we were performing together again."

Their grim expressions don't change.

"Is everything okay?"

"Hardly." Juan venomously spouts the word.

Whoa. I take a step backward. What is their problem?

Val shoves a phone toward me.

I glance at the photo on the screen and clutch the back of the seat in front of me, afraid my legs might give out. It's an image of all the items I took, spread out across the white cover of a bed. Next to the items is the form congratulating me on moving forward in the competition, along with the gold dress I wore on New Year's Eve. Beside the photo is a text—*I've been busy.*

I look back at the four angry faces. "Who…" I clear my throat and try again. "Who sent you that?"

"You." Marco answers.

Me? I shake my head as I stare at the screen of Val's phone, uncomprehending. Above the photo is the string of messages that Val and I exchanged about my second song choice. Lamely, I pull out my phone to double check, just in case there was any doubt. But no. The picture was indeed sent from my phone. But how?

I glance at the guys. Why are they so angry? They can't possibly know these items are stolen. Right?

"Care to explain why the stolen items are in your room?" Marco sneers.

Wrong.

Carlos seems to read my thoughts. "Pictures of the stolen items were circulated to the staff in case we happened to come across them. Many staff members tried to come to Rosaline's defense, so it was decided to send out a flyer. If the items could be located, then Rosaline would maybe be off the hook."

I sink into the nearest theater seat and face my firing squad. "I can't explain. But it's not exactly what it looks like."

Val leans forward. "It was you who stole the items."

"And you let them blame Rosaline," Juan hisses out the words.

I close my eyes. "I admit I took a couple items from other passengers, but that was before I met any of you. I honestly planned to turn them into a lost and found the night I met Rosaline. I even had them with me in my bag."

Val crosses his arms. "When you realized Rosaline was accused of stealing them, why didn't you go ahead and turn them in?"

My dry throat makes it hard to swallow. "I figured that if the items suddenly appeared after she had just been placed on leave, it would seem like she had turned them in, and it still wouldn't clear her name."

They stare at me with silent hatred, clearly not understanding my logic.

I try again. "Honestly, I was trying to help. I sent an email to the Brummels about the missing jewelry, hoping if they found it, that would be enough proof of Rosaline's innocence." Not one of them even twitches. "I felt bad that she was in trouble because of me and knew I needed to somehow fix the mess I'd created, so I resorted to something a little drastic."

Val's eyes narrow. "Let me guess, your big way of helping Rosaline was to steal even more stuff?"

"Yeah." What was I thinking?

The tension erupts in a slew of Spanish. I need not be able to understand the words to understand their meaning. I resist the urge to flee from their wrath but am determined to make them understand.

When their rant ends, I present my case. "I figured if other passengers complained about missing items, and the authorities knew it wasn't Rosaline since she was not on duty, then they'd assume someone else was behind it all and change their minds."

Val leans in, his finger inches from my face. I prepare for another onslaught of anger, but instead, he clamps his mouth shut and lowers his hand.

My gaze drops to the phone in my hand, and a new thought stops me cold. Someone was in my room, rummaging through my things, and snapped photos of the items with my phone. Which means Dad probably didn't take the items from their hiding spot. Someone else did.

"You're claiming that you didn't take this photo?" Marco demands.

"I swear I didn't send that to you. Why would I do that?"

"Because you're as crazy as your friend Josie." Juan shakes his head in disgust.

I ignore him and continue with my plea of innocence. "I rarely have the phone with me. It's been in my room for the majority of the trip."

Carlos looks completely unconvinced. "You have it now."

"I just grabbed it before I came to rehearsal." A new realization stirs. "When did you receive the message?"

Carlos glances at Val, who's still staring at me. "Val received it about forty minutes ago."

I shiver—the exact time I was down in my room.

"We knew you'd be rehearsing, so immediately came to confront you," Marco adds.

Could the person who took this photo have been in my room when I entered? Maybe the movement I noticed was more than just the wind blowing the curtain? I'm pretty sure I hadn't opened the balcony door. Did whoever it was hear me entering and dart out the door, then leave through Dad's room? An icy chill snakes down my spine. Who would do this? It could only be someone with a key card to my room. One of the stewards? Why were they searching through my things?

I push away the panic that's creeping through me. "Look, I know you don't believe me, but I really was trying to help. Maybe I can still fix this. Please just give me another day before you turn me in."

Marco's finger jabs at the phone. "We can't do anything with that. We couldn't care less about what happens to you, but that photo is not proof that Rosaline wasn't involved, and it could even make things worse for her now that there are more stolen items."

Juan levels his furious gaze on me. "We trusted you."

Those last three words cut through me. I've made a horrible situation so much worse. I swallow the huge lump in my throat. "I'll try to make this right."

"Don't you dare contact Rosaline or any of us again." The threat in Juan's words is terrifying.

Chapter 16

As I leave the theater and the quartet of angry Latin men, my phone pings with a message from Dad.

> Heard from Quentin in security. He's dealing with something and will need to postpone our meeting until tomorrow.

Good. That gives me a little more time to figure this mess out. I carefully word my response, hoping to discover if Dad was the one to take the items, without clueing him in to the fact that they are now missing in case he wasn't the one to remove them.

> Okay. I'm just leaving the theater now. Have you stopped by the room to get the items?

I stare at the phone, willing his reply to be—*Yep, sure did.* Finally, my phone pings. I take a breath, then read his reply.

> Nope. Haven't been back to the room since this morning. See you at dinner.

My hand shakes as understanding washes over me. Someone else took the items. As creeped out as I am that someone was in my room, I head there anyway. It's the only quiet place on board, and I need to think this thing through.

Once there, I push the door open and glance around for a moment before entering. Then mustering as much bravery as possible, I check the closet, bathroom, and balcony to make sure I'm alone. I lock the sliding glass door and the connecting door to Dad's room, then plop on the bed.

I can't believe this is happening. The items were here last night when I showed them to Dad. I distinctly remember gathering them from the bottom of my suitcase, then, after our heart-to-heart, placing them in my purse so I could take them to the security office. I can't believe someone was searching through my things. Who would do that?

The only people who should have access to my room besides myself and Dad are the room stewards. After Rosaline had told me the stewards work in groups, I started paying more attention to the staff and figured out which crew members work with Vincent. So, logically the suspects are Vincent, Janie, Jamal, and their supervisor, Rafael.

I glance at last night's towel animal. The cute elephant peers at me from the chair, practically pleading Vincent's innocent. The man is so sweet. It couldn't possibly be him. At least, I hope not. Janie is Rosaline's roommate and friend. She wouldn't want to hurt her. That leaves Rafael or Jamal, neither of which, I know anything about.

I focus on the fluffy white clouds drifting across the sky. Whoever it was, I must have surprised them when I came back to the room. Maybe they had the items displayed on the bed for a blackmail photo shoot and were going to replace them but heard me outside the door when I returned. They would have panicked and maybe taken everything with them. Then sent the message to Val.

Well, one thing's for certain. Lying here is not helping. May as well get ready for dinner. As I push myself off the bed, I notice a slip of paper near the door to the hallway. Someone slipped another note under my door. Well, that's not creepy at all.

I stare at it for a moment. Do I call security? That's ridiculous. The note could be from Cole, or, more likely, it's about the competition. But what if it's not. Should I pick it up by the corner, so I don't disturb any fingerprints in case it's something sinister? I shake my head. Reality check. Like there's a whole forensics team on board? In two steps, I'm hovering over it. With an empowering breath, I grab the note and, before I chicken out, unfold it.

We need to talk. Alone. Meet me on the front deck of the ship tonight at 8:30.

I stare at the slanted handwriting written on the ship's stationery, willing a clue to emerge. Is this from the person who's been sending me clues or from the person who took the items? Could these people be one and the same? Whoever set up the scavenger hunt knows me. Maybe they've been watching me and saw me steal the items.

As idiotic as it seems to be contemplating meeting the person sending mysterious messages, the front deck is a popular place for photo ops, trying to recreate the famous scene from *Titanic*. At 8:30, there should still be plenty of people around. I could safely sit in one of the lounge chairs in the center of the deck—far away from the railing. Do I go? Of course, I do—I need answers in order to help Rosaline.

~

Dinner could have been completely awkward after the whole Gwen-being-a-total-mean-girl thing, but Dad's friends are cool. They offer the right amount of support and indignation, then change the subject. Afterward, our happy little group proceeds to the evening show. The singers and dancers perform again, as well as an impressionist. Try as I might to enjoy the show, my anxiety grows with each passing minute.

Too soon, the applause dies down, and the house lights rise. It's rendezvous time. Before leaving the theater, I glance at Dad. "Don't forget we're meeting Cole and his family in the Starlight lounge in a half hour."

He salutes. "Wouldn't miss it."

Me neither. Unless this sketchy meeting goes terribly wrong.

I slide past him and make my way through the exiting crowd. No time to dawdle if I want to arrive first to scope out the area.

As predicted, families and couples are milling around the beautiful bow of the ship. It's hard to resist the front of the boat and the unobstructed view of the vast ocean in front of us.

While the sun has already set, the bluish-gray night sky is not quite dark enough to enjoy the millions of stars.

I spot two strategically positioned lounge chairs in the middle of the deck. Better to keep far away from the deck railing, as my mysterious note sender could be a psycho. "Accidentally" falling overboard would not be cool.

As I wait, my gaze fixes on an adorable couple holding hands and looking lovingly into each other's eyes. The twinge of envy turns to an unease that flickers through me as a shadow hovers over me.

Time for some answers. I look up, startled at the familiar face. "You?"

He glances around, then walks around me and sits on the lounge chair to my left. Even though I had no idea who to expect, I'm still surprised to see Val Consuelos.

I stare at him, waiting for understanding to wash over me. It doesn't. "You're behind all this? Did Josie put you up to it?" Maybe my best friend knew what cruise line they worked on, and when she realized we'd be on the same ship, talked them into helping her create the scavenger hunt. It definitely sounds like something she would do.

His face reveals nothing. "What are you talking about?"

"The notes, the clues, the church."

He continues to stare at me. Clearly, he's not going to admit to anything.

I sigh. "Fine. But, why all the secrecy with the note to meet you here? Why didn't you just text?"

"Since our last conversation was a little tense, I wasn't sure you'd actually meet me, and I couldn't leave things the way they ended yesterday. And besides, you told me you didn't always have your phone."

Well, he's got me there. "So, what do you want to talk about?"

His eyes shift, taking in all the guests around us before his gaze lands on me. "You know, when I received the photo on my phone, we didn't actually think you were involved. We figured someone was trying to set you up. It wasn't until you confessed that we realized you were the thief."

Way to go, Liz. I study his face but can find no trace of anger. "But you believe me that I was actually trying to help Rosaline?"

He rubs his perfectly stubbled jaw. "Your claim that you were trying to help Rosaline by stealing more stuff is the most ridiculous thing I've ever heard."

Well, when presented like that—it does sound a little dumb.

"But then I realized I had heard an equally idiotic plan once before. Josie also had a hair-brained scheme last summer that nearly ended in disaster." He releases a deep sigh. "I figure since you're best friends, maybe you both just think in totally obscure ways that make absolutely no sense."

"Um…thanks. I guess."

"Anyway, I suppose I believe you."

"Good." Now, how do I break the news to him? There's no easy way. Better just rip off the Band-Aid. "I hate to have to tell you this, but the items are gone. I can't turn them in to security."

His eyes squeeze shut.

"Whoever took that photo must have taken them from my room. I was hoping maybe they gave them to Rosaline?"

"No." The shake of his head dashes my faint glimmer of hope.

"I'm so sorry I made such a mess of everything. I should've just turned myself in when I first figured it all out."

He doesn't respond, kindly keeping his agreement silent.

"I just can't figure it out," I continue. "Sending you the photo makes it seem like they wanted to help Rosaline. If that was true, why wouldn't they turn me in and tell Rosaline where to find the items? On the other hand, if they want to continue framing her, why did they send you the photo?"

He continues watching me, one eyebrow cocked.

My mind continues scanning possibilities. It's nice to have someone to brainstorm with, even though I'm the only one contributing any theories. "So, since the person didn't give Rosaline the items to clear her name, it must be someone who wants her gone. Is there any reason Vincent, Raphael, Janie, or Jamal would want her fired?"

"Jamal?" Those bushy black eyebrows furrow.

"Yeah. He's one of the stewards who takes care of my room. Is he bad news?"

Val's jaw twitches. "Maybe. Juan doesn't trust him. He's often hanging around Rosaline."

My eyes widen. "If he has a thing for Rosaline, maybe he wants to split her and Juan apart."

"Maybe." His hands clench.

I reach out to touch his arm, but the hard look in his eyes stops my hand in midair. "I haven't given up. We still have a day to figure this out."

He stands, peering down at me, his expression once again hard as chiseled granite. "Forget it. Listen, the only reason I wanted to meet you is to tell you that I believe your intentions were good and that you genuinely feel bad. The truth is, ever since Josie helped us escape unscathed from the huge mess we found ourselves in over the summer, I've wished I could repay her somehow. Exonerating you from your guilt is my attempt to cover that debt. This is partially our fault for asking for your help in the first place. However, my cousins don't share that view and would be furious if they knew I was talking to you. You've done all you can and now you need to stop interfering. Your good intentions have caused more harm. I'll take it from here." He turns and strides away.

His harsh words sting for a moment, then I brush them aside. I started this mess. I've got to keep trying to fix it, whether the Consuelos boys want my assistance or not.

Chapter 17

By the time I scurry into the Starlight lounge, it is already filled to capacity. Wow. This piano man is popular! I knew he drew a crowd in the little side lounge, but this space is much larger. He has quite the fan base. I scan the room and spot Cole waving at me. His smiling face causes my heart to do a little flip. His family, Linda and Matt, and my dad have squished into a circular booth.

I slide in next to Cole just as the popular entertainer takes the stage.

"Welcome. I'm so glad you all could join me tonight. That little lounge was getting a bit crowded." The audience laughs. "For those who don't know me, I'm Don Juan. If you have any requests, jot them down on the papers on the table and hand them to the wait staff. Shall we get started?"

The audience cheers in response.

"Great! I think I'll start with a song made popular by the great Nat King Cole." He sits on the piano bench, then begins playing and singing.

Not knowing who Nat King Cole is, I'm surprised I know the L-O-V-E song and am soon singing along with the rest of the table. It was in one of the movies Dad had rented when I was little. I glance at him, and we share a knowing smile as we belt out the lyrics.

The whole room sings along to a few more songs, then Don Juan moves on to an 80s tune by the Police.

Dad nudges Linda's husband. "Remember how often we listened to this album in middle school?"

"Oh, yeah. We wore out the cassette."

"Every Breath You Take" is a catchy tune, if not rather creepy. Sounds a bit more like a stalker's anthem than a love song. As Don Juan smoothly croons about watching someone's every move, I realize I've been living my own version of this song—the scavenger hunt. The clues are obviously from someone I've met who has been watching me. But who? My gaze scans the crowded room in search of familiar faces.

I recognize most of the people but only because we've been on a ship together for the past week—not because I've had any interactions with them. So, I focus on those I've actually met. Leaning against the back wall are Mr. and Mrs. High School Sweethearts, singing their little hearts out. Gwen is too absorbed in a conversation with a group of women to be paying attention to the music. I resist the urge to march up to her and dump my drink over her head. *Let it go, Liz. We're thinking good thoughts, remember?* My scan continues. Cozied together at a front-row table are our original tablemates who were too good for us. Two tables from us sit Tank and Renee. Renee strokes her new necklace like it's a pet. Tank glances up and catches me looking at them. With a smirk, he raises his glass as if to toast me and winks. I roll my eyes in return as a shiver runs down my spine—what a creep.

I continue my visual search and notice tiny little Midge and an elderly gentleman that I don't recognize sitting together at the bar. She touches his arm and leans toward him to tell him something. He smiles and nods. That suave silver fox is most definitely not her dancing partner. Who knew Midge was such a player?

"You okay?" Cole asks.

I turn to look at him and realize that the piano music has stopped. Don Juan must be taking a short break. "Sure. Why?"

His eyes narrow as he searches my face. "You seem distracted. And I should know because I've become somewhat of a Liz expert, and usually when music plays, you have a hard time controlling yourself and end up singing along."

A little laugh bubbles up and escapes. "A Liz expert, huh. Well, you aren't wrong." I lower my voice. "It's just I keep wondering who sent me all those clues. Who would do that and why? It must be someone I've come in contact with this week."

"Any suspects?"

I raise one shoulder in a shrug. "I haven't met that many people, and I keep thinking how the last clue led me to a church on an island. How would a passenger know about that church and know they could leave a clue there with the priest?"

"Maybe they had been on the island before? Or maybe they got some assistance from a staff member?"

"Or maybe it is a staff member." It's nice to have a comrade to help me consider possibilities.

Cole's gaze shifts. I turn to see a man approach. He doesn't say anything but does some complicated handshake with Dad, then repeats it with Cole's dad. They finish with a hearty "Booyah."

Cole leans close, his body heat sending spastic bursts of energy through me. "Is it only me or is it really weird to see your dad acting like a teenager again."

I couldn't agree more. "I know. It's like watching our parents enacting a parody of my high school."

Cole laughs. "And here I thought stupid cliques were unique to my school. I guess some things never change."

"Thank goodness styles do. We may be doomed to repeat the actions of the past, but at least we look much better in the process."

The audience's chatter dies down as the lights flicker and Don Juan makes his way toward the baby grand piano for the second half of his show. "Okay, this next number brings back so many memories. It was my great aunt Miriam's favorite song. She used to play this record over and over when I'd visit. She'd take my hand, and we'd dance around her living room, belting out the lyrics. This one's for Aunt Miriam."

～

After the show, Cole's family bids us goodnight. Knowing that there's only one day left on this trip, one final day of seeing Cole, fills me with overwhelming sadness. Watching him walk away with his family tugs at my heart. How could I have become at-tached so quickly? Linda and Matt also depart, leaving Dad and me alone at the table.

"That was a fun evening." Dad still looks a little tentative, like he's unsure of what to say to me.

"Yeah, it was."

He rubs his jaw. "So, we're set to go to the security office to-morrow, bright and early?"

"Um…about that." How do I tell him that all the items are missing?

"Wade! There you are." One of his buddies strides toward us.

"Hey, Pete. What's up?"

"A few of us were trying to get a late-night basketball game going. You in?"

Dad's gaze shifts toward me. "Um…no. I don't think I can make it."

"Dad, I'm heading to bed soon anyway. You go and have fun."

"You sure?"

"Yep." Thank you, Pete, for the reprieve from sharing the bad news.

Pete grins. "Excellent. Meet us on the sports deck in twenty minutes." He walks away.

Dad's forehead creases. "Are you sure?"

I flash my most reassuring smile. "I'm sure. Just don't get hurt. I need a dance partner for that prom thing."

His eyes widen in surprise. "Okay, I will do my best not to get injured." He slides out of the booth. "Ready to head back to the room?"

"I think I'm going to take a quick stroll around the deck before heading down."

He hesitates, then tentatively leans toward me and kisses my forehead. "Okay. Goodnight. See you in the morning."

As he leaves, I'm left wondering how I'm possibly going to help Rosaline. And if I can't—how am I going to live with myself knowing I had a hand in getting her fired. If I'm unable to figure out who is behind this, I'll just have to plead my case to whoever will listen before we dock and try to make someone believe me, even without any proof.

I'm tempted to just curl up in the booth and forget the situation but refusing to give up, I slide out. Several groups remain in the lounge, chatting and laughing with loved ones, including Midge and her gentleman friend still sitting at the bar. As I walk toward the exit, she waves me over.

I take a detour. "Hi, Midge. Did you enjoy the show?"

"Absolutely. I'm a big fan of Don Juan's. I guess you could say I'm his biggest fan and groupie." She turns to her gentleman companion. "This is my dear friend Liz."

His smile is warm, making him look just like the grandpa of my dreams—loving, kind, and full of wisdom. "Wonderful to meet you. I'm Arnie. Are you having a nice vacation?"

What a rollercoaster of emotions this trip has provided. "Well, it's been memorable; that's for sure."

Midge pats Arnie's arm. "Arnie brought his children and grandchildren on this vacation."

Arnie nods. "Vacations are such wonderful memory creators, don't you think?"

I ponder the statement. "Yeah, I guess so." This trip will most definitely provide new, positive memories for Dad and me.

Midge reaches out and touches my arm. "I'm so glad to see that you and your Dad seem to be getting along better."

My eyes widen. "You knew we weren't getting along?"

Equal parts insight and mischief tint her smile. "If you take time to observe, you can discover all kinds of things."

I wander aimlessly, thinking of Midge's words. If only I'd observed more things, maybe I could've discovered the answer to my various quandaries. The clock keeps ticking. To help poor Rosaline, I need to figure out who stole all the items from my room—now. There's not much time left for observation.

My meandering journey through the ship ends at the front deck where I met Val. Due to the late hour, the deck is much quieter, but there are still a few canoodling couples. Pushing away the spasm of jealousy, I plop myself in the same lounge chair as before and lower the backrest so I can lay flat and gaze at the endless blanket of stars above me.

This trip has been amazing in so many ways. I really hate to see it end. First, and foremost, was the reconciliation with Dad. Not sure he'll ever be the one I turn to first for advice or to share my problems with, but at least we can now spend a week together without me wanting to tear my hair out—or pilfer items from unsuspecting bystanders.

Then there was meeting Cole and realizing that nice guys do actually exist. And then the biggie—my faith. I finally understand why Josie felt so different when she returned from her summer in South Carolina. I can't help but feel bad for rebuffing her numerous attempts to invite me to youth group with her and Ryan. Or for not throwing my support behind their effort to make the school cafeteria a space of inclusion. Well, it's not too late. I may be a few days late, but I've finally figured out my New Year's resolution: to continue my faith journey and reach out to others.

I stare at the millions of shining stars. Now, if I could just figure out how to help Rosaline.

"Is this the section for bored teenagers who have been forced to attend their parent's high school reunion?"

My gaze shifts from the brilliance of the stars to the handsomeness that is Cole. I smile, remembering the first night we met when he used that same line. "Yes, it's an exclusive club. Only room for one more." I pat the lounge chair next to mine.

He lowers the backrest and lays down. "Just to be clear, I was not following you. I found my way to this deck for a little stargazing, certainly not for any stalker-esque intentions."

"Well, that's good to know." Although, I certainly wouldn't have minded if he had been seeking me out.

"You do seem a little lost in thought, though. Any big issues on your mind? World peace? Saving the planet? What songs to include in your cruise memories playlist?"

I roll my head toward him, contemplating a witty reply. But a moment of clarity strikes—I'm tired of hiding my thoughts. Cole was my scavenger hunt cohort; maybe he can help me puzzle out this Rosaline problem. My body cringes, realizing that would entail telling him all my deep dark secrets and admitting my sins. As much as I'd love for him not to see my serious character flaws, what does it matter? In a few days, we will part ways and most likely never see each other again. While I hate the thought of him learning the truth, I have to try everything in my power to help Rosaline.

Here goes nothing. "Well, since you asked…" I continue talking, telling him everything. When, how, and why I began taking and hiding Dad's things, and how I reverted back to my childhood mischief, snatching items from people on board this ship. I explain my original plan of returning them, and how, after the Consuelos guys approached me, I didn't think it was possible to turn them in without making things worse for Rosaline. I tell him how I reconciled with my dad and about my ruined plan to turn in all the stolen items. I admit that the items are now gone and that I don't know how to help Rosaline. With a final deep breath, I finish and look into his unreadable brown eyes.

His jaw twitches. Is he going to flee? Is he going to tell me what a horrible person I am? Is he going to pull me into his arms and tell me it will all be okay?

His eyes narrow, then he bursts out laughing.

Not a response I considered.

Once he controls himself, he looks at me, a grin plastered on his face. "You had me going there for a minute before I caught on to your whole *Pygmalion* reference. Although, I don't remember Ms. Doolittle being a thief, just a poor working girl."

It's now my turn to gape with bewilderment. He thinks I made all that up? It's tempting to go along with his assumption. He has provided me a way to save face, but something stops me—time to stop pretending. Maybe Eliza Doolittle and I do have something in common—we've both made a transformation.

I look into his dark brown eyes. "Cole, I'm being serious."

He grins, obviously anticipating the punchline.

I patiently wait while the realization sinks in that the girl he has been spending time with all week is not who he thought she was.

His expression transforms from joviality to stone-cold sober as his face hardens and his eyes narrow. "You're serious."

I nod, then attempt to add a little levity to the moment. "I can picture it now. Your friends ask about your trip, and you respond with 'I met the girl of my dreams, but it turns out she was a wanted criminal.'"

He rolls to his side and props himself on his forearm. "Why did you tell me all that?"

I focus on the twinkling canvas above us, gaining courage from the celestial wonder. "Believe me, I didn't want to, but I need help. I can't figure this out, and I've got to try and make things right for Rosaline." I turn back to look at him. "I don't know how I'll live with myself if she loses her job. She has children back in Haiti who live with her sister. She supports her entire family with this job."

He lets out a deep breath. "Then we better figure it out. Do you have any suspects in mind?"

I close my eyes. A smile spreads across my face. *Thank you, God, for bringing this stand-up guy to me. You have totally restored my faith in teenage boys.* "I keep thinking it has to be one of the room stewards. No one else has access to the rooms. They might also have recognized Val's number. I'm stumped though as to why they wouldn't give the items to Rosaline to help prove her innocence."

He bites his lip and looks off to the right as he concentrates. "Thank you." Cole breaks the silence. "For trusting me enough to tell me this."

"Now you know how tragically flawed I am." My attempted joke falls pathetically flat.

He holds my gaze. "Everyone has problems. I know that better than anyone." The sympathy in his eyes is almost too much to bear.

"That's hard to believe. You don't seem much like the mischief-making type."

The corner of his lip twitches. "My parents adopted me as a baby, and I guess I never questioned why I looked different from them—that is until I started school. It's amazing how cruel kids can be. There was a group of little punks who made fun of me. I didn't tell my teacher or my parents. I just started acting out." His jaw twitches. "Let's just say I went through a bit of a destructive streak."

"Really?" Hard to imagine. I search his face for any hint of rebellion but find none.

He nods. "Sure. See, you're not the only one who didn't know how to deal with a painful situation." He reaches out and takes my hand. My breath catches as his fingers interlace through mine.

"And I don't think I'd admit this to anyone else, but there are times when those thoughts still pop into my head. But then I remember my dad's words, that everyone has their crosses to bear. It's how you learn from and deal with problems that shows your true character. You made up with your dad, plan to take responsibility for your actions, and are risking a lot to help Rosaline. Those are all good things. Don't be so hard on yourself."

I squeeze his hand. "Thanks."

His thumb rubs the back of my hand. "Anytime. That's what cruise ship buddies are for. Now, let's puzzle this out together." He gives my hand two quick squeezes, then lets go.

Though disappointed by our disconnection, I couldn't be happier to begin brainstorming ideas with the sweetest guy I've ever met.

Chapter 18

I pull the door shut behind me, feeling more devastated than before. Well, that was a colossal waste of time. I plop onto the bed. Quentin, the Security Deputy, said nothing as he listened to my story, however, I could see the disgust in his eyes. He told us he would pass the info on to the personnel department but couldn't guarantee that Rosaline wouldn't lose her job. We didn't have the items and there still was the unresolved situation with the Brummels missing necklace.

Dad was sweet and said he was proud of me for trying, but his kind words failed to make me feel any better. I'm not as convinced as he is that Rosaline probably would have lost her job anyway due to the Brummel case.

A glance at the clock shows I only have an hour until my final dress rehearsal. The morning is already ticking by. Tonight's performance should be the only thing on my mind, but Rosaline's future is so much more important than the stupid vacation singing competition.

Refusing to spend that precious hour cooped up in my room, I venture out to the balcony. The tranquil ocean works its magic and soothes my stress. I breathe in the clean, salty sea air. Why did I ever want to stay back in Minnesota rather than come on this trip? I wasted so much of it sulking, and now it's almost over.

Nestling into the deck chair, I decide the best thing to do is to pray.

I say the final prayers of Josie's novena, then close my eyes.

Dear Lord, thank you for this trip. Um...can you thank your folks for their added prayers? Also, thank you for the chance to reconcile with Dad. Thank you for opening my eyes to the bleak future I was heading toward. Thank you for the chance to meet Cole and to realize there are great guys out there—somewhere. Thank you for blessing me with such a good friend, in Josie, who never gave up on me and kept trying to lead me toward You. Thank you for all the beauty You have created. Please help me to not fall back into my old ways once I return home. Help me to keep growing in faith. And, please let me find a way to make things right for Rosaline. I pray this all in Your name. Amen.

Now time to focus on the task at hand—proving Rosaline's innocence. Tomorrow, we arrive back in Miami. The only way to save her job now is to solve this mess.

Too bad Josie's not here. She loves a good mystery. Time to call on my inner-Josie. Where would she begin? Maybe with the motive?

Okay, so why would someone take the items? Considering that the staff all knew what the stolen items look like, whoever took them also knew that I couldn't report them missing without implicating myself. So, they might have removed them just because they could get away with it? But then why would they take a photo and send it to Val?

Or maybe the person actually wanted to help Rosaline. That would explain why they would send the photo to the Consuelos guys. Sort of. If the thief is trying to help Rosaline, shouldn't they either turn in the items or show them to her?

I stare at the endless blue ocean before me. The most likely scenario is that the person wanted Rosaline to be fired. Is there anyone who would benefit from her losing her job? Juan said these cruise ship jobs are competitive. Could someone be that cutthroat to poor Rosaline, whose entire family is depending on her? I picture the various crew members that I've met. Every one of the employees probably has family members relying on them. Desperate people do desperate things.

And how did this mysterious person even know that the items were in my possession? Did they see me swiping them? Were they just randomly searching through my belongings? The window of opportunity was pretty narrow—sometime between when I placed them in my purse after showing them to Dad and when I went to retrieve them for our meeting the next afternoon. Which brings me to the question of who.

The most obvious suspect would be Victor—my outstanding room steward. As much as I hate to admit it, he is, undoubtedly, the person with the most access to my room. It seems impossible that someone so nice could do something underhanded. But really, what do I know about him? Besides the fact that he makes adorable towel animals. Could there have been any incriminating clues in our brief conversations? Doubtful. He never said anything remotely personal except that his day off was when we were in Bonaire.

Then there's the rest of the cleaning crew—Janie, Jamal, and Raphael. They all had fairly easy access as well. Maybe one of them wanted to get rid of Rosaline to create a job opening for a friend or relative. It seems that Raphael, as head steward, would be risking way too much to steal the items. Janie also seems unlikely since she's Rosaline's friend. She'd have to be cold-hearted to do that to her roommate. That leaves Jamal, who may be interested in Rosaline. Maybe he was so angry that he couldn't have Rosaline that he decided to sabotage her chance of happiness with Juan. The man does have a bit of a temper, as I witnessed during his argument with Janie.

Rounding out my list of suspects are the Consuelos guys. No. At least, very doubtful. They are trying to help Rosaline. It was them who asked me to assist her in the first place. It's just not logical for them to be involved.

I squeeze my eyes shut. None of it makes sense. Even if I had more ideas, there's no time to continue my contemplation—it's time for my rehearsal, and I definitely don't want to be late today.

～

I step out of the auditorium feeling even more frustrated. It was a decent enough rehearsal, but my heart just wasn't into the song. The Rosaline situation makes it hard to concentrate on anything else. Wanting to spend as much time as possible near the water, I begin wandering the deck, willing my brain to uncover some missing clue.

"There you are."

I glance up to see Cole approaching. Warmth floods through me. "Hi. I figured you'd be busy with your family on this last day at sea—another day of family games or something."

He walks alongside me. "They're spending the day at the pool. I'll meet up with them in a bit. But first, I want to spend some time with you."

He flashes that high-wattage smile of his. Oh, my breaking heart. I'm so very thankful for my time with Cole, but how am I ever going to say goodbye?

"How'd the meeting go this morning?" he asks.

As I tell him about the useless meeting, he offers a compassionate smile.

"I'm sorry. Now what?"

The weight of the dilemma causes my shoulders to sag. "I've been doing a lot of praying but so far God's been less than forthcoming with any guidance."

Cole taps the table with his index finger. "You know, God is a busy fella some days. Maybe he sent this lowly servant to give you a hand."

I love how this guy always knows how to improve my mood. "You seriously want to spend the last day of your vacation dealing with my problems?"

"I can't think of a better way to spend my time." He stops at a bench and makes himself comfortable. "What details are there to focus on?"

I slide in next to him. "The only physical clue I have is the message sent to Val from my phone." I rummage through my bag for the phone and pull up the text and photo. I hesitate for a moment, embarrassed to show the image to Cole.

Oh, well. After tomorrow, he'll never see me again. I hand the phone to him. He stares at the photo of all the stolen items splayed across my bed, accompanied with the text—*I've been busy.*

He concentrates on the image, and I begin to fiddle with my bracelet. His eyes narrow as he concentrates on the screen. "So, why would the person send this to Val, then take all the items?"

I resist the urge to pull my hair out. "I have no idea."

He double taps on the phone, then, using his fingers, enlarges the photo. Shame bubbles up within me as he scans across all the items I took, which are now in someone else's possession and may never return to their rightful owners.

Cole's brown eyes peer at me from below furrowed brows. "How'd you manage to get the necklace?"

His words stop me cold. "What necklace?" I lean further in to look at the phone's screen. My blood turns to ice when I see the glimmer of colored jewels peeking out between the iPod and the romance novel. "That's Tank's wife's necklace." I manage to say amid my cloud of confusion.

Cole tilts his head and peers at me like I've lost my mind. "Uh, yeah. One of his many anniversary gifts."

I sit up straight. "But I didn't take that."

Cole's eyebrows furrow, and he stares back at the photo.

My mind starts churning with confusion. How did that get in the photo?

Cole rakes his fingers through his dark hair. "The plot thickens. Do you think we should talk to Tank's wife to see when she last had the necklace? Maybe she doesn't even know it's missing. I saw her a few minutes ago. It looked like she was enjoying all the sale items at the stores."

I glance at the time on my phone. "Okay. I should be able to squeeze that in before my spa appointment with Linda."

⁓

"I'm telling you—my necklace is safe and sound in the safe in our room." Cole and I follow an unsteady Renee Jones down the hallway, past my room and Dad's, to her stateroom. "Safe in the safe." She lets out a snort.

I glance at Cole and roll my eyes. I think the woman has been enjoying the cocktails this morning already. The alcohol has thankfully made her helpful. "We have reason to believe that several passengers have had items stolen."

She braces one hand on the doorframe then slides her key card in the reader with the other. She pushes open the door with a bump of her hip. Her room looks identical to mine except for the larger, king-size bed and the ginormous bouquet of roses on the desk, and the lingering sweet smell of her perfume. She tosses her shopping bags on the bed, then turns her attention to the closet and the built-in safe. Her long, polished nail taps on a few keys, then she twists the handle to open the metal door. As she reaches in and pulls out a velvet pouch, I sneak a peek and notice that there is nothing else in the safe.

She slides a hand into the pouch. Her plump fingers pull out the necklace, multicolored jewels surrounding a diamond pendant. "See, I told you. My sweet Tank had this designed especially for me. I keep it safe in the safe." Another unladylike snort follows a hiccup.

More confused than ever, my face scrunches into a frown.

"Thanks for checking," Cole tells her, then reaches for the door, holding it open for me.

"Yeah, thanks," I call over my shoulder. The door clunks shut behind me. "How can that be? It's clearly in the photo."

Cole shrugs. "Maybe it's not a one-of-a-kind piece. Maybe he bought it here on the ship or at one of the ports."

I slowly trudge behind him. "Yeah, I suppose that makes sense. I just thought we finally had a lead of some sort."

Cole stops walking and turns to me. "Don't worry. I have a feeling we'll still figure this out. Now, you go have a relaxing spa day. While I go meet up with the family.

"If you insist."

"I do. Time to turn you into a star for tonight's performance." I grin. "My *Pygmalion* makeover?"

He raises his hands. "Just for the record, you said that, not I."

"Duly noted." I add a salute for good measure.

"Because I wouldn't change a thing."

He winks, then continues walking, leaving me with my pounding heart and a fervent wish that I didn't have to say goodbye to him in less than twenty-four hours.

When I turn around, I nearly collide with Jamal who's carrying a handful of towels.

"Excuse me, miss." He ducks past me and into one of the rooms.

I eye him suspiciously, but he seems fairly innocent as he expertly rolls and folds the towels into some kind of animal.

It's not until I'm in the elevator when realization strikes. The towel animal. I quickly pull up the photo of the stolen items.

Every time I'd looked at the photo I'd concentrated on the items, not on the background.

The bed is perfectly made, and in the chair next to the bed sits the singing swan and her adoring fans. I've been so enthralled with the towel animals and have become a bit of an expert. Every night, I place them in the chair before I go to bed so they can watch over me as I sleep. They stay in that chair all the next day, even after the room is cleaned. Vincent doesn't remove them until he comes to turn down the bed in the next evening. At that time, he takes away the previous night's animal and leaves a new creation.

In my exhaustion, I fell asleep on New Year's Eve with all those animals still on the bed. In the morning, I finally moved them to the chair before heading off to Bonaire. Which means that photo had to have been taken on New Year's Day—not the day after, when it was sent to Val.

I click on the photo app and sure enough, there's a date next to the photo—January 1st.

But how did they discover the items if they were in my suitcase? I close my eyes, trying to remember. I was in a hurry the next day to visit the church. Did I leave the items uncovered with the suitcase open and the clothes still piled on the floor? No way. Probably not. Possibly?

Well, two things are for sure. First, Vincent is in the clear since he went ashore that day. And second, whoever took that photo didn't send it to Val or take the items until the following day.

While the second realization leaves me completely baffled, the first gives me a new clue.

I text Val and beg for his help with one more thing—to find out who cleaned my room that day.

Chapter 19

Ahh…I lean back in the massage chair and close my eyes. For the first time all day I'm feeling hopeful. Finally, I have my first clue. "Thanks for setting this up, Linda. This is amazing." While my feet soak in a warm bath, awaiting their pedicure, the technician massages my calf muscles with hot rocks. While it may sound like medieval torture, it feels heavenly.

Linda lets out a contented sigh. "I'm glad we found a time to use our prize."

"Me too. I also wanted to thank you for being my friend. I don't know what I would've done without you this week. I wasn't sure how I was going to survive the trip, surrounded by all of Dad's classmates and not knowing a soul."

"It might not have been Wade's most thought-out plan, but I still think it was sweet that he wanted to spend time with you."

It actually was kinda sweet. "Yeah, I suppose."

"I'm so happy that the two of you patched things up."

"Gotta admit I never saw that coming." Josie will be so excited to find out her novena worked.

"Liz." Linda's voice takes on a we-need-to-have-a-serious-talk tone. "I've been wanting to tell you how impressed I am with you. I know a thing or two about absent fathers and how devasting it can be."

One eye peels open to look at her. "Really?" It is comforting to know I'm not the only one in the world.

"Absolutely. But it took me much longer to come to terms with the situation. It wasn't until I was out of college and met Matt that I was finally able to realize that even though the hand I was dealt was pretty crummy, it didn't need to define me. I was determined to learn from the past and create a different future for my own family." She reaches over and squeezes my hand. "I'm glad you were able to work through it. All those negative feelings don't help. They only compound the problem and make things worse."

Such true words. "Well, don't give me too much praise. I didn't exactly handle things very well over the years."

She squeezes my hand one last time, then returns her arm to her armrest. "I'm sure you didn't, but that is not exactly surprising. You were a child. It is how you handle things as you mature that speaks to your character."

My new friend closes her eyes, enjoying the massage chair. *Thank you, God, for this week and for bringing all these amazing people into my life, even for a short time.*

Her eyes flutter open. "Did I tell you how excited I am for your performance tonight?"

"Thanks. Even though it's just a silly vacation competition, I can't wait."

"You know who is probably even more excited than either of us?"

"Who?" I ask as the technician lifts my left foot out of the warm water.

"Your dad."

My eyebrows raise. "Really? Even after the last fiasco?" After patting my leg dry, the technician begins lathering it with lotion.

Linda nods. "Apparently, after the big basketball game, the guys stopped for a nightcap. Your dad couldn't stop raving about you. He told anyone who would listen that they need to come to the show. He even talked someone into playing the video he'd recorded on his phone on the big screen TV in the lounge."

A warm, gooey feeling floods over me. I didn't even know he recorded it. Well, his attention is better late than never. "I'm sure everyone was thrilled to have to watch that."

"As I heard it, everyone cheered—except for one person. Tank. Your dad didn't seem to notice, but I was worried the vein in Tank's forehead might burst."

"Think those two will ever get past their rivalry?"

"Maybe in another thirty years."

We lock eyes and simultaneously answer. "Nah."

Speaking of Dad's nemesis reminds me of the necklace. "Hey, you know that special necklace Tank gave his wife? Do you think it could be something he picked up at one of the many jewelry stores at one of the ports?"

Linda lets out a hearty laugh. "I never thought of that, but it wouldn't surprise me. Can you imagine Renee's reaction if she ever found that out?"

I picture the loud, brass woman going postal on her husband. "Yeah, it probably wouldn't be a pretty sight."

"She threw a big enough fit when he didn't present an impressive enough gift to her on their actual anniversary." Her eyes widen. "Hey, maybe your theory is right, and to appease her, he found something suitable in port."

My eyes narrow. "He didn't give her the necklace at their big party?"

She rolls her head back and forth. "Nope. At the party, she made a comment about expecting more gifts than just the diamond tennis bracelet he'd given her. He then claimed that the bracelet was just the start of their anniversary celebration and he'd be lavishing her with more gifts throughout the week. I thought it sounded like an excuse. So, you may be onto something."

I watch as the nail technician expertly brushes the bright red nail polish on my toenails. "Do you happen to remember what day he gave her the necklace?"

Linda leans back and closes her eyes. "I think it was the night of our last stop."

I picture Tank finally going ashore to shop for jewelry. That would fit with Cole's theory that the piece was not unique. I can worry about that later. But first—time to enjoy this moment with Linda.

⌣

"There are our girls!" Matt is the first to notice us when we join him and Dad at the pub for lunch. Tantalizing smells cause my stomach to growl in anticipation.

Dad beams when he turns and sees me. "Did you enjoy the pampering?"

"Yes, it was wonderful. But now I'm famished." I slide onto the stool and reach for a menu.

Linda leans in and kisses her husband on the cheek. "How was the poker tournament this morning? Still on your winning streak?"

"Nah. We're out," her husband answers.

"But at least we lasted longer than Tank." Dad grins.

"What was his problem?" Matt asks. "I thought I might have to break you two up like in the old days."

I set the menu down. "Did you guys almost get in a fight?"

Dad shakes his head. "The guy's off his rocker. He grabbed my arm as we were walking out and uttered some dumb warning."

"A warning?"

"I guess that's what you'd call it. I think his exact words were, 'I'm still going to get the last laugh.' Whatever that's supposed to mean."

As much as I'll be glad never to see Tank again, I sadly will be heading back to school and dealing with my own obnoxious bullies. I can't wait to tell Josie that I'm ready to help her and Ryan with their lunchroom safe-space idea. If there's any way to actually make a difference, I suppose we should try.

⌣

After lunch, I once again pull out my phone to check for a text from Val. This poor neglected device is certainly getting a workout today. Finally, a message appears.

If you get a chance, come by the pool deck. Our break is at 2, and I can give you an update.

Perfect! And while I'm there it would only make sense to spend a little more time with Cole.

After a quick detour to my room to change, I join the masses around the pool. The Consuelos guys are entertaining the crowd with one of my favorite Latin-vibe pop songs. As I walk past, Val takes a moment to nod at me as his smooth, sultry voice croons to his enamored fans. My aimless wandering through the rows of vacationers soaking in the last few hours of sunshine doesn't last long before Mia finds me.

"Liz! Come join us!" She pulls me in a new direction. Soon I'm standing in front of four lounge chairs piled with towels, bags, and sunscreen. Mia and Cole's mom is perched in the fifth chair, reading a book. She lowers it when she senses us hovering over her.

"Hi, Liz. How are you?"

Before I can answer, Mia speaks. "You can leave your stuff here and join our water volleyball game."

From the pool, Cole sends a quick wave my way, then turns his attention back to the game at hand.

"Mia, maybe Liz would rather relax."

I glance at my newly painted nails. "Yeah, maybe I'll just watch for now and cheer you on."

"Awesome!" She scurries toward the pool.

Her mom shakes her head. "That girl. Please, move some of those towels and take a seat."

I leave an open seat between us, thinking it would be a little weird to lounge right next to her. "Thanks." I adjust the reclining back to make myself comfortable. "What time did you have to come out this morning to get this prime piece of real estate?"

"Mia woke up early and insisted we come claim our spot. We hadn't spent much time at the pool so far, and I promised her today we could spend the day here."

I pull out my sunscreen to lather up my pale skin. "It's awesome how you all do so much together. You seem to really enjoy being together as a family." Do they know how lucky they are?

She adjusts her sunglasses. "Well, the kids can get on each other's nerves. But overall, we do have a good time together. We've always made it a priority to have a lot of family time."

A little twinge of jealousy zips through me. Remembering Linda's advice, I shake it off. *Don't dwell on what you can't change. Just make the future different.* "Well, you've done a great job. You've got some amazing kids." Especially that handsome son of yours.

"Thank you, that's sweet of you to say." She looks toward the pool where her husband and children splash in the water. "I think they all will miss you next week." She pauses for a moment. "Especially Cole."

My heart flutters. "I'm going to miss them, too." I lean back and watch as Cole leaps to hit the volleyball coming his way. Instead of smashing it back across the net, he bats it toward his sister to let her take the shot.

The raucous game continues for a while, then the two sides meet at the net and shake hands. Soon the dripping family members join us. I scooch over and let Mia share my lounge chair and hope my sunglasses hide the fact that my gaze is fixated on Cole's chest. "Did your side win?"

"Yes!" Mia beams with excitement. "Although, we lost the first game, so after a snack break, we'll resume for the championship battle."

Cole shakes his head, spraying me with drops of water.

"Hey!"

He grins. "I think you're our lucky charm. We were losing until you showed up."

"Well, I guess I'd better stick around then. I wouldn't want to be the reason for your loss."

"Hey, let's go get some ice cream." Connor slings his towel over his shoulder.

"Sounds good," I heartily agree.

"Actually," Cole says, "I'll get your cone. You need to chat with someone."

I turn my confused gaze toward him. His chin lifts in a nod toward where the Mambo Boys are set up.

So enraptured by the intense volleyball game, I hadn't noticed that the band had finished their set. Val stands to the side, drinking from a water bottle. His intense gaze aimed at me. Must be two o'clock.

"Oh. Would you mind getting me a twist cone?"

"Your wish is my command." Cole grabs his towel, then follows his siblings toward the soft serve machine.

I pull on my cover-up and head toward Val.

"You guys sound fantastic, as usual," I tell the group of cousins as I pass.

Not that I expected anything more, but their reaction to my compliment is less than gracious. Marco shoots a glare my way while Carlos mumbles something in reply. Juan doesn't even acknowledge my presence.

I sidle up to Val. As usual, he is not the conversation starter. "Did you figure out who cleaned my room that day?" I prod.

He nods. "Janie."

My shoulder's sag. "I was hoping that wasn't going to be the answer. She and Rosaline are roommates and best friends. There's no way it could be her." Back to square one.

His intense gaze shifts to the left. "It gets worse."

Oh no.

"When we discovered Janie was the one who cleaned your room that day, Juan confronted her."

"And?" I brace myself.

Val runs a hand through his hair. "Janie admitted to taking the items from your room."

Competing emotions battle within me, keeping me quiet. I'm glad to have finally figured it out, but I can't help but feel horrible for Rosaline. Some best friend. I can't comprehend Josie ever betraying me.

"Did Janie give a reason?"

His serious face grimaces. "She didn't have one. She just started crying and said she was sorry."

"So, did she hand over the items?" Time to turn them in and put this whole nightmare behind us.

"No. She said she can't and refuses to say anything more."

My gaze travels back to the rest of the cousins as understanding washes over me. "So, Rosaline is still going to be blamed?"

His steely gaze is all the answer I need.

My shoulders sag with the weight of the truth. Poor Rosaline. "It definitely hurts when someone you love betrays you." Or doesn't live up to your expectations. "Well, Janie admitted it once, so we just need to record her confession."

His arms cross, indicating our friendly discord is no more. "Just leave this alone."

His irritation is no match against my determination. "What are you talking about? We have an answer now. We can save Rosaline's job."

"Rosaline's not like you. She doesn't want to fight."

That doesn't make sense. "What about her job? Her kids? Juan?"

"I think this has all just been too much for her. She wants to put it all behind her and move on."

I square my shoulders. "Sorry. But I've got to keep trying to make this right."

Our standoff of wills ends when he rubs his forehead. "You know, you really do remind me of your best friend, Josie. Just like her, you won't take no for an answer."

I smile in triumph. "Her crazy idea worked in the end. Maybe mine will as well."

The smirk on his face makes me pretty sure he doesn't completely agree. "Good luck. It's going to take a miracle."

"Hey, one last question." I may be pressing my luck with his patience, but I need to know. "Are you sure you didn't work with Josie on setting up that scavenger hunt? Come on. You can finally fess up."

His eyebrows furrow together then his face suddenly relaxes, and he lets out a breath. "Let me guess; you found a series of clues that led you on a hunt around the boat."

His response makes me pause. He knows about the clues, yet it doesn't seem like he's involved. I glance toward his cousins. "So, it was one of them?"

He runs a hand through his thick, dark hair. "I didn't realize you were her pet project."

"Who are you talking about?" My turn for puzzlement.

"Midge."

"*Midge*?" Sweet, little Midge? "But…how do *you* know?"

"Because she does that on almost every cruise."

Confusion sweeps through me. "What're you talking about? Isn't she a passenger?"

"A perpetual one." His nonchalance makes it seem like that's perfectly normal. "She prefers cruising the Caribbean to being cooped up all winter in her retirement home."

"She, like, lives on the boat?" That has got to be the strangest thing I've ever heard.

He nods slowly, as if I'm the one spewing nonsense. "Her nephew is one of the staff members. Each cruise, she finds what she likes to call her 'little project.' Someone who she feels she can help somehow. Guess you were the lucky recipient this trip."

Her "little project"? She must have noticed my anger at Dad and thought she could help. Amazingly, it worked.

"Not everyone bothers searching for the clues or successfully unravels them, and I have no idea if she's actually ever helped anyone, but it gives her something to occupy her time." He glances at his watch. "Time for our next set." He takes a stride toward his cousins, then stops and looks back at me. "Hey, I stopped by and saw part of your rehearsal. The song sounds pretty good, but can I give you a piece of advice?"

"Sure."

"Sing it to someone. Your other performances had so much emotion in them, probably because you were envisioning someone, right?"

He makes a good point. I poured my feelings about Dad into the previous songs.

"I don't know if you have someone that would fit, but I think that would make it really special."

"Thanks, Val, that's great advice."

Chapter 20

I try to savor every moment of the afternoon with Cole's family at the pool, but the Rosaline/Janie situation never leaves my mind, making it hard to pay attention to the final round of the intense volleyball game. Finally, as Cole and his siblings bask in their win, I bid them farewell and wander around the ship, contemplating my unanswered questions. How could Rosaline just give up? How do I coerce a confession from Janie? Do I confront her? Trick her? Spy on her?

No answers come to mind; however, I do spot Midge at the coffee shop. She's enjoying a pastry and latte while chatting with the barista. When they see me approach, the staff member bids the tiny, elderly woman goodbye and resumes her place behind the counter.

"Liz, so good to see you." Midge motions for me to join her, so I sit down. "Can Constance make you something, dear?"

I shake my head. "No, thank you."

"Are you ready for your big night tonight?" She takes a sip of her coffee.

"Not really. Honestly, I have a few things on my mind which have been distracting me. If I could maybe solve those, I'd be able to focus all my attention on the song."

She sets down her mug and focuses on my face. Her intense gaze seems to penetrate through my body, directly to my soul. Uncomfortable, I can't help but shift in my seat.

"What is on your mind, my dear?"

"Well, for starters. You."

Her eyes widen as her mouth forms a little O shape. An odd sense of satisfaction washes through me for catching her off guard.

"Me? What do you mean?"

I lean forward ready to lure her in. "Are you the person who sent me on a scavenger hunt?"

Her features pinch together.

Satisfied that I've surprised her, I lean back.

She hesitates for a moment but doesn't resist. Her smile and the twinkle in her eye provide the answer. "How did you figure it out?"

"I wish I could take the credit, but Val told me, after I assumed it was him."

Her head tilts. "Really? No one's ever revealed my secret before. I may have to have a chat with that boy."

"Don't be too hard on him," I quickly answer. Midge is probably not someone you want on your bad side. "He's had a tough week." Thanks to me.

Her eyes narrow. I can feel the curiosity oozing from her.

"I want to thank you." Not wanting to discuss the whole matter, I keep her focused on the subject at hand. "You made this trip fun."

Her manicured nail taps her coffee mug. "Well, I'm glad, but entertainment wasn't really the goal. Did you discover anything to help the situation with your father?"

"Yes. I had a long chat with the priest at the St. Bernardo church and then with my dad."

She smiles, looking proud of her accomplished mission. "I'm so glad to hear it."

While she may be satisfied, I'm not. "Val said you live on this ship and on each cruise, find someone to help. Why did you choose me?"

A little laugh escapes her mouth. "I have always prided myself on my observation skills, but the hostility between you and your father was as obvious as a neon sign." She motions to the barista and points at her mug.

I look away, embarrassment flooding through me. Was I that transparent?

She places her warm hand over mine. "Don't feel bad. Each week, hundreds of families and couples arrive on this boat. It's amazing how many pretend to be happy, but if you observe, you can see the cracks beneath the veneer. You were one who didn't feel the need to hide your true feelings."

Openly translucent, apparently. "How do you know what each person needs?"

My wise friend leans back as she shares her technique. "I just recognize that there is some kind of divide between the family members or a deep wound of some sort. Sometimes, I try to help couples reconnect. Sometimes, I come across a grieving person who recently lost a loved one and try to encourage them to cherish those memories but also to move forward with their lives."

Despite my decline for a beverage, the barista delivers fresh drinks to both of us.

"Are all your scavenger hunts the same?" I take a sip of the warm, chocolaty mocha.

She wraps her hands around her mug. The veins and sunspots reflect the years that have made her so insightful. "No. I like to change things up. For instance, on the last cruise, there was a couple that just seemed to be going through a difficult time. I sent them an anonymous card with a reservation at the most romantic restaurant onboard. There, they were presented at dinner with a couple's massage coupon." One thin shoulder rises. "It keeps me busy."

"Are you some kind of counselor?" I ask this little angel-on-earth.

She takes a sip of her drink before answering. "No. But I learned a lot from my three favorite men. My father was a deacon who showed me that faith is the most important aspect of life. My sweet husband, may he rest in peace, was a detective who showed me how the powers of observation can speak louder than words. And my nephew, who is like the son I never had, has shown me that small kindnesses can make all the difference in the world."

I stare at the brown creamy liquid in my mug, thinking about her words.

"Those keen skills of observation might help you with whatever your other situation might be."

My gaze lifts to look at her. "I wish, but I think it's too late for that."

Her bony little shoulder rises in a shrug. "You never know. Most people just go about their lives, focusing on themselves, missing out on all the clues around them. For instance, I immediately recognized the strife between you and your father. I just wasn't sure quite how to fix it. Then I saw you reading a prayer card and realized you had a least a small bit of faith, so I knew the church in San Bernardo would fit in perfectly. I don't know what you are still trying to figure out, but my advice would be to concentrate on the details, observe everything, and ask God for direction."

Midge finishes her drink then makes her exit. I concentrate on her wise words. If it weren't for her leading me to the priest, would Dad and I ever have started down this road to reconciliation? Midge has truly been an answer to my prayers.

～

Too soon, I'm headed back to my room to get ready for the evening—our final night on the ship, and what a night it will be. Despite the trip nearing its completion, and my failure to help Rosaline, I can't help but be a little excited about the evening—between the final competition and the prom.

I wait for the elevator, contemplating what to do with my hair. Everything needs to be perfect. My transportation's presence is announced with a loud ding. The doors slide open, and I'm suddenly standing face to face with Gwen. I hesitate, tempted to wait for a different elevator, but the slight panic in her eyes bolsters my confidence, so I step in.

The doors shut, and I turn to her. "Gwen, I never had a chance to tell you what I thought of your performance the other night."

She takes a deep breath. "Listen, Liz. It was nothing personal. It's my job to poke fun at things."

I take a step closer, which causes her to step back against the wall. "Poking fun? Is that what you call it? Because I think purposefully humiliating someone in front of a crowded auditorium is cruel. Maybe what he did to you thirty years ago was a jerk move but hanging onto your anger and plotting your revenge after all that time is not the answer. Believe it or not, I want to thank you. You made me realize how important it is to let go of the drama of high school because I certainly don't want to end up like you in thirty years."

Her gaze remains on me until the elevator stops moving and the doors open. Glad to see it's my stop, I walk away wishing I'd told her that thanks to her, Dad and I reconciled. Oh, well. It still felt good confronting her.

As I make my way down the narrow stateroom corridor, replaying the elevator drama, I see Janie up ahead, straightening the cleaning supplies on her cart. Anger flashes through me. How could she betray her friend like that?

Calm down. Now's my chance to confront her. But what do I say?

Needing a moment to gather my thoughts, I push open my door. Before I can formulate a plan, my gaze lands on a large white envelope propped up on my pillow. My first reaction is to glance around to make sure I'm alone—knowing people can come and go as they please has made me a little paranoid.

After confirming that I'm alone, I secure the security lock on the door, then venture over to check out the envelope. My name is written on the outside. I pull out the contents. The first sheet is a handwritten note.

The following message was received. The sender asked for it to be delivered to you.

The second page is a printout of an email addressed to me.

Liz,

Thank you for reaching out to us. We were still traveling so did not receive your email right away. We responded as soon as we could but realize that if you are at sea, you might not receive our reply until you are back in Miami. We don't know if we can be of any help, but since you seem to be working on our behalf, we wanted to share any relevant information.

We were indeed on the cruise before yours. And, yes, my wife did lose a valuable piece of jewelry. It was a piece that I had just designed and created for her to represent the many years we have been together. All the stones had significant meaning to us. She had it at the beginning of the cruise, then it disappeared. My wife's memory is not what it used to be, so we don't know if she misplaced it or if it was taken. We did report it missing, but we did not know until your email that Rosaline was suspected of stealing it. This distresses us greatly, as Rosaline was so gracious to my wife on numerous occasions, helping her find the correct room and locating misplaced items. While we don't know this young woman very well, we do not believe she had anything to do with the lost piece. I am also writing a letter to our contact at the cruise line to express these same feelings. I do hope you are able to prove her innocence. I have attached a photo taken on board the ship of my wife wearing the item in question.

In kind regards,

W.M. Brummel

I squeeze my eyes shut, so thankful that he responded. Surely his letter, along with my statement, will help Rosaline. I flip to the final page of the document—the photo. The image is of an elderly couple posing in front of one of the ship's many backdrops. The man is in a gray suit, his wife in a sparkly, long black dress. Around her neck is the missing piece of jewelry. I stare in disbelief at the same necklace that Renee Jones pulled out of her safe just hours ago. While the photo printout makes the image slightly grainy, there is no denying the unique shapes and colors of the stones. I was wrong; this necklace is not something found at a tourist jewelry store. Tank was telling the truth. It is one of a kind. Just not created by him, but by Mr. Brummel.

I sink onto the bed. How can that be? If Janie stole it during the last cruise, how would Tank have gotten his grubby hands on it? Maybe she didn't steal it, and Tank somehow found it? Could his room be the same room the Brummels stayed in? But my mind flashes to the image on my phone. Either way, it was definitely in the picture sent to Val—which had to have been Janie, since Tank doesn't know Val. So, how did Tank end up with the necklace? Someone has some explaining to do.

I grab my phone, shove it in my pocket, then rush out to the hallway and scan the area, hoping to find Janie, but it's deserted. Not about to be deterred, I head to the storage area and peek inside. Janie and Vincent are both there, sorting through the carts.

Vincent is the first to see me. He straightens, a smile quickly forming.

"May I help you with something, miss Liz?"

Janie looks up. Her face seems to drain of all color as she stares at me.

I hold her gaze. "I was just hoping to chat with Janie for a moment."

Janie breaks eye contact and glances at Vincent, who looks a little hurt and confused.

"Everything is perfect as usual, Vincent. It's just that…" My mind races. "I could use a female's help with something."

His cheeks color, and he glances away. "Of course."

I feel bad for embarrassing the poor man. He's the best room steward anyone could want; I didn't want him to think otherwise.

Janie doesn't move until Vincent shoots her a look. The passengers' needs come before all else—she really has no choice but to speak with me.

She finally nods.

"If you could just come to my room for a moment."

She bites her bottom lip, then follows me.

Once we're in my room, I turn my back on Janie to close the door. I pull out my phone, push the video button on the camera app to record our conversation, then shove it back in my pocket. I take a deep breath then turn around to face her. Time to end this thing. "This won't take long, but I need to ask you a few questions."

She clasps her hands and stares down at the floor, clearly uncomfortable. Which she should be.

Now that I have her here, I have no idea what to say—didn't think this move through. *Please Lord, a little help here?*

"Janie, I think we need to talk. Obviously, you know that I stole some items from other passengers."

Slowly her eyes lift to look at me.

"What you don't know is that it was a stupid, childish way to get back at my dad. I was planning on turning in all the items."

Janie's gaze shift toward the door. Is she planning on making a break for it? Better tread carefully before she leaves.

"It's obvious now that you came across the items before I had a chance to return them. I won't tell anyone that you took them from my room if you give them back to me or turn them in to the head of security yourself."

"I can't." Her words come out in a whisper.

"Janie, I know you are friends with Rosaline. I'm sure you don't want her to lose her job."

Her eyes narrow. "I cannot lose my job either."

"No one has to lose their job." I keep my tone calm and even, pushing away my frustration with this woman. "The items can simply be 'found,' no harm no foul."

Her gaze darts to the left, then back at me. "I cannot give them back. I sold them."

I flinch. She might as well have just sucker punched me because that's what it feels like. "You sold them? Why? How could you betray your friend?"

"I needed the money." She rolls her shoulders back. "My papa needs to have surgery, and this was the only way I could raise money to save his life."

What do I say to that? She stole for something real, unlike my pathetic reason. I try to imagine how desperate I would be if I was poor and had no way to save a loved one's life. "So, that's why you sold the Brummels' necklace to Tank Jones?"

She stares at me, betraying no emotion, but doesn't answer.

"I know you stole the necklace from the Brummels on the last cruise." I thrust the photo toward her. "Did you sell it to Mr. Jones, down the hall?" She probably heard Renee screaming at Tank that he had forgotten their anniversary and realized she could capitalize on the situation.

She breaks eye contact and focuses on the photo. Finally, she offers a sharp nod. "Yes. That is right. The rest of the items I took to a shop in town for resale."

A pawn shop. I squeeze my eyes shut as realization hits. The items are indeed gone.

"If that is all, I will leave now."

I look up. "That's it? You're not going to even try to save Rosaline's job?" How could this stone-cold woman and sweet Rosaline ever have been friends?

Her face hardens. "I cannot."

Janie walks past me toward the door.

"One last thing," I say before she leaves. "I just don't understand why you took a picture of all the items and sent it to Val."

She stops in her tracks, then turns back to look at me, her expression unreadable. "I cannot answer that."

This lady is really ticking me off. "Were you hoping he would somehow make me back away from investigating? Because it's almost like you wanted Rosaline to know. I just don't get it."

She glances down at the floor again, then looks me in the eye. "Sometimes things that cannot be explained are a plea for help."

She turns and walks out of my room, leaving me staring at the door as it shuts. What does that mean? Was she hoping Val and Rosaline would discover her secret? Maybe she's so full of remorse she wanted to get caught. I can certainly understand how guilt can eat at you. But I can't understand why she won't tell the truth to save Rosaline's job.

My frown turns to a smile as I pull the phone out of my pocket. I now have a recording of her confession.

Chapter 21

"Are you ready?" The backstage coordinator sidles up to me.

I nod and let out a deep breath. I'm next. Time to sing my last song in this competition. For this final night, they have the large stage set up like one of those TV singing shows. The three-person panel offers thoughts and encouragement, but once again, the audience has the final say. As the audience entered the auditorium, each person was handed their own control pad to choose their favorite singer. The person with the most votes wins the Siren of the Sea trophy. I've been reminding myself all week that this is just a silly cruise ship event, but the sudden butterflies prove I've done a lousy job of convincing myself.

I shake off the nerves and watch as Grandma Millie takes her final bow, then exits into the wings on the opposite side of the stage. From across the way, a smiling face comes into focus. Val. He's watching from the wings. I smile my thanks, hoping he knows how much his support means to me. He nods, then pats his heart. His gesture is loud and clear—reminding me of his advice to sing from the heart, dedicating this song to someone in particular. I offer a thumbs up in acknowledgment. I know exactly who I'm singing this song to—Cole.

For my final song, I've chosen to sing one of my favorites— *Can't Help Falling in Love*. My mom loves the Elvis version, but I prefer the more bluesy, recent renditions. I wasn't sure about my selection or focusing on Cole during this particular song. But since this is the last night, I might as well use my emotions for a dual purpose: to make this song as perfect as possible and to let one special guy know that I have feelings for him. Bold move, but I've had enough regrets—I don't want any more.

Completely lost in my thoughts, I don't even hear my name when Miles announces it. The backstage coordinator nudges me and motions for me to make my grand entrance.

I close my eyes. *Dear Lord, please be with me. If this song can touch someone and somehow make a difference, please guide my voice. And, if it's not too much trouble, don't let me make a fool of myself.* After a deep breath, I stride toward center stage, my silvery dress making me feel like a star. I flash a smile at the debonair cruise director, then turn and wave at the audience as they politely clap. Despite the blinding stage lights that obscure the auditorium, I can make out the first few rows. A beaming Dad is front and center, flanked by Linda and Matt on one side and Mr. and Mrs. High School Sweethearts on the other. Cole and his family sit in the row behind them. Cole gives me a thumbs up.

"Liz." Miles smiles at me, looking rather dashing in his fitted tuxedo. "You have been a crowd favorite all week. Do you think you can continue that trend tonight?"

I raise the microphone that I'm holding. "We'll see, but the competition is tough. Grandma Millie is a hard act to follow."

The audience laughs.

"Yes, indeed," Miles replies. "And since her family seems to consist of half the passengers on board, getting more votes than Millie is an uphill battle."

More laughter.

He smoothly continues. "One thing that has made your performances stand out is the emotion that you add to them. You shared with us earlier in the week that your relationship with your father was what made one of your songs so powerful. Are those same feelings behind tonight's song choice?"

I glance at Dad. He's looking down at his lap.

"No, tonight's song is one of my favorite love ballads."

The audience oohs in unison.

Miles grins. "Ah…So, is there a certain young man that is the recipient of this song?"

I give him my most coquettish smile. "Maybe." Something about being on the stage always brings out my inner actress. Might as well give the audience a bit of a show.

The aahs join the oohs.

I bravely shoot Cole a smile. No regrets.

His eyebrows raise. He looks surprised at my boldness, but then he smiles and winks. Suddenly, we're the only two people in the whole auditorium. With any luck, I can hold on to that feeling during the song.

"Okay then." Miles laughs. "As a special treat for you all, Liz will be joined by our very own piano man, Don Juan—and one of our talented violinists!"

The audience cheers their approval. I still can't believe the talented pianist agreed to accompany me.

"Without further delay, here is Liz—singing her final song of the competition."

The audience claps.

Miles lowers his microphone and leans close. "Break a leg, kid."

I perch myself on the lone stool in the center of the stage. The bright lights dim, and only the warm glow of a single spotlight encircles me. The first piano chords of the song pierce through the silence of the room.

My eyes close, and I picture Cole's handsome face. I'm not fooling myself that what I'm feeling is love. Even if we weren't about to say goodbye forever, it's much too soon to mention the "L" word, but Cole's a special guy, and he deserves to know how I feel. Singing is the best way to express those feelings. With one final deep breath, I begin slowly and deliberately singing the words.

I'm soon lost to the song and my emotions. The violin joins in, and the beautifully haunting melody carries me away. Each word, each note, resonates in my soul.

Too soon, I sing the last phrase. With my eyes closed, I hold it, savoring the moment, while Don Juan and the violinist play the final few notes.

The eruption of applause startles me. As usual, I was so into the song that I lost all sense of reality. I open my eyes. Dad is standing and cheering. So are our tablemates and most of the first few rows. Those harsh stage lights make it impossible to see further into the auditorium, but the loud applause and cheers tell me that the audience enjoyed my song choice. But I do notice one couple that has remained sitting—Tank and Renee. The sneer on Tank's face is almost comical. Renee, looking bored, lightly claps her hands together. I turn my attention and bravely sneak a peek at Cole. Our gazes lock for a moment, and my cheeks flush.

I wave my thanks to the crowd, trying to show my appreciation for their applause.

Miles joins me. "That was simply beautiful."

"Thank you. It's always been one of my favorite songs."

The panel gives their thoughts and praise, but all I can think about is facing Cole after the performance and my unique PDA.

Miles places a hand on my shoulder. "Well, we will know soon whether it was enough to win the trophy. But first, we have one final competitor." He turns his attention to the audience. "Let's hear it one more time for Liz and our very own Don Juan."

With a final wave, I head toward the grand piano to thank my accompanist.

He stands and offers his hand, but I wrap him in a hug, much to the audience's glee. "Thank you. You helped make the performance special."

"I don't think you needed me to make it great."

We exit the stage together.

Once we're off stage and standing in the wings, he looks at me. "Now I finally understand why my aunt chose you for her special project."

My eyes bulge. "Midge is *your* aunt?"

He grins and nods, then disappears behind one of the thick black curtains.

I turn toward Val and give him a playful punch. "Why didn't you tell me about Don Juan and Midge?"

He shrugs. "Wasn't my secret to tell. By the way, great job. Seems like you took my advice."

My cheeks flush again. "Yep. Thanks, coach."

He laughs. It's nice to see that this usually serious man has a softer side.

"And thanks so much for coming." I lower my voice as Miles introduces the last contestant. "I'm really glad you're here because

I've got some great news." I quickly update him on the Brummel necklace and recording Janie. Despite all that Janie's done, I can't help but feel for her. "She told me about her father. I guess her desperation pushed her over the edge."

His brows furrow. "Her father?"

"Yeah, his upcoming surgery."

A flash of annoyance transforms his face. The man has no poker face. His emotions show so easily. Maybe that's what makes him such a great performer. "You can't believe anything she says. Her father is deceased."

"Are you sure?" She seemed so sincere and sad. Janie's words swirl through my head. *Silence is a plea.* A plea for what? What was she trying to say?

"Yes. She took time off a few months ago for the funeral and to help her family."

Wow. She's one convincing liar. I guess no one really knows her or what she's capable of. "But at least we have her confession. It should be enough to save Rosaline's job."

The final contestant starts his song, a country classic.

Val rubs the back of his neck. "We'll see. Listen, thanks for trying, but I don't want to get anyone's hopes up. This whole mess has really been tough on the whole staff. We're having a farewell gathering for her in the crew lounge at eleven. Everyone wants to let her know how much they care."

If only there was an explanation that cleared both her and Janie. Why can't there be a real villain? Like Gwen or Tank? They play the role exceptionally well.

I sneak a peek toward Tank and Renee. Her necklace reflects the stage light.

The audience claps as the last performer finishes his song.

There's still one thing that I don't understand—why Janie sent the photo to Val. It just doesn't make sense. What was she thinking? Midge's words about noticing the details come to me. Did I miss a critical clue?

The cowboy's interview ends, and Miles asks Grandma Millie and me to join them on stage while the audience votes.

The next ten minutes are a blur. Grandma Millie, the cowboy, and I stand together on the stage as the panel shares their final, unnecessary thoughts. Behind us, on a large screen, a video plays clips of our previous performances. Finally, an envelope is brought out to Miles with the audience's final tabulation. While I should be nervous or excited, I'm just anxious for it to be over. This silly trophy is not important. All I can think about is the Rosaline/Janie tragedy.

"And the winner of our first Siren of the Sea competition of the new year is…"

Miles' dramatic announcement is followed by a literal drumroll.

Come on, get on with it.

He flips open the card and smiles. "The voice of an angel— Liz!"

As confetti rains down on us, the audience cheers, and my fellow contestants congratulate me. I graciously thank them and bow to the audience.

Miles hands me the surprisingly heavy and awkwardly large trophy then holds his microphone in front of me. "Thank you so much. You've all been so kind."

My gaze lingers for a moment on Dad and his obvious pride. I don't think I've ever seen such a massive smile on his face.

I hold up my trophy. "I have the perfect place of honor for this beautiful award. That is if I can figure out a way to fit it in my luggage."

The audience laughs.

Miles nods. "Yes, it is rather large. Well, once again, congratulations!"

The next few moments are spent shaking hands with Miles and the guest panel. Then I slip into the wings.

I grab the arm of a passing stagehand. "Is there an exit I can use besides through the auditorium?"

The stagehand takes one look at my ridiculously sized trophy and nods in understanding. "Take the hallway, then your first right, and you'll get to a service elevator. You can take it to your floor. But if someone asks, you got on it by accident."

"Sure thing. Thank you."

I shoot him an appreciative smile, then hurry down the hallway and soon find the elevator. The stark contrast between the passenger and the crew parts of the ship is somewhat shocking. After spending a week surrounded by opulence and grandeur, the plain white walls and metal doors seem very out of place.

Soon the elevator doors open onto the 9th floor, and I make my way toward my room. Suitcases line the hallway, each passenger's belongings waiting to be taken away until they're reunited with their owners in a warehouse after tomorrow's departure from the ship. Did everyone have as much trouble with this process as I did? Packing most items while leaving the essentials out for tonight and tomorrow in my small carry-on bag proved quite challenging for me.

As I pass the rooms, I see a few doors are open as stewards are turning down the beds one last time for this set of passengers.

When I get to my room, I watch sweet Vincent creating one final towel animal for me. I'm going to miss being pampered by that guy. He glances up when I walk in.

"Oh, Miss Liz!" His eyes shift to the trophy in my hands, and he flashes me a huge smile. "Congratulations on your win! How very exciting."

"Thank you." I hold up my prize. "But, how on earth am I going to get this home?"

His eyes crinkle as he laughs. "I am an expert packer. I would be happy to offer my assistance."

"That would be wonderful."

He disappears into the hallway for a moment, then lugs my giant suitcase back into the room. I watch as he deftly lifts it onto the bed and unzips it. In a matter of moments, he moves enough of my items around to miraculously make room for the trophy.

I shake my head in amazement. "You're a lifesaver. I'd never have fit it in."

He nods as he begins replacing the items he removed around the prize. "It is one of the services I provide. There is usually a passenger or two who needs some assistance." He pauses his work to look at me with a crooked smile. "There is one passenger down the hall who had me pack everything single item while she sat and watched."

"Let me guess, Mrs. Jones?"

The slight twitch of his mouth confirms my guess. He quickly regains his smooth composure as he holds up one of the souvenirs I hastily stuffed into my luggage. "Do you mind if I wrap this a little better? I wouldn't want it to break."

"Thank you."

He examines the piece. "Did you get this at our stop in Haiti?"

"Yeah. I couldn't resist the locals, so I ended up buying quite a few things." Good thing I had extra room in my luggage. I hand him one of my sweaters to use as wrapping material.

"Which stop did you enjoy the most?" He wraps the delicately carved wooden piece, then finds it a snug home.

"That's hard to say. All the islands were beautiful. Have you visited them all?"

Satisfied with his work, he rezips the suitcase. "I have but almost always choose Bonaire, like this week, because I have friends who live there."

I think of the beautiful island and the beautiful church that made such a difference in my life—the last stop of our trip.

Vincent lifts the suitcase off the bed. "Goodbye, Miss Liz. It was a pleasure meeting you."

I stand, resisting the urge to hug him, knowing that would be inappropriate. "Thank you so much for everything. You helped make this trip very special."

He makes a quick little bow, then rolls my suitcase out of the room. Time to head to the dance. And to Cole. I refresh my makeup with the few items I kept out for tomorrow.

As I reapply my blush, something hits me. Vincent always gets off the boat at the last stop. That is the day that Janie found the stolen items in my room. Which means she couldn't have sold the items to a pawn shop like she claimed. She wasn't allowed off the boat, and there have been no stops since then. I freeze, staring at my reflection as a new thought takes shape. That means the items are still on board! But where?

Chapter 22

Alone in the elevator as I head up to the prom, I send Val a quick message.

> Did Rosaline ever search her and Janie's room for the stolen items? I believe they are still somewhere on this ship.

A reply comes quickly.

> Juan had her check days ago. There was nothing.

The pulsing music greets me as the elevator doors open. The event is already underway.

A shiny disco ball provides extra flashes of light in the dimly lit room. All of Dad's classmates are dressed in their finest. Many ladies wear their hair up, and a few are adorned with corsages. As I enter, I realize that this might be the only prom I ever attend—a depressing thought but seeing as not one boy at our school interests me, it's a definite possibility.

Circling the crowded dance floor, I soon spot Dad and his friends. As I approach, they start cheering.

"There's my girl!" Dad pulls me close for a hug.

"You were sensational!" Linda hollers over the music.

"Outstanding!" One of Dad's old tennis teammates lifts his drink in emphasis.

Dad releases his bear hug. "And I thought Elvis' rendition was my favorite version of the song."

I curtsy and give my best Elvis impersonation. "Thank you, thank you very much."

"That trophy was almost as big as you," Matt comments.

"Yes, I needed some help to fit it in the luggage."

They all laugh, probably thinking it was a joke. Between the congratulations, I scan the room for Cole but don't find him.

The DJ shifts to a slower song.

Dad reaches out his arm. "Care to dance with your old man?"

I smile. "I'd love to." I loop my arm around his.

He leads me to the dance floor, and I wonder when we last danced together. I shake the thought from my head—no dwelling on the missed moments in the past. We have the here and now.

He stops at an opening and turns to me. Noticing the awkward hesitation in his eyes, I place one hand on his shoulder and hold out the other. He takes my hand and places his other on my back.

We start to move, and he finally relaxes. "I was so proud of you this evening. You were amazingly poised on that stage."

"Thank you. It was fun."

His smile fades a degree or two. "It makes me sad to think of all the performances I've missed."

"Remember, we're not focusing on the past."

"Ah, yes. Forward is the name of the game."

"Thank you so much for bringing me on this vacation. I know I was not the most pleasant companion at first, but it has been amazing. And I'm glad we were able to work things out."

His heads dips slightly. "I'm sorry the meeting with the security officer didn't work out. I'm proud that you tried to right your wrong."

I grin. "Well, as a matter of fact, I have an update." As we sway to the music, I quickly fill him in on what has transpired.

He stops moving and drops his hand from my waist. "You're serious?" Fury flashes in his eyes. "You think Tank had something to do with all this? And that the items are still on board?"

I take the lead and keep us moving. He reluctantly follows suit, and we resume our dance. "Don't go doing anything crazy. Janie won't confirm he was involved. If I could only find the missing piece to the puzzle."

He grimaces. "That guy has never been anything but trouble."

"I still want to try and make things right for Rosaline. I hoped to figure it out before the cruise ended, but I failed. Do you think we could talk with that Quentin guy again tomorrow before we fly home?"

He pulls me in for a hug. "Of course. We can push our flight back if necessary."

"Thanks, Dad."

We continue our dance amid his classmates.

"Did you enjoy spending the week with your old friends?" I query.

"I'm offended you just called me old," he jokes, then lets out a deep breath. "Well, it's been an interesting trip. I mean, I had fun reconnecting with friends but could have done without seeing Gwen or Tank."

"Yeah. It's sad that they both are still holding grudges after all these years." Although, I can see it happening with my classmates. Too many hard feelings during a tough period of life. It's hard to get over.

"Speaking of, Gwen actually apologized."

I pull back. "Really?"

"It seems she received a lot of negative feedback from her little performance." He grins. "And I hear that a certain someone told her off pretty well."

I lift one shoulder in a shrug. "Only I have the right to humiliate you in public."

He throws his head back with a laugh. "And as for Tank, at least I made it further in both the poker and golf tournaments."

I pat his shoulder. "Good job."

The song ends, and he drops my hand and takes a step away. With his hand on my back, he starts to lead me back to our group. I stop walking as his words settle in my brain.

He turns to look at me. "Want to keep dancing?"

I shake my head. "Did you just say that Tank participated in the golf tournament?"

"Yeah, why?" He draws the words out, unsure of what I'm getting at with my question.

"The tournament on Bonaire that started early in the morning and lasted so long it delayed our departure?"

His eyebrows furrow in confusion. "It was a long drive to the course. Whoever set it up mustn't have realized it was on the other side of the island."

"So, there was no way to run back to the ship in the middle of the tournament?"

"Impossible."

"Hey, I've got to do something real quick. I'll catch up with you a little later."

His forehead creases. "Um…everything okay?"

"Yeah, I just need to find Cole."

I turn and dart through the crowd. However, I don't make it far when a warm hand grabs my arm. "Liz."

I turn and smile, thrilled to see him, especially looking so handsome in his dark-gray suit. "I was just searching for you."

"And I was looking for you." His smile widens. "You were amazing this evening."

"Thank you." I brush the compliment away. There will be time to talk about the song later. "I actually need your help. I think I figured out this whole mess."

His eyes light up. "Okay, boss. What do you need?"

"To find Janie." Again.

~

"So, where are you dragging me?" Cole asks as he strides along beside me.

"Val mentioned the crew is having a farewell gathering for Rosaline in their lounge area." I glance at him. Maybe he doesn't want to miss the party. "You know, I can handle this by myself. You don't have to come with me. Feel free to head back to the dance."

His arched eyebrow conveys an *are-you-kidding look*. "Nice try, but you're not getting rid of me that easy." He smirks. "Who knows what kind of trouble you'll get yourself into without my presence."

As we make our way to the back of the ship, we pass numerous passengers strolling the decks, enjoying their final evening on board.

When we round the corner, the faint strains of music waft up from the staff lounge nestled below us.

I peer over the metal railing to the stairs heading down to the crew quarters.

Cole unlatches the "Crew Only" sign for me. "Are you sure about this?"

"Yes. Kinda. Maybe."

He laughs, then takes my hand. Together we head down the metal stairs into the staff lounge.

Chapter 23

A long bar is anchored to one wall of the staff lounge. Tables and chairs fill the rest of the space. At first, no one notices us. I barely recognize the crew that has served us all week. They all look so different out of uniform, laughing and relaxing. My eyes scan the room, stopping at a table across the room where the Consuelos guys sit with Rosaline. Jamal is hovering nearby.

Carlos is the first to notice me and says something to his cousins. In unison, they all turn to look my way. Soon the whole room quiets down as everyone shifts to stare at Cole and me. My heels click across the tile floor, punctuating our unwanted presence.

One man approaches. I recognize him as one of the waiters from the dining room. "I'm sorry, this area is for crew only."

Val strides forward. "It's okay. She's with me."

The guy gives us one more questioning look, then turns away.

As people resume their conversations, we follow Val to the table. He gestures for me to take his seat. I lower myself into the chair and glance around the table at the hard, unfriendly faces staring at me. Cole squeezes my shoulder, and I'm suddenly so thankful he came with me to face this less than friendly group.

"What are you doing here, Liz?" Val speaks for the group, taking charge as usual.

"I need to find Janie."

He mumbles something in Spanish under his breath before switching to English. "I told you earlier to forget it."

"But I'm pretty sure I finally figured it all out and am sure we can save Rosaline's job."

Rosaline and Juan share a look. She gives a barely perceptible nod. Juan's jaw twitches as he turns his sharp gaze my way. "Well, we have nothing to lose, I suppose."

Relief washes over me. "Thank you. Do you know where we can find her?"

The cousins all shake their heads, but Rosaline sits up a little straighter. "Maybe. Since all this has happened, she's been spending less time in our quarters and more time in the chapel. I hoped all her prayer time would help her realize she needs to tell the truth, but I think it's the only place she can go where people will leave her alone."

The grief of her friend's betrayal is evident in Rosaline's sad eyes and weary expression.

Juan abruptly stands, his chair screeching in protest along the tile floor. All eyes once again turn our way. "Fine. Let's get this over with."

The group follows him through a door and down a plain hallway, Jamal bringing up the rear. No wonder Juan doesn't like the guy—he's a little stalkerish. It's so strange to discover a whole new section of the boat—like we're entering a secret underground, under*water*, world.

"Will you all be in trouble if someone sees us with you?" Maybe I should have thought about that before we began our journey. The last thing I want is to cause more trouble.

Marco shakes his head. "Don't worry about it. Anyone with authority who would care stays on their own deck."

Reminds me of my high school. Upperclassmen avoiding the underlings as much as possible. The cool kids isolating themselves from others. Does that class hierarchy exist everywhere?

As we journey further into the bowels of the ship, I reach for Cole's hand. Thank goodness he didn't take me up on my suggestion to head back to the dance. I think I can trust these people, but what do I really know about them? Nothing.

Finally, we stop outside a door with a metal sign bearing a single word: "Chapel." Juan pushes it open, and we all traipse into the small space.

Janie sits alone in one of the chairs, staring at the plain wooden cross on the altar in front of her. She glances our way, then jumps up, fear in her eyes.

Rosaline takes a step toward her roommate. "Don't be afraid. Liz just had something she wanted to ask you."

Janie's eyes narrow, burning hatred blasts toward me. "I told you that I have nothing more to say. Leave me alone!"

I take a step back, not even recognizing this usually mild-mannered person. Silence fills the room. I'm apparently not the only person surprised by her outburst.

Cole squeezes my hand, which gives me the courage I need. I squeeze back, then let go and take a few timid steps toward her.

"Janie, I'm not here to accuse you. I needed to find you because I want to help Rosaline—and you."

Her eyes dart around like a caged lion. She must feel trapped with our entourage staring her down.

I turn back to the group. "Can we just all sit for a moment?"

The Consuelos guys don't budge until Rosaline pulls on Juan's arm to sit in one of the upholstered chairs. Jamal, Cole, and the cousins all dutifully follow suit.

I turn back to Janie and motion for her to sit again as I settle into the chair next to her. I glance at the cross on the altar. *Please, Lord. Give me the words and wisdom to fix this situation.*

Janie glances at the room full of former friends, then looks at me. "Miss Liz, I told you all that I can say. I have decided to submit my resignation tomorrow."

"Janie, no." Jamal's voice is surrounded by surprised murmurs.

"If you're going to resign, first clear Rosaline's name," Juan pleads.

Janie's eyes brim with tears. "I can't."

I shoot a look toward our audience to silence them, then turn back to Janie. "I know you are scared and think you have no options. I've been thinking a lot about all you have told me. There was one thing I just couldn't understand—who sent the photo to Val. But now I believe I finally know what happened."

Janie wipes away a tear.

I take a deep breath before continuing. "My last guess was pretty close, wasn't it?"

Janie remains speechless, which I take as confirmation.

"Why don't you stop me if I get something wrong, okay?"

She gives a slight nod.

"Good." I glance at my captive audience and decide to start at the beginning. "Okay, this is what I believe happened. As you know, my anger at my dad caused me to revert to a childhood crutch that used to make me feel better, and I snatched some items from unsuspecting passengers. I was on my way to turn them in at the front desk when Val and the guys told me about Rosaline's situation and asked for my help. I was afraid if all the items suddenly showed up, it would look suspicious and harm Rosaline rather than help her." I suck in a quick breath. "For some reason, I thought if I took even more things that were not from rooms Rosaline cleaned, it would show that she wasn't responsible.

"But the morning of our Bonaire stop, I hurried off the ship and I'm guessing, in my haste, I forgot to re-hide the stolen items. Vincent had the day off, so Janie was in charge of cleaning my room that day. I believe she came in and saw the items, and because of the circulated photos, knew they were the missing belongings. Before she could decide what to do, another passenger came into the room. Maybe this person wanted to ask Janie for something, but when they saw Janie standing above them, they threatened her. In fear of losing her job, Janie pleaded with them and gave them the Brummels' necklace to keep quiet."

Rosaline gasps. "You had the necklace?" Tears fill her eyes.

Janie doesn't look at her roommate. I continue. "I assumed it was Tank Jones who'd somehow figured out I'd stolen the random items, and knew he'd found the perfect opportunity to get back at my dad through me."

"But it wasn't Tank?" Cole asks.

Janie shakes her head.

"No," I explain. "It couldn't have been Tank because he was at the golf tournament that day."

"Then who?" Juan asks.

Janie bites her lip.

Juan throws his head back in frustration.

"I believe it was Renee, his wife." I watch Janie, who glances down at her hands but remains silent.

"Okay," Val says. "But why would she send me the photo and text?"

"That had me stumped as well. Especially since it wasn't until the next day that the message was sent, and the items were taken. I think Renee waited a day, trying to figure out how best to use the information. My guess is she decided to take the items and send the photo and message to my dad to cause trouble. But there was only one number in my texts—yours. She must have assumed it was my dad's number."

"Fine," Marco jumps in, "but it doesn't change the fact that Janie stole the Brummels' necklace and let Rosaline take the blame."

I let out a sigh, wishing I could fix that deception as well.

"Janie didn't steal the necklace."

All eyes turn to a voice in the back of the room. Jamal.

My eyes narrow. "You stole it?"

He glances at Rosaline, whose lip is quivering. "I found it in the laundry bin. I didn't know whose it was." He clenches his hands. "I'd been saving money for months, hoping to buy Janie a Christmas present to show her how I felt. But I couldn't scrape together enough to buy what I wanted—what she deserved."

Oh. He liked Janie and was chummy with her roommate in order to get to know her. Did not see that one!

Various expressions pass amid the crowd as realization hits.

Jamal clears his throat and continues. "Then this necklace shows up—an answer to my dilemma. Obviously, the owner didn't care enough to be careful with it. I figured if they missed it, they would alert the staff, but I never heard anything. I wasn't aware of Rosaline's initial situation—only the missing items from this cruise. Maybe I should have figured it out, but I guess I was so excited to give the necklace to Janie that I didn't care."

The dam bursts as tears roll down Janie's flushed cheeks and words tumble from her mouth. "I didn't know it was the missing necklace either. It was a very sweet gift, but I knew Jamal had feelings for me that I couldn't return." She takes a deep breath, then continues. "A couple days ago, when we were docked in Bonaire, I had the necklace with me in order to give it back to

Jamal. I was cleaning miss Liz's room and noticed a pile of sweaters on the floor of her closet. I bent down to tidy them up and saw all these loose items on the bottom of her suitcase. They looked like the missing items that we'd been asked to watch for. I'd been keeping the printout of the photos and descriptions of the belongings in my pocket, so pulled it out to compare. I couldn't believe I'd discovered the items that could clear Rosaline's name. Mrs. Jones must have walked in through the open door to ask me something. I didn't know she was standing above me until she said, 'Well, what do we have here?'. When I turned, she snapped a photo of me, kneeling next to all the stolen items, holding the compact. I knew how bad it all looked and panicked. Even though she wouldn't know they were missing passenger items, she might assume I was about to steal them from Liz's suitcase. I assumed she was going to turn me in for stealing and since my father passed away, my family needs my income more than ever. In exchange for her silence, I offered her the necklace. She agreed, as long as I also kept quiet, then she left."

Janie pauses and looks at me. "I thought she was a relative or friend of yours and was protecting you. I hoped if I remained silent, she wouldn't show that photo to anyone." She squeezes her hands together. "But I felt so guilty. I couldn't let Rosaline lose her job when I had proof that she wasn't a thief. Yesterday, I planned to show our supervisor, Raphael, the items but when I went in to double check on them, they were gone." Her shoulders sag, then her gaze returns to me. "I don't know how Mrs. Jones got back in your room."

"It probably wasn't very difficult." I picture all the things Dad leaves lying around. He could have easily left his room key laying on the poker table or on a bar. Renee could've swiped it, snuck down to my room, and returned it before he was any the wiser.

Juan clenches his fist. "But you still remained quiet."

Janie shakes her head. "No. I went to the head of personnel, but he wouldn't listen. He thought I was just making up a story to protect Rosaline." Her eyes fill with tears again. "I knew I couldn't save her job, but I could protect her reputation, so I let everyone believe that I'd taken the items and sold them." She covers her face with her hands, her anguish on full display. "I'm so sorry."

Jamal rushes to her, kneels, and takes her hands. "No, it is my fault. I put you in a terrible position by giving you the necklace in the first place."

"How could you be so selfish?" Juan looks like he might throttle the guy.

Rosaline places a calming hand on her boyfriend's shoulder before sitting next to Janie and pulling her close for a hug. "Thank you for sharing the truth. It never made sense that you would purposely hurt me."

Cole's eyebrows furrow in concentration, puzzling out what I've already determined. "So, Renee Jones took the items."

I nod. "Which means they have to still be onboard—somewhere."

"But where?" Desperation tinges Rosaline's words.

Probably in her suitcase about to leave the ship." Carlos voices what we're all thinking.

"Vincent told me he helped Renee pack. I wonder if he came across them," I say, thinking out loud.

Rosaline shakes her head. "Vincent knows enough about all this that if he'd come across the items, he'd have let us know."

"Wait." Val's deep voice fills the room. He turns his intense gaze toward me. "Did you say you thought Mr. Jones wanted to cause problems for your father?"

I nod. "Yeah, they have this weird rivalry thing going on."

"Why would his wife care about any of this?" Marco asks.

I flash on the time I saw him leaving his room and her yelling at him, "Get over it." "Maybe she feels he can't move past their dumb high school feud—you know, always feeling inferior or something?"

Cole shrugs. "Pretty pathetic, but it makes sense, I guess. He's been trying to show off his wealth during this whole trip."

A horrible thought begins to form. "Oh. What if she's setting Dad up?" I turn to the crew. "What happens to the luggage that we left in the hall tonight? Are they scanned before leaving the ship?"

Jamal's head bobs in affirmation. "Yes. If anything sets off the scanners, the luggage will be opened and checked."

"Or if there is any suspicion, they will be checked," Juan adds. "Miami police are called on occasion."

A horrible vision comes to me. Dad, surrounded by all his classmates, innocently retrieving his luggage and being confronted by police. The final humiliation. "Is there a way to check my dad's luggage?"

The crew members exchange looks before Jamal slowly nods. "Maybe. Let me call in a few favors."

Before we know it, we are venturing further into the belly of the ship. Jamal leads us to a room filled with monitors showing various video feeds from the ship's security cameras. Every few moments, the clips change.

A tall, dark-haired man in a crisp white uniform stands when we enter. "Good evening." He greets us with a salute and a sharp British accent. "I'm Steven. Jamal filled me in a bit. You are looking for a video of a woman placing something in luggage that didn't belong to her?"

I peel my eyes away from the monitors. "Yes, my father's bag. I'm worried that whatever it is will cause him to be detained."

His scrutinizing gaze travels among our group, then he gives a curt nod. "Can I see your room key to verify your story?"

I hand him my key, tell him Dad's name and room number, Renee's room number, and her description. After a few moments of typing on a keyboard, a black-and-white image of our hallway appears on the large screen in front of us.

Jamal leans over Steven's shoulder. "The luggage in question will be the third set in."

People zip in and out of the shot as the video speeds along. Then I spot her.

"There! That's her."

Steven slows the video, and we watch as Renee slowly walks toward Dad's luggage. She glances both ways then unzips the top of Dad's suitcase. She reaches into her purse and pulls out a small plastic bag which she then slides into the luggage. She rezips the suitcase and continues on her way.

Cole looks at me with a smile. "Got her."

Steven provides a form for me to list the contents they will find in the bag and which passengers they belong to—the identical list that I provided Quentin this morning. I also tell him about the Brummels' necklace that Renee Jones is currently wearing and show him the printout of the email and photo I recently received from the elderly couple. With any luck, everything will be returned to its rightful owner by the time we reach Miami.

Steven glances at what I wrote. "Thank you for your assistance. We will take it from here. We will investigate the luggage and determine how to proceed." He turns to me. "You and your father will need to meet with Quentin and myself before you disembark. But for now, you may enjoy the rest of your evening."

We offer our thanks to Steven, then troop back to the staff lounge.

Rosaline wraps her arms around me. "Thank you so much."

I return her hug but know I don't deserve her thanks. Her job could still be in jeopardy. "If it hadn't been for my stupid actions, none of this would have happened. I'm so sorry."

Janie hugs me as well. "Jamal and I will join you in the meeting tomorrow to help explain everything. Thank you for being so persistent. I owe you so much."

Val crosses his arms, forming a barrier—making it clear he does not want a hug. "Yes, thank you. But can you and Josie *please* stay away from us?" A grin sneaks through his serious expression.

I laugh, despite the fact the rest of the Consuelos cousins are nodding in agreement.

Cole turns to me. "Ready to head back to the prom?"

I grasp his outstretched hand. "Absolutely."

Chapter 24

My eyes are still adjusting to the dark ballroom when the DJ ends the late 80s song he's playing—can't say I'm sorry we missed the journey back in time. I glance toward the DJ, mentally trying to send him a message. *Please play a slow song.*

The man leans close to his microphone. "I've had a request for something a little more romantic."

Yes!

"Although, this one might take a little more skill. Rumor has it that a few folks in our midst have been learning the tango."

Cole grins, then reaches out his hand. "Shall we?"

I tentatively place my hand in his. "But we haven't been rehearsing."

"Come on." He leads me to the dance floor.

Most people clear the floor, leaving just a few couples I recognize from our dance class. Most eyes in the room are focused our way, ready to be dazzled by our smooth steps or entertained by our hilarious attempt at grace. Hopefully, our feet don't tangle so we end up in a pile on the floor.

I place my hand on Cole's shoulder and hold my other hand up, which he clasps. He then rests his other hand on the small of my back. The music begins, and I look into his eyes. My heart beats in time to the sultry music.

Our gazes lock as Cole leads the dance with confidence. The basic steps come back to me as we glide across the floor. Our swivels are nearly flawless, and we miraculously make it through the ocho steps, the most complicated move we learned.

The moves begin to flow naturally as we repeat the steps. We gracefully circle the dance floor like we're the only two people in the room. I savor every moment of the dance—Cole's strong embrace, his handsome face, the unspoken message in his eyes.

When the song ends, everyone watching claps for us all.

Cole squeezes my hand and pulls me in for a hug. "Thank you for the dance."

"Thank you for everything." I'm about to celebrate when his body stiffens.

"Ready for more fireworks?"

I pull back and follow his gaze. Steven and two other uniformed men enter the ballroom.

Oh, boy. "Think they're looking for us or Renee?"

"Only one way to find out." Our fingers interlace as Cole leads the way toward the intimidating trio.

Steven nods in greeting. "We located your father's suitcase, and the items you listed were in the bag that Mrs. Jones appeared to place in the luggage."

I release the breath I was holding. This whole ordeal is finally over.

Steven scans the room. "Can you please point out Mr. and Mrs. Jones?"

"Here? *Now?*" While I knew they would need to confront Renee, I wasn't expecting them to do in front of everyone.

Steven gives me a curt yet understanding smile. "I'm just going to ask her to leave the party to come chat with me so we can clear up a misunderstanding."

"Um…Okay." I certainly don't want to cause a big scene and ruin the special ending to the reunion. "They are at the table closest to the bar. He's the big bulky dude, and she's wearing the long black-and-white dress." I don't bother adding the description of the skin-tight, plunging neckline. They have eyes of their own.

Steven strides across the room while Cole and I remain with the other two crew members. We cannot hear the ensuing conversation above the music, but Steven appears calm and professional. Tank and Renee exchange a few words with the man, then stand, drinks still in their hands.

All seems peaceable until Renee's gaze lands on me standing by the other two uniformed men. She stops in her tracks and begins shaking her head back and forth. The song emanating from the speakers ends. The brief moment of silence is shattered by Renee's shouts.

"No! I'm not going anywhere with you!"

Tank turns his bewildered look toward his wife while the entire room is drawn into the unfolding drama, including the DJ, who neglects to start another song.

Steven reaches out a hand to calm Renee, which has the opposite effect.

"Keep your hands off of me!" she screams, pointing her manicured finger in my direction. "You can't believe anything that lying minx says!" She then tosses her drink into Steven's face and begins running—toward me or the exit, I'm not sure. Although, her hurried departure in high heels and form-fitting dress resembles a penguin waddling across the ice rather than the great escape she may have planned.

Steven wipes the alcohol off his face with the sleeve of his jacket, then, in two quick steps, reaches out to grab Renee's arm.

This sets Tank in motion. "Keep your hands off my wife!"

He plops his drink down on the nearest high-top table. With a clenched fist, he lunges toward Steven. Two of Tank's buddies grab onto him, trying to hold him back. But proving his nickname still fits, he continues barreling forward, dragging his friends along.

The two security members next to me jump into action and rush toward the melee. Gasps fill the air as the uniformed men restrain Tank and Renee. Well, this certainly isn't the calm, quiet confrontation Steven expected.

As the crew tries to move the Joneses toward the exit, Renee begins berating her husband.

"This is all your fault! This cruise was supposed to be your shining moment, showing your stupid classmates that you've become successful! But you couldn't even do that without screwing up! Why do I have to do everything for you!"

"What are you talking about?" Tank continues to squirm, trying to break free of his captors' firm grip.

Renee turns her sneering face toward her husband. "I finally found a way to help you get past your stupid juvenile rivalry!"

"What did you do?" Tank growls through gritted teeth.

"I only tried to make you the man my father wanted you to be!"

As the group passes us, Steven shoots a less than friendly look our way. Another crew member who will be happy to have us off this ship.

Tank and Renee's bickering diminishes as they are escorted from the room.

Shocked silence quickly turns into a buzz of excitement.

Dad suddenly appears at my side. "What was all that about?"

My head shakes in disbelief. "It's a long story. Let's just say, all is finally right in the world."

The DJ attempts to bring order back to the event by playing a song—a slow one. My lucky night.

"Dad, can you excuse us?" I squeeze his arm, then boldly lead Cole toward the dance floor.

"Well, that was an exciting ending." Cole draws close for our dance.

"And here I thought this would be an excruciatingly boring ten days."

He grins. "Definitely not boring. Entertaining seems a more fitting description."

"Intriguing," I counter as we sway back and forth.

His head tilts slightly closer. "Romantic."

"Magical."

Cole's smile shifts from playful to indescribable. "There's something I've been wanting to tell you all evening."

I try to read his more serious expression to prepare myself but am unsuccessful.

He clears his throat. "So, um, that was some song you performed earlier tonight."

My mind conjures up some sort of witty reply, but I change my mind. After all that we've been through, complete honesty seems like the best path. What do I have to lose?

"It's always been one of my favorites, but I never really had someone in mind when I sang it—until now."

His silence makes me wish I'd stuck with my original joking reply, but I can't turn back now. "I…I mean, don't take the lyrics too literally. I just wanted to let you know how much I care for you and what a great guy you are." My cheeks burn.

His smile doesn't quite reach his eyes. "I completely understand because I feel the same way."

"If only…"

"If only…" He raises our hands, leading me in a twirl.

His strong arm pulls me back in. "Remember when you did that impression of me—for when my friends ask about my trip?"

"Yes." I remember every moment we've shared.

"Well, you were a little off. I think it might go more like this: 'Hey, Cole, how was your trip?' 'Great, I met the girl of my dreams, but sadly she lives in another state.'"

His words send my heart racing. "It's so unfair. If only you didn't live in Virginia."

His face scrunches. "Virginia? I don't live in Virginia. I mean, I did when I was a kid, but not anymore. The tragedy is that you live in Chicago."

My eyebrows furrow. "I don't live in Chicago. Only my dad does."

We stop moving.

"Where *do* you live?" we ask in unison.

He's the first to answer. "We moved back to Minnesota when I was in middle school. We're in Rochester."

My eyes widen. "My mom and I live in Lake Forest."

We stand there staring at each other, slack-jawed, as the realization that we live twenty minutes apart sinks in.

His open mouth turns into a smile. Then he pulls me close and continues swaying to the music.

"Well, this changes everything." His breath tickles my ear as he speaks.

"Indeed. We live close enough to see each other again." I pull back to see his face. "So, is this good news or bad news?" A vacation romance is quite different than an actual relationship. Better to find out what he's thinking now. "I mean, I'd hate for you to be worrying all the time that we might accidentally run into each other. Awkward reunions are the worst."

"True. But what if instead, I asked you out on a proper date."

A proper date. My insides warm, but I play it cool. "I might accept."

"Or"—I hear the teasing lilt of his voice—"you might keep making excuses until I finally get the hint that you aren't actually interested."

"But you're forgetting my New Year's resolution of continuing my faith journey, which includes telling the truth."

"You know, I didn't make a resolution this year. Instead, moments after midnight, I made a wish upon a star."

After I cowardly ran away. I push the thought aside. "And what was that wish?"

"To get a second chance."

"A second chance at what?"

He pulls back to look at me. "A second chance at showing you how amazing you are."

I offer a coy little smile. "And how do you propose to do that?"

"Say yes to my invitation, and I'll show you."

"I don't believe you have actually asked me out as of yet."

He thinks for a moment. "You make a good point." He stops moving. "Liz, will you go out with me?"

I tap my chin. "Can you top a day on a Caribbean beach? Or tango lessons? Or traipsing around on a scavenger hunt?"

"Oh, I see. You're one of those girls who's hard to impress." His head shakes back and forth. "Never mind. I'm not sure I'm up for the task."

My head cocks. "Why, Mr. Cole, are your true colors shining through? Do you run when the going gets tough?"

His eyebrows raise. "Ah, a test of my true feelings. Well, just for your information, it takes a lot more than a challenge to scare me away."

I try to continue our playful bantering but am completely unable to control my smile. "Good to know."

His head lowers. "So, is that a yes?"

"Absolutely."

"This new year suddenly looks promising."

"Indeed." My smile widens.

Our gazes lock for a moment, then he pulls me close, and we resume our dance. I lean in close, resting my head against his chest.

Thank you, Lord, for the chance to change the direction of my life and get it back on course.

About the Author

Leslea Wahl lives in beautiful Colorado and is the author of several award-winning teen novels. She strives to write stories that encourage teens to grow in their faith through fun, adventurous mysteries. Leslea is often inspired by her family, their travels, and real-life adventures. She particularly enjoys including the furry, four-legged members of her family in her novels.

Besides writing, Leslea also reviews faith-based novels on her website and is a founding member of CatholicTeenBooks.com. For more information on her novels please visit www.Leslea-Wahl.com.

Acknowledgements

There are a few people I must thank for helping get this novel published.

To God, for leading me down this writing pathway. All my success is because of Him.

My husband, for his unwavering support in every venture I try.

The Mental family, for giving me so many moments of joy and inspiration.

Tressa Lindsay of Bird's Eye Edits, for making the story shine and dealing with all those punctuation nuisances.

My author friends at CatholicTeenBooks, who are more than co-workers as they have become mentors and friends.

And to all the readers, thank you for taking the time to read this book.

If you enjoyed the story, please take a moment to post a review or share with a friend.

Author's Note

Liz's faith continues to grow in the short story, *Finishing the Journey*, which can be found in the anthology Ashes: Visible & Invisible by CatholicTeenBooks.com authors.

You can discover Josie's story in the first book of this series, *Into the Spotlight*.

For more fun facts about this story, my playlist of songs, and to learn which details are based on true incidents from my life, visit my website: www.LesleaWahl.com.

Dear Reader

If you enjoyed reading *Charting the Course*, I would appreciate it if you would help others enjoy this book, too. Here are some of the ways you can help spread the word:

Lend it. This book is lending enabled so please share it with a friend.

Recommend it. Help other readers find this book by recommending it to friends, readers' groups, book clubs, and discussion forums.

Share it. Let other readers know you've read the book by positing a note to your social media account and/or your Goodreads account.

Review it. Please tell others why you liked this book by reviewing it on your favorite ebook site.

Everything you do to help others learn about my book is greatly appreciated!

Leslea Wahl

Reader Guide/Questions

1. Liz and her father have a very difficult relationship. Through the story, they slowly find a way back to each other. Do you have any strained relationships in your life? Can you think of a way to move past the difficulties and journey forward? Is there someone in your life that you have had trouble forgiving? Have you turned to God to help you with that relationship?

2. At the beginning of the story, Liz is reluctant to pray the novena that Josie had given her. With nothing to lose, she gives it a try. As the relationship with her dad improves, she starts to see the beauty of asking heavenly friends to pray for her. Do you turn to any specific prayers or novenas? Has God ever answered your prayers in a unique or surprising way?

3. Forgiving her father is only part of Liz's journey. She must also forgive herself and acknowledge the choices she made. Do you feel it's more difficult to forgive others or yourself? Why?

4. Through the course of the story, Liz realizes that her actions have severe consequences. Do you ever think about how your actions could affect others?

5. Liz comes to understand that she's not the only one with a complicated family situation. Everyone faces difficulties in life. Is there a way to not become so focused on our own problems that you fail to recognize other people's hardships?

6. Liz turns to music to work through the pain of her childhood. Do you have an outlet for releasing your fears and frustrations: poetry, exercise, music, journaling? Or do you tend to keep painful things locked inside? Do you feel channeling your energy through an activity is helpful? Share other methods one can use to cope with trials.

7. Were you surprised that Liz ended up being the thief? Making her an Unreliable Narrator offered a surprising twist to the story but also provided an opportunity to highlight her vulnerability. Have you seen this technique used in fiction before?

8. Can you relate to Liz falling back into her childhood coping mechanisms? Why do you think this is a common reaction? What would have been a better way for Liz to handle the situation?

9. One message of this story is owning up to your mistakes and taking responsibility for your actions. How hard is that to do? Why?

10. Liz discovers her faith through the help of her friend Josie. Is there anyone you might be able to invite to church or share a novena with? Have you ever offered to pray for someone?

11. The books in my Finding Faith series are about teens who struggle in their personal lives. Sometimes we have to experience those moments of desperation before we can open ourselves to the beauty and grace of Christ. When you face difficulties, do you have a friend to turn to? Or can you be that friend for someone in need? Like Liz, don't be afraid to seek out a priest to talk to. Through Jesus' loving mercy, a priest can offer counsel and forgiveness.

www.ingramcontent.com/pod-product-compliance
Lightning Source LLC
Chambersburg PA
CBHW050734230626
47052CB00002BA/187

* 9 7 9 8 9 8 6 9 0 3 7 6 7 *